# Praise for Bianca D'Arc's
## *Hidden Talent*

"D'Arc's first novel about the StarLords is riveting and fascinating. She paints a colorful world where psychics are the norm and sexual pleasure is explored and cherished. Love blooms between her main characters as their worlds collide and lovers of both the paranormal and erotic genres will be enchanted."

~ *RT Book Reviews*

"In the first book of the Starlords series, Bianca D'Arc sets the stage for exciting new stories guaranteed to be winners...non-stop action, strange psi powers, and sex scenes that explode off the page."

~ *Sensual Reads*

# Look for these titles by
## *Bianca D'Arc*

## *Now Available:*

*Dragon Knights*
Maiden Flight
Border Lair
The Ice Dragon
Prince of Spies
Wings of Change
FireDrake
Dragon Storm

*Tales of the Were*
Lords of the Were
Inferno

*Resonance Mates*
Hara's Legacy
Davin's Quest
Jaci's Experiment
Grady's Awakening

*Brotherhood of Blood*
Forever Valentine
Sweeter than Wine
One and Only
Rare Vintage
Phantom Desires
Wolf Hills

*Gifts of the Ancients*
Warrior's Heart

*String of Fate*
Cat's Cradle

*Print Anthologies*
Ladies of the Lair
Caught By Cupid
I Dream of Dragons Vol 1
Brotherhood of Blood

# Hidden Talent

*Bianca D'Arc*

SAMHAIN PUBLISHING

Samhain Publishing, Ltd.
11821 Mason Montgomery Road, 4B
Cincinnati, OH 45249
www.samhainpublishing.com

Hidden Talent
Copyright © 2012 by Bianca D'Arc
Print ISBN: 978-1-60928-785-6
Digital ISBN: 978-1-60928-639-2

Editing by Bethany Morgan
Cover by Angela Waters

First Samhain Publishing, Ltd. electronic publication: October 2011
First Samhain Publishing, Ltd. print publication: September 2012

# Dedication

This one is for the fans who have waited so patiently while I got back on my feet after losing someone so very dear to me. Thanks for standing by me in the tough times. Thanks also for your patience and support. Most of all, thanks for understanding.

And though he will never read this book (for obvious reasons), I'd like to thank my Dad for his love and support of my writing career.

# Chapter One

The Tribal Mother's distinctive whistle summoned Jeri, though she had tried her best to walk from the paddock to the safety of her tent without being noticed. The Mother was talking with a tall male who wore the garments of an outworlder.

"Jeri, show the trader our herds," the Mother instructed as Jeri walked closer to her. "Take Broome and Asper and ride with him to the south paddock. Give him a good look at the breeding stock, then bring him back to camp."

Retracing her steps toward the horses, she saddled Broome and Asper. Both were sturdy examples of the fine steeds bred by the Hill Tribes. Jeri led them to where the Mother waited with the outworlder male. The tall stranger watched her with almost sad eyes, she thought.

Something about the man made her wary. And when Jeri was wary, she became silent, as her early life experiences had taught her. Silence and a tightening of her mental shields came naturally to her now after so many years spent hiding from the Wizards of Mithrak.

They used the antiquated name to conjure a sense of fear in the simple people who lived on the mostly agrarian worlds they controlled. They tried to inspire awe by making folk believe they were somehow magical, but Jeri knew better. Her father had taught her and her sister about the old times, when democracy had ruled Mithrak, not the self-proclaimed Wizards.

Just because some people could do incredible things with their minds didn't mean they were better or worse than anybody else, he'd always said. These Wizards though—they subverted otherwise good people's Talents for their own use. They were evil through and through, he'd taught his daughters. And they were to be avoided at all costs.

They'd come for her when she was barely a teen. They'd searched for her, over and over. But she'd hidden well and learned to be as silent as the grave, not even a glimmer of her inner power revealing her hiding place. She'd hidden deep in the ruined tower that had been her family home before the Wizards came, until she'd found a way off planet and eventually made her way to Pantur.

Now, Jeri was far from Mithrak, a refugee taken in by the famous Hill Tribes of Pantur. She was welcome among them— able to do the work she was born to, and able to hide her inner power among a people who had none. The Hill Tribes were known throughout the galaxy for their fine horses. They were descended from tribal peoples of old Earth, but they had little psi energy among them. It was a perfect place for her to hide. She'd been born a horse tamer, and her adopted people could neither feel nor understand the powers that made her a natural to the profession. They would also never turn her in to the so-called Wizards, or any who sought her only for her power.

From time to time, traders came to the Hill Tribes seeking horses. She was a minor trainer among the tribes, having proven her worth over the two standard years she'd been with them, but she'd never been entrusted to show a potential buyer around before. Such tasks were given to the older and more skilled trainers, and if truth be known, she wanted nothing of it. She wanted no contact with outworlders who might be able to sense the differences about her.

But the Mother had asked, and so Jeri complied. Silently, she jumped on Asper's back, the big mare welcoming her presence with a whicker. Jeri watched the muscular outworlder spring lightly onto Broome's back and was inwardly pleased by his show of skill around her friends, the beautiful horses of Pantur.

The trader was another story. The man made her nervous in a way she did not fully understand. He was by far the most handsome man she'd ever laid eyes on, and his piercing gaze did something to her insides that set them jingling. She tried to avoid his too-knowing gaze, but she could feel it like a laser, following her every move.

His size intimidated her too. Well over six feet tall, he looked down at her with those all-seeing eyes from a face that was ruggedly masculine, with incongruously long, flowing hair. Her fingers itched to comb through those wavy locks.

She knew about the goings-on between males and females. After all, what horse tamer didn't know these things? But never before had she met a man who made her feel the things she'd heard the girls of the tribe speak about in hushed giggles while the boys weren't around. This man, however, by his very presence, was teaching her about the feminine responses she thought she somehow had been born without.

Somewhat reassured that she could actually be attracted to a male, she was nonetheless disconcerted that it would be an outworlder. Outworlders were dangerous. Among the tribe, she could be sure no one would pick up on her energies, but she had no such reassurances with outlanders. For all she knew, he was a Wizard, though she hoped she would have already sensed such power in him, if he had it. She'd let down enough of her shields when she first saw him to satisfy herself that he wasn't showing any Wizard tendencies, but then, her experience was limited to the times when they were actively hunting her. For all she knew, the Wizards didn't give off telltale energy when they weren't hunting. She didn't know, and she didn't dare take a chance of finding out.

They rode to the south paddock. Jeri limited her speech to short descriptions of the horses they saw on their way. She answered his questions, but she didn't look at him if she could help it and he got the distinct impression that this little tribal horse tamer didn't like him.

That didn't sit well with Micah, Mage Master of Geneth Mar. Of course, aboard his beloved ship, the *Circe*, and while on the planet of Pantur, he was known only as the trader Micah. Few people knew his true rank as one of the rare StarLords, authorized by the Council to act on their behalf while out among the stars.

He'd done nothing to this little scrap of a woman, and her terseness was getting on his nerves. He'd never traded directly with the Hill Tribes before, leaving that task to his Executive Officer, Darak, but he'd heard only good things from his XO, who was also his cousin, and had expected a smooth transaction with this female-dominated tribe.

The girl's coldness irked him, and he looked for ways to tease her, hoping to put her in a better mood, or perhaps to tease her out of her icy chill. Even anger would be better than the way she was treating him.

Micah could scent her essence on the breeze and while it was not the perfumed elegance he was used to in the more civilized places he frequented, her scent was honest, primal and it sounded a heated call to his own starved senses. He hadn't had a woman since leaving on this mission and the lack was telling. He could have joined any of his crewmembers in their pleasures. They would welcome him with open arms.

Pleasure was shared freely in his culture, but he had found himself dissatisfied lately with most couplings where there was not at least some basis for deeper affection and some kind of equality of Talent. True, he loved his little family on the *Circe*, but he was a solitary man of late. At least he had been since the awful circumstances that had forcibly pushed his psi Talent to the next level, and he didn't want to inflict his growing melancholy on his friends if he could help it.

Micah had been on a mission to a fledgling world that had recently joined the Council. He'd been undercover to investigate rumors of slave trafficking. Slaving was forbidden on Council worlds and the Council took allegations of such business very seriously indeed. When Micah discovered that not only were they trading in human slaves, but Talented human slaves, he'd needed to gather evidence and free those people he could. He'd never expected the backlash.

The captives he freed didn't trust him and didn't understand what was happening to them. Without the stronger minds and Talents of the slavers controlling them, they'd released a series of mental shrieks that had knocked Micah off his feet. The wave had rolled over him—had been aimed at him. Hundreds of soundless waves of psi energy battered his shields. He survived, but just barely. And when he revived, he was able to calm the traumatized Talents only by sheer force of his will and an unexpected spike in his own powerful Talent.

He'd gone from Mage to Master in that moment when he stepped up to the task of calming and controlling—to a certain extent—the chaotic Talents he'd released. After that, the former slaves realized he was there to help them and calmed down. They'd gone eagerly to the *Circe* for resettlement on the world of their choice, far away from the memories of being a slave to unethical Talents.

The entire crew had received special commendations for

their work, but Micah had unexpectedly risen in power. The things he'd heard from the traumatized minds before he managed to subdue them, however, had changed him forever. He'd seen things through their eyes. Learned things about the way these poor people—mostly women—had been treated. It ruined his faith in his fellow man and made him pull into his own shell more than ever. Being suddenly so much more powerful than his friends and crewmates started a rift that had only grown deeper as time went on. Instead of healing, Micah had closed himself off, unable to deal with the scarred emotions that had been forced upon him.

He was ranked Master now and there were few women of Talent who were his equal. He was afraid he'd never find a partner that he wouldn't have to hold back with, as he had to do with every psi Talent ranked Mage and below. The rankings were defined levels of ability and power. He'd held a seat on the Mage Council for several years, working steadily at improving his control until recently, when he'd made the jump from Mage to Mage Master.

Everyone on his crew was below Mage level. Young Talents to be nurtured and older Talents who had perhaps already reached the limits of their abilities. None would be an equal to him, and he would always have to hold back some part of his power lest he inadvertently cause them pain or even damage.

But his cousin Darak had no such worries. Ranked Dominar, the level just below Mage, he was only a bit younger than Micah and still randy for any woman willing to give him some action. In fact, he'd left Darak with the women on the ship, taking the trading mission to the planet himself, though bargaining with the locals was usually not something he did. He simply wanted time away from the confines of the ship and he knew from shared psi images that Darak was having the time of his life. Micah didn't want to interrupt the three-day orgy they'd been enjoying since setting orbit around Pantur.

Darak had rejoined the crew recently, after a long and arduous mission, and he'd earned his pleasure. Micah didn't mind giving him a few uninterrupted days of recreation before he'd have to settle back into the responsibilities of being the Executive Officer on a trader ship that was oh-so-much-more.

Few knew about the secret missions the trader-*cum*-spy-vessel accomplished on behalf of the Mage Council. Only a handful knew that the Captain of the *Circe* was one of the rare and powerful Mage Masters and a respected member of the Council. They would hardly believe that a Talent such as he would even bother trying to tease a psi-blank native of Pantur. What pleasure could be gained from such a woman but the ease of his body alone? There would be no sharing of psi power, no mixing of Talent to titillate and tease the ethereal senses. Only a base coupling that would ease a physical ache.

At this point, even that would be a welcome change to the disenchanted Mage Master. At least he wouldn't have to worry about singeing her senses, for these people had no Talent among them. It was just not in their genetic make-up. Perhaps without the added burden of dampening his psi abilities, he could just lie back and enjoy a carnal interlude.

And he'd truly enjoy having the lithe and muscular Jeri ride him the way she did her steed. He would settle under her and slap her rump to make her go faster, reveling in the purely physical for once. He could almost feel it as he watched her thighs clutch against the saddle. He felt himself clench as he fell back to watch her.

"We must be moving if you wish to review the sale herd before mid-noon."

Her voice was gentle as she called back to him. He took it as a good sign. She was clearly flustered by him. It was enough for now.

They stopped about an hour later at a small stream and dismounted to allow their horses to drink and stretch their muscles.

"We are on the south paddock grounds," Jeri said softly, trying desperately to stay out of reach of the outworlder male. But he seemed to want to always move closer to her in the most disconcerting way. "The sale herd will be here soon to drink, and you can get a good look at them."

Micah looked down at her from his superior height, his gaze surprisingly warm as she stood transfixed, unable to move away. Her skin tingled, and she realized she was in serious danger of allowing him too close. Since she'd sought refuge with the free-loving Hill Tribes, she'd had to reject a few men and even some women who wanted to share her body, but once she made her stance firm, she was left alone for the most part—except for the odd looks and some of the other girls' cutting remarks about her strangeness.

This man tempted her as no male had ever before. He was tall and broad of shoulder, built well and heavily muscled. His eyes shone with intelligence and a snapping sort of wit that made her long to discuss all kinds of things with him.

But it was impossible.

She was in hiding. Anonymity was her way. It was the only way to keep her safe from the Wizards and their ilk. Wizards who wanted to tap into her soul's power and make it their own.

That she would not allow.

She found it hard to move away when this outworld trader's handsome face blocked the midday suns, leaning down and moving closer.

Before she knew it, his lips were on hers, she was in his arms and he was kissing the breath out of her body. How had that happened? One minute she'd been staring up at his attractive eyes, the next, she was in his embrace, his lips hot on hers as his tongue sought entrance into her mouth.

Jeri had never been kissed in such a way and didn't quite know what to do. She felt warmed by the light of a thousand suns from within as his hands swept her close to his hard body and his mouth sipped at hers. She opened to him on a sigh of pleasure and let him do as he willed for the moment. She would drink in the experience, she decided rashly, to hold against the cold, empty, lonely days ahead. Just this once, she would find out what a kiss was all about and why the tribe's girls went on and on about their lovers' kisses.

His hand moved upward to cup her breast and she was jolted by an almost electrical charge that led from her nipple straight to the growing wetness between her legs. It shocked her out of her reverie, and she realized that she had let the kiss get out of hand. He would think she was inviting him to more, when in fact she had known she would stop him at a kiss and not let this go any further. She didn't want him to think she was a tease.

She tried to push him away, but her hands were weak, trembling with excitement and new feelings she'd never experienced. She tried to speak, but his tongue tangled with hers in the most delicious way.

She knew she had to do something. This couldn't go further. She couldn't give her body to this man any more than she already had. It wouldn't be wise.

She did the only thing she could, and sent out a silent call to the horses that were nearby, coming for a drink at the stream. Reaching out to them with her mind, she used her gift to call them to her side faster, unsurprised when a big, wet nose came between her neck and his chest, seeking to drive them apart.

The horses had come, and they were claiming her for their own.

Micah laughed as he jumped back from the stallion who'd had the temerity to push his nose between him and the little horse tamer. He let her go with a heated glance, promising more, but she avoided his gaze and turned her attention to the huge horses that were now crowding around them.

It was odd, really, how they swarmed her, staying near even when they realized she didn't have treats of food or sugar for them. They nuzzled her small body, careful of their force, treating her with an amazing love and respect he could almost feel vibrating through him.

"They must love you." He eyed her, stroking the nearest neck of a pretty young mare.

She smiled but didn't meet his eyes. "They are my friends," she said shortly, unwilling to look directly at him. "Aren't they lovely?"

He watched her enjoyment of the huge beasts and how they licked and stroked her with their soft muzzles.

"Lovely," he agreed, but he had yet to really look at the horses. It was the horse tamer who had caught and held his full attention.

She moved away from him, allowing the herd to separate them, and he turned his attention to the business he'd come here to conduct. He made mental notes of the horses he would bargain for with the tribal Mother, making his decisions easily and quickly. Really, there wasn't a bad one in the bunch and any of this herd would do well on the agricultural world to which he would transport them.

He pretended to watch the horses, but he really watched the horse tamer. She slipped among them and they each seemed to reach out to touch her as she passed. It was like nothing he'd ever seen. These horses seemed to want to be near her—all of them—as if she were special in some way that only they understood.

It was a puzzle, and Micah was a man who enjoyed deciphering puzzles. It was also something he was very good at.

He worked his way over the herd, always keeping the small horse tamer in his sights as he studied her while pretending to study the horses who practically worshipped her. He remembered the searing kiss they'd shared. Or rather, the kiss he'd given her and she'd accepted.

He could tell from her lack of practiced response that she was a novice compared to him when it came to bestowing pleasure through a kiss. Perhaps that was just a cultural thing peculiar to the Hill Tribes. Many isolated worlds like this one had odd customs when it came to pleasure and male-female interaction.

Still, he knew she'd been a willing participant until he tried to take the kiss further. If he'd had a few more minutes before the horses interrupted, he knew he could've convinced her to continue with him, partners in the pleasure they could find together.

It was an odd twist of fate that the horses chose that moment to come between them. But then, perhaps the horse tamer had some way of controlling the beasts that he knew nothing about. He'd never known horses to behave this way. Even now they followed her wherever she went, watching her with their eyes when they couldn't get near with their bodies. Indeed, the entire herd seemed focused on the small woman, giving him a respectful distance, but they wanted to be next to her, touching her in whatever way they could.

It was damned odd.

If he didn't know better, he would think that the woman had some hidden or latent Talent with which she enthralled the beasts. But the inhabitants of Pantur had no discernable psi Talent to speak of and as a newly made Mage Master, he knew he would be able to detect even the faintest glimmer of raw Talent.

Still, he watched her and questioned his own thoughts. The whole thing was damned odd.


They rode back to the summer camp in the quiet time before dusk, speaking little as he worked over the puzzle of the little horse tamer.

Working on the tangle in his mind, they arrived at the camp almost before he knew it. He dismounted and moved to help her with the saddles and tack, but some of the younger Tribesmen took the task from him. He stood there, watching the silent woman remove the large saddle from her mount while another girl took the saddle from the horse he had ridden.

He sensed some animosity between the two young women as they worked—Jeri silent and alone, the other girl surrounded by a small crowd of her followers. She was pretty, but full of her own selfishness. Micah wasn't surprised when the other woman's words turned to taunts as he observed, using a small burst of his Talent to direct the other woman and her friends to forget he was even there.


"So, little Jeri and the trader have returned at last. Did you have a *good* time today?"

"Leave it, Sheli," Jeri said softly, ignoring the taunting tone of the other girl as best she could.

"What's the matter, Jeri, too tired from spending all day in the south paddock bedding our visitor? I hope you didn't shame the tribe by leaving him stiff." Sheli's petulant voice grated on her nerves. The other girl was a bitch, and close enough in age to Jeri to cause constant torment with her practical jokes and barbed comments.

Jeri ignored her and continued to work unsaddling her mare, but the solid form of Micah stood in her path. Her gaze shot up to his, her shields clamping down tight as she felt a flicker of questioning from him on a psi level she hadn't felt in ages.

*He has Talent!*

Jeri shivered and redoubled her efforts at remaining calm under his scrutiny and his mental probing.

"Is this true? Were you expected to share your body with me?"

She couldn't answer his softly spoken words and probing gaze. She resolutely put her head down and moved around him to put the saddle away. Silence was her protection. Silence was her friend. It had kept her safe before, and she prayed to the goddess of all it would keep her safe in the face of this unknown threat.

And trader Micah was definitely a threat. She felt it in her bones.

He wasn't blatantly after her power like the Wizards had been, eager to add her to their ranks and consume her into their collective. She didn't think he even realized she had any Talent of her own. He probably assumed she was a native of the Hill Tribes and therefore without any psi power. If so, all the better.

21

She breathed a sigh of relief when he didn't follow as she went silently about her tasks, but she felt his gaze watching from the distance. His sad, almost dazed expression had followed her all day, and it was working on her senses like a drug. In desperation, she sought her tent on the other side of the camp, needing time alone. With any luck, the outworlder would be gone in the morning, and she could get back to her simple life with the tribe.

"Trader Micah," the Mother of the tribe spoke softly at his elbow as he watched the young trainer disappear in the distance, "go easy on Jeri. She is young and not used to our ways."

That piqued his interest, and he turned questioning eyes on the leader of the small band. "Wasn't she born and raised among you?"

The older woman shook her head sadly. "She is an outworlder, come to us some two seasons past. She was troubled and silent even then, but she has a natural affinity for our horses and will be one of our greatest trainers, given time and study. I thought to confer favor on her by having her escort you today, but I fear I have made a mistake. She was not ready, and did not understand the honor. Perhaps you would find one of the other girls more willing to be your companion in the bed furs tonight."

Micah jerked upright at the casual words. "It was expected that she grant me sexual favors?"

The Mother sighed. "If you desired it. We Hill Tribes women take our pleasure where we find it. Jeri has been among us long enough to know that. I was hoping you could entice her, since to the tribe's knowledge, she has been celibate since she came to us. It is not a natural state for us."

Micah considered that for a moment. "Perhaps it is to her," he said quietly. "If she is not of your world, perhaps her own code of behavior is different than yours."

The Mother sighed. "You are probably right, Trader Micah. Forgive my folly. I have grown so used to young Jeri that I think of her as one of my own. She is so gifted with the herd that I would make her my successor, if I could."

"She's truly that good, Mother?" He was surprised by the idea—though he had seen firsthand how she cared for the herd she had shown him that day—and how they cared for her. It was almost magical, how the horses responded to the small beauty.

The Mother nodded sadly. "But she will never be Mother here. It is not for outworlders to rule the Hill Tribes. Though her skills will help the tribe prosper for many years to come." She turned to him. "But come, we have business to discuss before dinner, and then the feasting and bedding can begin. You will find any number of young women ready to pleasure you and be pleasured in return."

Micah didn't know how he would handle the hours to come, but he suspected he'd want no other young lovely in his arms than the small, silent girl who had practically run from him and his mind probe. He realized in that moment that his probe had been well and truly blocked, not deflected by the absence of Talent, but deflected by a concentration of Talent.

Jeri was an outworlder. Suddenly it all fell into place. She had Talent of her own. She must have. And she was undoubtedly hiding among the Hill Tribes, for those with Talent were not many in the galaxy, and most held positions of great power. Young Jeri could have had a very pampered life on many of the planets he'd visited, with even just a glimmer of Talent. If she was able to not only deflect but camouflage from him, she must have more than just a little Talent.

Micah's own Talent was Mage Master level, and he still had many years' growth ahead of him. If he had not yet reached his full potential, perhaps in many years of constant work he might be able to reach Vizier level, though only a handful of that vast power existed in any generation. He was considered one of the strongest Talents in his family, which was dotted with strong Talent as far back as could be traced. There had even once been a Sha in his line—the highest level, gifted to only one or two in every generation. Micah didn't carry any illusions that he could ever be a Sha, but he knew deep inside, he had not yet reached his limits and he was already among the strongest Talents in the galaxy.

But this little horse tamer was able not only to hide her power from him, but almost make him believe she had none, which spoke of a Talent greater than average. Perhaps greater than his own.

He had no choice. He had to seek her out and learn more about her. The possibility of such power could not be ignored or left to wallow on this unprotected world for anyone to find and take. She needed to be protected and trained. Only then could she reach her potential—whatever that was. Only then could she be free to aid in the fight against those who would try to enslave her and others like her.

He needed a strategy. Sitting at the Mother's negotiating table, he thought out what the night would bring. Lord Micah of Geneth Mar wasn't known as the most outrageous StarLord in the sector for nothing. He would have young Jeri with him when he left, in addition to half the sale herd of the Hill Tribes. Both would turn him a tidy profit—one in credits, the other in the much deeper currency of satisfaction.

# Chapter Two

Jeri trembled as she sank onto her bedroll. She had a tent to herself, mostly because no one else wanted to sleep with the tack. She was more than happy to spend her extra time mending the bits of leather and metal, so no one seemed to notice much when she made the tack shelter her own domain. She'd simply moved her bedroll inside along with her few possessions.

Jeri wrapped her arms around her upraised knees, settling her head down and trying hard not to tremble in fear. That man had unsettled her. He was handsome and scary and filled with an odd power that frightened her almost more than his physical presence. She knew, deep down, if she ever let her guard down around him, he would know her deepest secrets. She would not be safe until he left camp. Perhaps not until he was gone from Pantur completely.

Yet he stirred something inside her that had never seen the light of day. She had watched him this afternoon as his powerful thighs commanded the horse to do what he willed and it had made her mouth water with unaccustomed desire. She knew the Hill Tribes women were free with their favors and had learned that they took pleasure where they wished, but it had never been her way. Still, she could admire a well-built man and this man was the most well built she had ever seen. He made her think of things better left alone.

She heard the gong sound when the feast began, but she wasn't hungry and feared facing the trader again. She stayed in her tent, surrounded by the implements of her chosen trade, and hid. She busied herself with the endless repair tasks that filled her non-training hours, making good progress on several harnesses that had been damaged the week before.

Time sped by and before she knew it, the sounds of the camp were quieting down for the night. She labored by the light of her sole little lamp. The rest of the tribe was used to seeing her light burning late into the night. She slept little compared to them, but they'd never remarked on it.

She focused so tightly on keeping her shields in place that she was caught off guard when a polite knock sounded on her tent pole, followed almost immediately by an impolite opening of the flap.

The trader stood there, a knowing smile on his face and a covered thermo plate in his hands. She had no idea what to say. She just stared at him with wide eyes. He apparently took her silence as an invitation and stepped inside, letting the tent flap close behind him.

"I took the liberty of bringing you some dinner since you missed it," he said, bending close to place the thermo plate in front of her.

There was little in the way of furniture in her crowded little tent, but he didn't seem to mind. He folded his knees and sat opposite her on the tail end of her bedroll, smiling in a way that made her stomach clench. She had no idea how to take his actions. He'd been respectful of most of her boundaries up until that moment and in the two years she'd been with the Hill Tribes, she had never had anyone cross the barrier she placed between herself and the rest of the world.

"Aren't you going to thank me?"

Her eyebrows rose in surprise. She was processing information as quickly as she could amidst almost debilitating fear, but she still didn't know what to make of him or his actions.

And she had no idea what she was supposed to thank him for. For disturbing her peace? For barging into her tent uninvited? For making her crazy?

"For bringing your dinner," he prompted when she still didn't speak. He uncovered the thermo plate and sniffed at the generous helping of meat and tubers. "Smells delicious. And I brought enough to share."

He produced two forks from a pocket and handed her one with a courtly flourish as his eyes danced in amusement. Her breath caught as his eyes seemed to sparkle at her.

"Thank you," she said softly, accepting the fork.

"There. See? That wasn't so hard. Was it?"

He seemed to be teasing her, and it made her heart flutter. No male had ever paid her this much attention. Especially one that looked like him. He was stirring her senses with his dark eyes and bold looks. He was powerfully built and no stranger to hard riding and physical exertion.

"You shouldn't be here," she said softly in protest as he speared a piece of meat and brought it to his lips.

"I think you have it wrong," he countered. "Your tribe Mother told me it was expected that when you were chosen as my escort, you would also be my bed partner." She gulped, her eyes widening in panic. "Since there has been no other accommodation made for me, I've decided I will sleep here, with you."

Jeri gasped. The brute had a lot of nerve. She immediately

27

saw that he'd put her in an impossible situation. She couldn't kick him out with the strict hospitality laws of the tribe. She couldn't leave the tent herself, though she longed to do so, because then she would never hear the end of her failure from not only the tribal elders, but from the jealous girls like Sheli who coveted even her low rank as trainer.

She was well and truly stuck with the big oaf. But what would transpire within the tent was in her control—at least she hoped it was. He was bigger than she was, but if he harmed her, he would be killed by the tribe. All she had to do was scream for help and the elders would come to her aid. She would prefer not to have to resort to such dramatics, but she held the option in reserve should this outworlder overstep even further.

"Good then," he said shortly, touching a sequence on his wristcomp. With a flash of light, some of his belongings were transferred from his ship to the interior of the tent, startling her. Her family had never been able to afford the newer technologies and ion transport was just one of the things she'd heard about but never seen. The thermo plate was put aside as he brought his belongings to the side of the bedroll.

"A few comfort items from my ship," he said shortly, rifling through the small pile before pulling out a small box that had her jumping to her feet, terror in her eyes. He switched it on and immediately her senses were swimming in her Talent, awash with her own power. And she was in great, great pain.

"Turn it off. Please," she cried as she crumpled to the floor, her fists clutching at her temples as he stood over her, concern warring with rigid determination on his face.

"Drop your shields," he said softly. "The reflective field won't hurt you if you drop your shields as I have. I want no more secrets of Talent between us, Jeri."

She started to sob, the pain almost too much to bear with the shield's force being turned back onto her own mind. She knew about reflective field generators and had feared them perhaps more than any other weapon in the Wizards' arsenal. She'd learned to withstand the soft hum and reflection of her own power over time. It was just a matter of practice and control, but she hadn't used the skill in over two years and it was obvious to her now that she would pass out and be even more vulnerable should she refuse to lower her shields to this outworlder. Besides, he obviously knew her secret. The game was up, well and truly.

With a cry of fear and resignation, she lowered her shields and stared at him with rage. "Why are you doing this to me? All I ever wanted was to be left alone." She cried as she huddled in an almost fetal position. "I won't become a Wizard. I won't let you steal my power."

Strong hands surrounded her, pulling her against the trader's warmly muscled chest. He soothed her as she tried feebly to fight her way out of his embrace, but she quieted when he took no further aggressive action. The reflective field still hummed, trapping all their combined powers within its perimeter, effectively hiding them from any who might happen to scan in their direction. The reflective field was a way to unearth hidden Talent, but had been primarily designed as a way to train it and shield it from detection, which is what it was doing for both of them at the moment.

"I won't hurt you." His voice was soft in her ear as he slipped his hands up under hers, tugging her close to his chest as he lay them both down on her bedroll. "I will never harm you. Quiet now, for me, and we'll talk this through."

He turned her in his arms when she didn't resist, bringing her face into his chest as she cried silently. She was shaking in reaction and her head had to hurt like the dickens, he knew, but he had to make her reveal herself in whatever way he could. He didn't have much time left on this planet and when he left, he wanted her with him.

"Let me help you, sweetheart. I know you got a jolt from the field, and you must hurt. I'm sorry. Let me help you." He raised one hand to her forehead, touching lightly as he spoke, trying to calm her. Gathering his own Talent, he sent out a tendril of power, seeking to take the pain from the places that hurt inside her mind, having a good look around while he was there and her barriers were down. What he saw impressed him and tugged at his heart. This little horse tamer had been through a great deal in her young life and, if he had anything to say about it, she would be given the respect due her level of power from here on out.

As the pain lessened, Jeri's unease grew. She was held fast in the arms of a virtual stranger and was sharing the extent of her Talent with him. She fought back, knowing enough not to try to shield with the field still on, but her watery gaze met the outworlder's steadily.

"What have you done?" she whispered, jarred to her soul.

He bent and kissed her forehead, removing his hand with a final caress. "I did only what was needed. You cannot hide here forever. Others will find you, and they may not have your best interests at heart."

"And you expect me to believe that *you* do?" Her gaze spoke of her distrust.

Micah laughed. "Not yet, sweetheart. Not yet. But in time, you'll learn that I will always speak truth to you."

"You're leaving tomorrow," she reminded him.

He nodded. "And you're coming with me."

"Why should I?"

He stroked her hair and cuddled her against him as she sighed. "The horse trade has helped me amass a fortune with which I fund just a small part of the Resistance on non-Council worlds. I sit on the Mage Council of Geneth Mar. We're trying to put an end to forced recruitment of Talents on all worlds. Indeed, it's already against the law on Council worlds to interfere with the natural development of individual will." He stroked her hair gently. "I get the idea that you were not brought up on a Council world."

She was crying lightly again as he held her. "I was born on Mithrak."

Suddenly her cries about Wizards clicked into place for him. "I've heard of the Wizards of Mithrak. Believe me when I say you will never have to fear them or anyone like them again. At least not after you've completed your training."

"Training?"

"Yes, sweetheart." He placed a kiss on her temple. "I will take you as my apprentice." He kissed lower on her cheek, closer to her aching lips, drawing out the sensation as he strung his words out. "And I will take you as my mistress." He finally kissed her mouth as he had earlier that day, but deeper and sweeter than anything she had ever known.

His words registered through the fog of desire that was building so quickly she could barely breathe, but somehow she didn't want to argue at that moment. He'd awakened something within her that wanted to know the full extent of the pleasure he could bring.

She didn't resist as he laid her back against the furs, his hands roaming downward to caress her breasts and lower as he kissed her thoroughly. Her eyes closed on a sigh of sheer pleasure and he smiled inwardly, marveling at how responsive she was to his merest touch. It was rare among Talents that one should mesh so closely with another on short acquaintance, yet her energies fit like puzzle pieces into his own now that they were fully revealed. He wondered if their bodies could mirror the near perfect fit of their Talents as he kept her off balance with lingering kisses and long sweeps of his hands.

He undressed her slowly, savoring the first discovery of her lithe young body. She was muscled and sleek in a way the gently bred young ladies of his world seldom were. She was honed by her years spent mastering beasts much larger than her own small frame and living a relatively harsh life among the nomadic Hill Tribes. This was not the kind of posh life she should have had, but he didn't mind the sleek, hard muscles under her silky skin. He would have spared her the hardships if he could, but he was nearly salivating over her taut body and the thoughts of the way she would ride him, like one of her great beasts.

He'd spent a fair amount of time that afternoon watching her ass slide up and down in the saddle as they rode around, ostensibly looking at the herd. In reality he had been looking at her, fantasizing about her mounting him the way she mounted her large steed. He would give her the ride of her life and quite possibly, she would do the same for him.

It was time to find out the truth of those thoughts.

With a growl of need against the soft skin of her neck, he removed her top, flinging it across the small tent. Her hands dug into his hair, dragging his open mouth closer to her breasts.

And what breasts they were, he thought with some satisfaction. Firm and soft at the same time, they were larger than he'd imagined, full and round and pointy with desire. He cupped them in his hands, pinching her nipples and squeezing as he drew them closer to his waiting lips. She was whimpering, lost in sensation as he battered her with physical pleasure while at the same time one part of his mind stood back to watch the way her Talent responded to him and his physical assault.

The first joining of two Talents could be a dangerous thing. If they were incompatible the results could be explosive, so great care was taken. Most often the first joining was done under the guidance and supervision of a higher level Mage. Micah had witnessed many such joinings since he'd achieved Mage status.

But he had no other Mage here to oversee this joining, and he knew it had to be accomplished as soon as possible—both for his own sanity and as a way to convince this naïve young woman that her future lay with him and the Council rather than hiding in fear. He also had to admit, to himself at least, that this little horse tamer turned him on like no woman had in too many years to count. Her very walk made his mouth water and the little whimpers of pleasure she was favoring him with nearly drove him mad with desire.

Oh, it was no hardship to take this woman to his bed, no hardship at all. And she promised to bring him more pleasure than he'd felt in years, along with a powerful Talent that could be useful to the Council.

There was her safety to consider too, he thought as he sucked one of her tight nipples into his mouth. He gathered her breasts together so he could lick both at the same time, and she nearly rocketed off the bed. He soothed her with his hands and mouth, reaching up to swirl his hot tongue into the whorls of her ear, then swallowing the moan that came from her mouth, driving his tongue in hard and fast. He stroked her mouth with his tongue the way he would soon use his dick to stroke inside her pussy.

No, this beautiful treasure, this young Talent was too vulnerable here on a world where none of the natives had an inkling of power. She was in danger from any of the enemies of the Council who might stumble upon her, much as he had. She was lucky he'd found her first and given time, he would make her understand the truth of that statement.

He moved his hands lower, tackling the ties that held her britches in place, wanting inside her as soon as possible. From the way her power was rising along with her arousal, it was what she wanted too. He marveled again for a moment at the way their Talents meshed, growing stronger together in a way he'd never quite witnessed before. It was primal. It was almost feral. They fed off each other only to grow stronger. That was unique in his experience, but he wasn't questioning it. Not when he had her where he'd wanted her since almost the moment they'd met.

No, at this moment, he wanted to be inside her. He wanted to bathe in that glow and rush of power until it burned him and her both, driving their pleasure to a level he had never experienced.

He had her naked beneath him in moments. He knew he was rushing, unable to truly appreciate her fine form with the fierce drive of passion pushing him onward. He stripped himself with urgent need and took his place between her thighs. Her eyes were closed, but he wanted his new lover to see him and know he was the one bringing her such intimacy, such pleasure as he joined their bodies—much as their Talents were already joining.

"Jeri." He nipped her jaw. "Open your eyes, baby. Look at

me."

He pulled back to see her lids lift slowly, a dazed sort of caution in her eyes. "What's happening to me?"

He smiled down at her. "The same thing that's happening to me. You have awakened the beast within and it will claim you. Now."

He rubbed his straining cock against her soft folds, and she shivered.

"I-I've never been with a man." She nearly shouted as a sudden fear seemed to overtake her. "Please don't hurt me."

Micah stopped, letting his cock tease her opening but moving no further. He cursed inwardly and realized he should have guessed that his little refugee would be a virgin. She was far too innocent and had lived on the run, if his guess was correct.

He had to be more patient with her. Micah stroked her hair and soothed her with soft sounds. He could smell her arousal and the return of her shivers meant that she was responding to him not in fear but in continued arousal.

"I won't hurt you, sweetheart. I'm glad you told me it's your first time, but it must be done. You'll understand it all soon. For now, relax as best you can and let me in. I'll show you pleasure the likes of which you have never known. But, you have to let me in."

He pushed forward gently, settling just the tip of himself inside, then pulled out a bit, dragging her lubricating warmth with him, making her rife for further exploration. He repeated the process with just the very tip of his cock until she was more comfortable and his dick was wet from her arousal. He tested, then pushed a bit farther inside, nearly dying with pleasure as her tight, virgin channel bathed him and gripped him, clenching as she learned the feel of him and her body's abilities to respond. He groaned as she tightened her muscles.

"Good goddess," he whispered, coming over her to place a sliding kiss along her throat and up to her mouth. "Don't clench me so hard, baby. It's torture."

Her eyes grew worried. "You don't like it?"

He let out one harsh laugh and kissed her lips with a smack. "Like it? I love it. But it's too soon for you, sweet. This first time, just relax, but tell me if anything starts to hurt, all right?"

In truth, she wouldn't have to tell him for his own psi energies were so easily aligned with hers at this point, he could feel just about everything she did. She would have the same power over him, of course, once she learned a bit about how to read the psi waves and how to direct her thoughts. He shuddered with ecstasy at the idea of bedding her then, meshing fully mind-to-mind as well as body-to-body. It could be the ultimate high, if she would grant him that sort of access once she learned more about how to direct her Talent.

He would do everything in his power to keep her open and wanting him as he taught her about her Talent. Never in his life had he known such bliss inside a woman and he wasn't even fully seated yet. He would not give this up, and he would not let her deny them both this pleasure. He had to have her. Had to keep her. And he would do anything to make her his own. Forever.

Where that last thought came from, he didn't know, but it scared him a bit to be thinking in such permanent terms about a woman he'd just met. Still, he couldn't deny, it felt right to think of her at his side, in his bed, riding his cock, for all time.

He just had to get past this potentially dangerous first joining. He pushed forward a bit more, tensing himself when he felt her tense under him. She relaxed her grip on him a moment later, slowly acclimating to his entry. There was no real barrier. This girl had probably been riding horses all her life. Perhaps she was one of the lucky women whose barriers weren't too hard to breach. Or maybe she was so turned-on, she barely registered the pain as he pushed through, making her bleed just a bit, but bringing her pleasure that overshadowed the pain.

She was so open to him he knew without a doubt that this was the first time she had ever taken a man into her body. He felt a vicious sort of triumph at the thought that he was the first to take her. The first to show her the pleasure her body was capable of. The first to fuck her and teach her.

He knew it was a primitive thought, but he couldn't help himself. Among Talents, pleasure was shared and multiplied by their psi links. It wasn't uncommon to take multiple partners as a Talent grew, to master their energies, but this powerful little horse tamer was nowhere near in control of her power, nowhere near ready to try to mesh her Talents with others and he was glad of it. He would teach her and keep her tight pussy for himself while she learned. When she was ready, it would be he that watched over her joinings. The thought almost made him snarl, but if she wished to have another cock inside her, by the goddess, he would be there too, watching over her and joining the orgasmic frenzy.

He stroked her hair with a tenderness he hadn't felt in a long, long time. "I'm inside you, sweetheart. I'm part of you, and you are one with me." He rocked gently back and forth, moving inside her a tiny bit. "Feel me," he whispered as he stroked in and out, increasing the depth of his penetration, mimicking the action with his hot tongue in her mouth. She tasted of wonder and innocence and he drank her in on many levels. The physical rush was awesome in itself, but the rush of her power was even more phenomenal.

He realized obscurely that such vast flows of psi Talent coursing together could be dangerous, but he also felt the rightness of the joining. He felt her power flowing through him as his flowed through her in that timeless moment just before he pumped them both to completion, the psi current feeding the physical sensations of skin on skin, skin in skin and wet, hot need.

He didn't last long, but it didn't matter. She was with him and he knew it was best not to linger overlong during her first real experience with physical intimacy. He was bigger than an average man, and he didn't want her to be too sore when she came back to herself after the pleasure faded.

"Now, sweetheart. Come for me now," he called to her, and she responded with a screaming climax that made him smile even as he felt the first jets of his own pulsing orgasm.

He pumped inside her, filling her and claiming her. He didn't give a thought to tomorrow as he felt his psi Talent well up and join with hers in the most remarkable way. He knew in that moment that he wanted it again and again, as often as he could get it. She was an addiction—instantly forming and lasting lifelong. The twisting, twining energies bathed his senses, surrounding them both and making them stronger. He realized the overwhelming power posed no threat to them, but elevated them both.

He'd heard the legends of course, but he'd never seen a joining that seemed as full and complete as the one he'd shared with his little horse tamer. As he came down from the ultimate high of ecstasy, he kissed her cheeks and stroked her hair. He felt the tears that leaked out of her eyes and he kissed them away, soothing her with soft sounds as the aftershocks continued around them, the light of their power bathing them both in comfort, strength and joy.

Slowly, so slowly, ecstasy receded, leaving them as man and woman, joined in the most elemental way, the eddies of their power retreating, but still floating in their awareness. His drew back to look at her face, watching the wariness return to her beautiful eyes.

"You are mine now, Jeri," he said with some satisfaction, though he didn't like the fear that crept into her gaze. "I vow to you here and now that I will never hurt you either psychically or emotionally. I may smack your ass from time to time, but only if you deserve it. And I promise you'll like it." His expression spoke of lecherous delights that she could only imagine at this point, but he was gratified to see a spark of arousal enter her gaze.

He pulled out slowly, applying gentle pressure as her body sought to hold him within. She cried out and he stopped, looking at her.

"You have to let me go for now, sweetheart. I'll join with you again as soon as we can. You're undoubtedly going to be tender since this was new for you. Let me heal your aches so that when we get to my ship, we can join again without soreness." He swooped to lick her lips, then placed a lingering kiss on them. "What do you say to that, my Jeri?"

She made a humming sound, trying to focus on relaxing her muscles as he withdrew from her body. Already she was missing his hot strength within her, but she was comforted by the cushion of his warm, welcoming psi energy that surrounded her and seemed to permeate her being. She was aware of her Talent as she'd never been.

She hadn't allowed herself to drop her shields since the Wizards had killed her family all those years ago. It had been so long since she'd examined her power, it was strange to see how it had changed and grown over the years. And she saw the definite changes her joining with this outworlder had wrought. It was beautiful really, the swirling patterns meshing together in her soul that showed her how his power had meshed with hers as they climbed to the stars together. Even now, a bit of him remained joined with her as she remained with him.

She would ask him about that later. She was so new to the idea of learning about and harnessing her Talent that she was beginning to relish the idea of mastering her own power and being able to call it at will. It would be a welcome change from always running and hiding and shielding so tight that her head and heart ached with the need to break free for just a minute.

She'd learned from bitter experience that a single moment of freedom could spell her doom, as well as the others she held dear. But this outworlder had told her that it could be different. She had joined with him and suddenly she knew things about him that he hadn't told her. She knew things about his world and the truth of his words about the Council and the things he could teach her.

Suddenly, she wanted to learn from him. She realized that he had joined with her to convince her of just such a thing. She was saddened by the idea that he would use sex as a simple matter of expedience, but his ploy had worked better than even he realized and she drew some satisfaction from the knowledge that he had been totally unprepared for the way they were together.

She smiled a little as she allowed him to move her under the furs of her bedroll, spreading them wide enough to accommodate them both. She watched idly as he rifled through the little pile of stuff he had transported from his ship and came up with a soft box she recognized as a standard shipboard first aid kit.

He rolled the furs back to make a soft cushion that would fit them both, then put a thin thermal blanket from his ship off to the side within easy reach as he settled between her thighs and spread her wide.

"You bled here a bit, love. I'm sorry."

She was embarrassed by the words and heated by the small kiss he placed on her belly, as if in apology as he wiped her with a soothing cloth from the medical kit.

"Your nether lips are red and swollen," he said with seeming satisfaction. "You'll get used to me in time though, and be able to take more than the gentle joining we just shared." He moved his gaze from its intent study of her folds upward to meet her eyes, and grinned in a purely male way. "I look forward to it."

He refocused on her pussy as he lifted her with one hand under her butt cheeks, opening her more to his gaze. He reached again into the kit with his free hand and came up with a tube of clear gel. Uncapping it, he inserted the applicator up into her without so much as a by-your-leave, making her squirm and start in surprise.

"Not to worry," he said softly, caressing her clit with his knuckles as he positioned the tube within her. "This will take away the sting and help knit the tissues. It'll feel good, I promise."

So saying, he pressed down on the applicator and she was flooded with the cool gel that seemed to rocket straight to her womb as her senses ignited. He smiled in satisfaction as he rubbed harder on her clit, bringing her to a quick, hard climax. He patted her curls, removing the applicator and discarding it, before putting away his kit. He then settled beside her on her furs, dragging the thin thermal blanket over them and wrapping them in warmth as he pulled her into his arms.

"Sleep now, sweetheart. We have a big day tomorrow, and I'll want to taste you at least once more before dawn."

His words set a fire in her, but his arms snuggled her close, one hand cupping her breast, the other pillowing her head close to his heart. It was amazing that she felt so safe, so secure in his arms. She hadn't slept with another being in the same bed since her big sister had been taken when she was just a little girl. She wasn't sure she could sleep with someone in her bed, but after a few moments of basking in his warmth, she was unable to fight the lethargy she felt after the pleasurable releases he had given her.

# Chapter Three

Jeri woke to incredible warmth all around her and a hot, wet mouth sucking at her breast. She gasped, remembering the outworlder who had taken her to bed the night before and all that had transpired.

"Good morn, *dama*." Micah smiled at her in the dim, predawn light. "Would you share your pleasure with me before we have to leave?"

She was a little taken aback that he was asking formally after all that had gone before but she nodded, unable to deny the heat that was even now welling in her, waiting for the release she knew he could give her.

He went back to licking her breast, moving slowly upward, placing wet, nibbling kisses over her chest and throat before he worked his way to her ear, then her lips, tasting her at every turn. He stroked her sensitive nipples, plucking them with skilled fingers. She felt her temperature rise even as he threw the thin thermal blanket off them and rose up, touching her body with knowing hands.

"I have a fantasy I would like to share with you," he whispered as he moved back, staring with obvious enjoyment down the length of her nude body.

"What kind of fantasy?" she asked, barely able to string more than two words together as his hands raised all kinds of gooseflesh over her sensitized skin.

He grinned. "Something easy for you. Something I'm certain you will like and something that will drive me wild."

"What?" she breathed out as he cupped her pussy, much recovered from the initial soreness she'd felt the night before.

He leaned down to nip her nipple, moving back until the tight bud popped out of his mouth, gleaming wetly in the uncertain morning light.

"I'd give anything for you to ride me."

Smiling, she realized this was something she could do, if she didn't die of embarrassment first. She blushed as the thought of riding his muscled body excited her. She had to fight the urge to hide her eyes as she nodded and his whole expression lit up.

"I think I can do that, if you'll show me how."

He reversed their positions, eagerly lying flat on the bed of fur, positioning her legs to straddle him.

"There's one more thing, sweetheart." He reached out to the small pile of things he'd transported from his ship and grasped a red velvet pouch, opening the strings with near reverence. He let the contents spill into his hands as he sat up, positioning her on his thighs, her breasts full and round in front of his face.

The delicate gold chain that spilled into his hands surprised her. It was quite obviously old and finely wrought. It also glimmered with precious gems embedded in the intricate design. It was like no necklace she had ever seen, though she had seen little fine jewelry close up.

"What is it?" she asked, almost breathless now as she watched him move. His gaze narrowed on her breasts.

He leaned forward and licked, sucking one of her nipples to a sharp point. Moving slowly, he put one end of the chain over her distended bud, tightening a special loop as she watched.

"The chain is a token of affection and commitment among my people. It also heightens pleasure."

She felt the added stimulus already, even as he leaned forward to tighten her other nipple with his mouth before sliding the other end of the chain over and securing it tight enough to make her groan in pleasure.

"Will you wear my chain, sweet Jeri? I would have my people know you are mine when we get to the ship. This will tell them without need for words."

"If it pleases you, my lord." She didn't even have to think about it—not that she *could* think with the little zings of pleasure shooting from her nipples through her entire body.

Her words were subdued as she thought of the implications of her agreement. She had just agreed to more of this pleasure, true, but also to some degree of commitment between them. And what really did she know of this man except what she'd glimpsed in the wash of his power the night before?

He leaned forward to kiss her lips. "Call me Micah, sweetheart. I want to hear my name on your lips when you come."

"Yes, Micah."

She spoke softly as he lay back, his fingers playing with the nipple chain, sending a shiver through her as he moved his hand down her body to pull her forward, closer to his straining cock. But he didn't rush. He let his skilled fingers tangle in her soft curls, moving to the folds of her pussy to massage the tight nubbin of her clit. He swept into the dewy moisture that increased as he prepared her to take him inside.

"You are so wet for me," he whispered, pushing his fingers in while meeting her gaze. She blushed, and the color flooded her cheeks and down her chest to her upright nipples. "So warm and ready. Do you want to please me, sweetheart?"

She was trembling, her body swaying to the rhythm of his fingers. She thought she would go mad if he didn't move faster.

"Yes," she cried, a small explosion hitting her as he rubbed her clit.

He smiled. "Good, hot pussy. *My* pussy. Right, Jeri? You wear my chain and now you'll ride my cock."

She nearly screamed as he replaced his wide fingers with his incredibly hard cock. He moved both hands to her hips, but she needed little encouragement to ride him the way he wanted. Truth be known, it excited her no end to be able to control their joining in this way, even though her body was well out of her own control, screaming toward the ecstasy she knew waited for them.

She moved her hips faster, taking him deep then shallow, deep then shallow, her eyes held captive by his hot gaze as he watched her. His hands moved over her straining body, pausing to stroke her tight nipples or tug on the chain, making her gasp, then stroking down to urge her hips faster.

She rode him at a gallop, as fast as her pounding heart, until her body screamed for release.

"Please! Micah!" She didn't know what she asked for, but he seemed to understand. His hand began a fast, teasing rhythm on her clit and she exploded even harder than she had the night before.

He wasn't far behind, pumping his hips off the ground in his urgency as he pulsed deep into her hot sheath. He groaned as he came, sliding his hands around her shoulders and dragging her down for a lingering kiss as he began to come down from the heights, his cock still buried within her.

They were basking in the afterglow when she spoke into the dim light of dawn.

"Why do you want me to wear your chain? Is your crew so dangerous that you must mark me for my own protection?" Her tone was only half-joking.

He scratched the stubble on his chin as he considered how to answer her.

"My crew are like my family, sweetheart. They would never harm you. But the chain will tell them that you are under my personal protection." He stroked the slope of her breast with one hand, teasing the sensitive tip where the chain was attached, warming her. "Our culture is free and easy with our pleasure and my crew may not realize that you have lived quite differently. This little symbol of my protection will let them know that no sexual invitations are to be issued or accepted without my approval. You've a strong Talent, sweetheart he paused to kiss her temple, "—one that could cause harm to you or others if your first joinings are not carefully monitored. It is one of my duties to witness first joinings among those with Talent and if you desire to join with any of my crew, I will bear witness to be certain that all parties remain unharmed by the act."

"Will you also participate?" she asked, somewhat scandalized, but also titillated, he could tell from the little squirming movements of her body.

He tweaked her nose and nodded, grinning widely. "It's a hard duty, but one I must perform, I fear." She pushed at his arm playfully, but he relented from teasing her. "Yes, Jeri, I have witnessed and joined in many such first joinings since earning Mage rank. None of my crew are above Dominar rank, so they must be monitored when first joining with other Talented partners. Your Talent is so raw and so powerful it is excitingly unpredictable. I should be with you should you desire to experiment sexually with anyone else until you are better trained. I will also admit he seemed hesitant to proceed, but resigned, "—that I feel something with you that I've never felt before. I would rather keep you for myself than share you with anyone, even the trusted members of my crew. If you will have me, the chain I gave you can also symbolize our commitment to each other for as long as our time together lasts."

She seemed to consider his words carefully. "I'd like that, Micah. Right now I can't imagine ever wanting another man to do to me what you've done."

He groaned at her stark admission. "You haven't met my cousin Darak yet, the lady killer. Promise me you won't let him charm you into his bed. At least not right away. You're way too good for the likes of him."

His wrist comp chirped softly, and he glanced down with a rueful smile. "Speak of the devil." He touched a button and spoke into the device. "What do you want, Dar?"

"Is everything all right? I noticed you have a reflective field set up. I'm unable to read you."

"We're okay, Dar."

"We?" The disembodied voice sounded curious. "Who's we?"

Micah chuckled low. "We is me and my—," he stroked her cheek with affection, "—companion." His gaze told her the word meant so much more. "Expect me in about four standards with a passenger."

"We're taking one of the locals for a ride?" Darak was clearly curious now.

"You could say that, but she's not a local. She's joining our crew."

"A woman then." The voice on the other end of the

communicator grew suspicious. "Are you sure about this, Micah?"

"Sure as I've ever been about anything," he agreed. "Look, I'm taking the field down shortly. You'll see why. Now is there anything else to report?"

The crispness of his tone must have gotten to the other man. "Nothing to report, Captain. We'll await your return."

"Good then. Planetside out." He touched a button on the comp and the communication was cut off. He looked at her and smiled. "The speculation is already starting on my ship. You've accepted my chain, but will you keep it? Will you keep me? At least for a while?"

Smiling, she nodded and leaned upward to kiss his mouth. "I'd be honored." She wanted to say more, but the whole situation was too new and too insecure. She had no idea if she was doing the right thing in trusting him, but she had to follow her instincts and her heart. They had never led her wrong before. She would follow now, and see where this strange, powerful, sexy man led.

They dressed in the dawn light, working companionably together as she set aside the few personal possessions she wanted to take with her when she left. Her clothing wasn't designed to accommodate the nipple chain, he saw as she struggled to find some way to do up her lacings while keeping it on. He smiled to himself as he watched, realizing with satisfaction that she really wanted to keep it on—to keep the mark of his possession about her. It touched a deep, possessive chord in his soul that he hadn't known existed before meeting her.

He took pity on her attempts to dress though, and went to her, pulling the edges of her top apart to stare for a moment at the lovely sight of her hard nipples, pinched by his chain. He smoothed his hands over them, weighing her heavy breasts in his palms for a moment before bending his head to suck each hardened tip in turn, relishing her gasps of building excitement.

He stood back to look, pleased with the sight, but knowing he had to be a bit more practical for both their sakes.

"You have no idea how it pleases me to see you wear my chain, but you don't have to wear it so at all times." Gently lowering the tension on first one, then the other breast, he pulled the loops clear and took the glittering chain in his hands. He was inflamed by the look of dismay that crossed her face before she hid her feelings. "Not to worry, sweetheart. I would not abuse your tender buds so, nor would I want to cause you any discomfort. But I would still see my chain on your person."

"How?" He knew she had examined the chain in some detail as she struggled with her clothing, but she had evidently failed to find the hidden mechanism that would allow her to wear it always. He moved forward to show her the catch hidden in one of the links, pleased by her look of wonder.

"I would like to see this around the lovely column of your throat, sweetheart. The loops will dangle down, either between your shoulders or between your breasts. Either will signal to all who see this particular piece of adornment that you are claimed and chained. To me." He couldn't resist placing a kiss on her full lips as he thought how his chain would look about her throat. "Would you like that?"

She nodded, dazed by his kiss in a way that heated his blood, but they had work to do and many tasks to accomplish before he could seal them both in his cabin aboard the *Circe*. He put the chain about her neck, smiling as she pulled her hair up and out of the way. Tenderly, he closed the hidden clasp into one of the links, forcing it tightly, but not uncomfortably, against the satin skin of her neck. He took a moment to arrange the dangling loops over her breasts, then helped her arrange her top, lacing it up over her nipples and rearranging the chain so that it showed clearly.

He felt like his heart might burst out his chest, she was so sweet. He didn't examine the tender feelings too closely, just accepting them for later perusal. All that mattered was that she was wearing his chain, practically shouting her submission to him and his claim on her luscious body.

He was prouder than he'd ever felt, thinking about what his crew would make of her. She would stun them with her beauty and her amazing level of pure, raw Talent. But it was her wounded heart that had called to him in the moments of sharing the night before, and he felt an answering need within his own soul to heal her and bring light to the dark places in her soul.

Thinking again of his crew, he moved to disengage the reflective field, not giving her any warning. He had a suspicion she'd feel it the moment it was shut off, though any Talent below Dominar level would probably not be able to tell. True, she had not been tested and ranked yet, but he felt sure that she was at least Dominar level or above, though she lacked any training whatsoever and would have to be brought up to the mark before accepting any sort of official rank.

Still, he was gratified to hear her gasp as the field went down, then the sudden surge that told him she'd put up her incredibly tight shields.

"What did you do?" she turned on him, her face ashen.

He stood from putting his belongings together into a pile, then stepped back and used his wristcomp to transport them away with a little wink of light.

"I merely turned off the field." His eyes were mischievous,

but she looked really upset.

"Without warning me first?"

He moved toward her, apologetic now, though he was certain Darak had caught that amazing surge on his scanners right before she'd shielded so efficiently.

"I'm sorry, sweetheart. I knew you would feel it, so I didn't think it an issue."

He didn't tell her he wanted Darak to see what he'd found. He didn't tell her that he needed that reading to help him begin to classify her incredible level of power. He didn't tell her that he wanted his Executive Officer to know the kind of woman that was wearing his chain. *His!*

No, he didn't tell her any of that. He wanted her calm, and he also wanted her to realize that she could no longer stay on this psi-dead world. He'd effectively outed her, and she knew it. Further, he knew she knew and vice versa.

She didn't speak of it, but it was in her eyes. The short anger, replaced by resignation and then followed by the light of adventure he had hoped rested deep in her soul. When he saw that, he knew he had her. And by the goddess, he would keep her. As long as he possibly could.

Darak jumped out of his chair when the field went down. The rush on his sensors was almost off the charts for a brief moment before it suddenly winked out as if it had never been.

Someone was shielding *null* down there. Impossible! But it wasn't his cousin Micah. No, Darak could see the telltales he knew well of Micah's nearly flawless shielding, but still there was some indication of his presence. But this other entity—which had definitely not been Micah, though it was of a power level close if not above his powerful cousin's—showed no telltales whatsoever.

Amazing.

And they were taking this hidden Talent on as crew?

Darak had gotten the distinct impression from his cousin's words that his companion was of the female variety and he had probably bedded her already, hence the mellow tones of his usually stressed-out voice. Darak was glad Micah had found some female companionship to ease his tension, but he shuddered to think of what that first joining had been like with a woman so powerful as to nearly fry his scanners. Darak had always known Micah was brave, and perhaps a little crazy, but this went far and above the chances he'd taken before.

At least Darak knew that Micah and his companion had lived through the experience, and they were on their way back to the ship. This was one homecoming Darak had to see in person. He couldn't wait see the woman who could interest the jaded Mage Master who had made his crew's lives hell for the past months while he wallowed in loneliness. She was sure to be quite something, indeed.

When they left the tent, the tribal Mother was waiting for them. The small satchel of Jeri's few possessions did not go unnoticed as the Mother's eyes grew concerned, but ever gentle.

"So you will leave us, little horse tamer?" the Mother's voice appealed to her softer feelings, but Jeri needed to stay strong to say goodbye properly to these people who had been so good to her.

"I must, Mother. I'm sorry to leave you on such short notice."

"But why with this outworlder? What hold has he over you?" The Mother's eyes went to the jeweled choker, noting its placement though she probably did not know its significance in his culture.

"Mother," Jeri stepped forward hesitantly. "I am not what I seem. I've been hiding here among you and for that, I am sorry."

The tribal Mother looked on her kindly, but still a little worried. "I'm glad we could be there to comfort you in your time of need, child, but why would your differences cause you to leave us? Is he forcing you?"

Jeri smiled gently. "No. But there are those who would force me and my mere presence could bring death to your people. I cannot put you in danger like that. I've been selfish, thinking I would never be found out."

"But this outworlder has discovered your secret?" the Mother eyed him, then turned back to Jeri. "What is this secret that haunts you so?"

Jeri seemed to make a decision and turned to Micah. "What part of the sale herd did you agree on last night?" she asked quickly.

Micah's eyes narrowed with a suspicious smile as he guessed what she intended to do. "I can show you in my mind which ones," he said softly.

She nodded. "Do so."

He sent her a quick mental burst that showed her the choices he'd made and she in turn sent out her silent call to the horses who had moved closer to the camp. The Mother looked on with some confusion, but waited to see what would happen.

Jeri took the older woman's hand and led her to the outskirts of camp. "They come, Mother. This is my gift. And my burden."

"Who?" the Mother began to ask, when suddenly half the sale herd came over the small hill and galloped toward them.

Jeri started to laugh and cry at the same time, and Micah couldn't resist placing his arm around her.

"What is it?" he asked as gently as he could.

Her tear-streaked eyes smiled up at him. "They all came," she said breathlessly. "Every last one of the horses from miles around. They came to say goodbye."

And indeed, Micah could see a literal sea of horseflesh, drawing near to the small woman.

With a quick thought, Jeri directed the portion of the sale herd that would go with Micah to one side while she walked forward to go among the horses that had gathered. There were hundreds and hundreds, from the smallest foal to the oldest swayback. And she touched each one, sparing a pat for each velvety nose and a stroke for each strong neck as she walked among them.

Micah noted others from the camp coming to see what was going on and saw the slack-jawed amazement on their faces. His little horse tamer was a miracle to them, just as she was to him, and he was proud to see when they finally realized it.

"What is she?" the Mother asked him with some awe in her voice as she watched stallion beside stallion, causing no problems with each other—going against their nature to say goodbye to one small human woman. It was something she had never seen before and would probably never see again in her lifetime.

Micah smiled proudly. "She is a Talent the likes of which the galaxy has seldom seen."

"Talent?" the Mother asked with some dismay. "We have no psi powers here, but I've heard of such. Is that why she is hunted?"

Micah nodded with a sigh. "There are those who would seek to imprison her soul and steal her power."

"And you will not?" She eyed him suspiciously, but he was glad this strong leader would stand up for his woman.

He placed one palm across his heart. "I vow not, Mother. She is a rare and special woman, and I will protect her with my life."

The Mother grunted and turned back to watch the spectacle. "She was a good horse tamer, but I see now she was cheating a bit."

Micah laughed. "No, I assure you not. She comes by her work honestly. Her father was a horse tamer on Mithrak. The whole family raised horses, and she was set to follow in the family business before her parents were killed and her older sister captured. She lived wild among the horses for a long time, evading capture herself before finding a way off that planet and to yours."

"She told you all this? She has never spoken one word about her family to any of my people."

Micah shook his head. "No, I saw most of it in her memories. I just wanted you to know. She is a born horse tamer, though her methods are not like those of your people. She speaks to your horses, and they love her for it."

The Mother thought of that as she watched the small woman walk among the enormous steeds, touching each as if bestowing a blessing. And the horses seemed to truly enjoy her attention. They loved her. It was plain to see.

"She often called the horses her friends," the Mother remembered fondly.

Micah nodded. "And so they are. Her first and truest friends. They hid her from the men who would have imprisoned her. They protected her, and she protects them."

The Mother watched in awe, as did most of the tribe. Even young Sheli watched with fascination and not a little bit of respect.

The horses of Pantur made her cry. They gave her a send-off as she walked among them, taking time to speak with each of them in turn. They didn't speak in words as humans did, but in thought pictures and emotions and basic needs. She had always understood them and they her as she grew up among the small breeding herd her father had raised on Mithrak.

The horses of her father's herd had protected her out of love, helping hide her among them when the Wizards came seeking her. They had protected her and loved her, and said a quiet goodbye when she'd found a way to stowaway among them as they were sold and moved offworld after her father's death.

She had missed her friends when they'd gone to another tribe, farther south on Pantur, but she'd made friends among the Hill Tribes' horses and they warmed her heart as she took her leave of them. She thanked them silently for being there for her and for their silent, strong, loving support.

It took a bit of time, but she had to touch each of the hundreds that came to say goodbye. To do less would not be honorable and horses were a breed of honor, she had learned as a young child.

When she was done, the herds moved as one, trumpeting their voices together in one final goodbye before they started back for the fields and paddocks they had left. Jeri watched them go with love radiating from her heart until the last had left her sight.

She felt a warm presence at her shoulder and didn't have to look to know it was the Tribal Mother. The woman had a strong presence, and her warmth was unmistakable.

"I have never thought to see the like, horsemistress."

Jeri gasped at the title, one of immense respect given her by the tribal Mother. She was shocked into looking at the woman who stood just a bit taller than she, but the older woman was focused on the sale herd, waiting patiently where Jeri had directed with nothing but a thought.

"Go with the trader and find your destiny. But know that you will ever be welcome here among the Hill Tribes."

The tears started again, though she tried to suppress them. "Thank you, Mother," she said softly, watching the horses as the woman left her. It was all she could manage.

The rest of the tribe obeyed the Mother's command to give her space, but a few of her friends did come up, one by one to say goodbye as Micah coordinated transport of one horse at a time into the hold of his ship. Jeri stood near to calm the horses as they left Pantur for the orbiting ship, telling them without words that she would be with them again soon.

She had a few friends among the tribes and those few she would miss, but she had formed no special attachments. She'd learned not to extend her heart easily after her family had been ripped from her. Only with the horses was she free to love. And love them she did in the simple, uncomplicated way that they returned her affection.

But now there was the outworlder. Lord Micah touched something inside her that was fragile and easily hurt, but she had no control over it. She would prefer to keep her feelings under tighter rein, but she would think of that later. For now, she had an adventure to start and a new life among the stars to embrace.

With one last long look at Pantur, she gave Micah a nod and he touched the control on his wristcomp that transported her to the orbiting ship. In a flash of light she was suddenly with her horses again, inside a relatively dark hold.

She had barely a moment to gather her bearings when

Micah materialized beside her. Only then did she see the startlingly blue woman and tall, muscular man who watched her with suspicious eyes.

Micah stepped forward. "Loadmaster. Status?"

The blue-skinned woman stepped forward with a datapad and handed it to him. "The herd is loaded and settled. Amazingly fast, as a matter of fact. What did you do to them?" Her tilted smile and flashing eyes swept between the Captain and Jeri, making her suddenly feel a bit uncomfortable.

"Ah, that is the gift of our guest. She has a way with the beasts." He swept one palm down to the base of her spine and pushed her forward to meet his friends. "Jeri, this is Trini Chertuse. She is loadmaster on the *Circe*."

The two women greeted each other with smiles. Trini's was wide and welcoming and while it made Jeri feel a bit better, she was still quite shy at meeting these people.

"And this," Micah gestured toward the large man leaning against a bulkhead, "is my cousin, Darak. He's also my Executive Officer or XO for short." The man straightened and moved close to her. "Darak, this is Jeri."

"Chained already, cousin?" Darak's gaze went from the telling glitter at her neck to Micah's face. "You work fast."

Jeri couldn't tell if it was envy or anger in his tone, but suddenly this huge man frightened her a bit.

"It's a pleasure to meet you, my lady," he said with an almost courtly flourish as he took her hand and kissed it with more warmth than she was comfortable with. She tugged on her hand and his eyes widened with seeming surprise as she moved away from him. Apparently the handsome brute was unused to women resisting his dubious charm.

# Chapter Four

"Back off, Dar," Micah said with a warning growl when his cousin would have pursued the shy woman.

Darak's eyes widened with something close to shock. This was not the same melancholy man who had gone to the planet with such resignation only days before. This was not the man who had moped around even after achieving Mage Master status—something every Talent envied and admired about him. No, this was a territorial man who was a stranger to Darak. He'd never seen his cousin behave like this over a woman.

Darak held his hands up, palm outward. "No offense intended, Mage Master. I am merely surprised and...intrigued."

"Well, save your intrigue for some other time, Dar." He handed the datapad to the loadmaster who watched their interaction with some interest. "Since everything's settled, I'm going to show Jeri around the ship. Meet me on the bridge in one standard."

"Aye, aye, Captain." The sarcasm in Darak's voice wasn't lost on his cousin. They'd grown up together and had shared many women between them. Never had Darak seen Micah act this way.

If Micah weren't a Mage Master he'd think the female had some kind of nefarious power over him, but he knew with certainty that there were few beings in the galaxy that could best his cousin. Still, he would watch developments carefully to guard his beloved cousin's interests and safety.

Micah and Jeri passed into the companionway, leaving the hold and the two crewmen behind. As they stepped into the service lift that would take them to the crew deck, Micah smiled at her.

"Don't mind Darak. He can be an ass at times, but he's a good man. Just don't ever tell him I said that."

Jeri chuckled at his teasing tone and marveled at the ship. She had only been in one other ship in her life, but she had never seen more than the hold of the tramp freighter that had taken her from Mithrak to Pantur with her father's herd. She'd hidden among the horses and they'd protected her from the few crewmen who had stopped by once in a while to make sure the automatic care systems were giving the stock enough water and feed and that the waste removal systems were working properly.

Already she had noticed the hold of this starship was better appointed than the one she'd seen before. And the corridor they traversed after exiting the lift was brightly lit, clean and painted in a charming shade of light periwinkle blue.

As they neared the living areas for the crew, the colors became brighter and the furnishings more cushy. This was no tramp freighter. They passed a rec room with all kinds of exercise machines, presumably used to help keep the crew from losing too much muscle mass while cooped up in the ship for weeks or months on end. There was also a variety of gaming tables for amusement, as well as a large entertainment unit with a big rack of vid discs secured neatly beside it. Next to that was a food dispenser, and the whole area was upholstered in luscious-looking fabrics that probably cost more credits than she could imagine.

He led her past a few hatchways that had the names of the crewmembers on them, but didn't spare any time to really explain. She realized those were probably private quarters and she presumed he would not invade their privacy. If she wanted to see how they lived, she would have to be invited inside by the resident of those compartments, which was not something she wanted to contemplate just yet.

As they neared what appeared to be the end of the corridor, he stopped at one of the side hatches and opened it.

"We'll get the lock keyed to your palmprint as soon as possible," he said absently, indicating how the lock released when he pressed his hand to the surface of the door.

She walked in when he gestured her forward and was amazed by the view out the long viewport across the room. He noted the direction of her gaze and smiled.

"That's Pantur," he said easily, moving them to the viewport. "Darak will have us breaking orbit any moment, I think. Do you feel the drives rumbling up to full power?"

She realized then that she did feel a low vibration in the soles of her feet that was growing steadily as she thought about it.

"It's beautiful," she said as she nodded toward the hazy green of the planet below.

Micah seemed to share her fascination. "It really is," he said quietly, putting his arm companionably around her shoulders. "I never get tired of watching the planets and the stars. You're going to enjoy your time on the *Circe.*"

She took a moment to look around at the rest of the large room. The door slid shut behind them, enclosing them in the rich interior of what had to be a private bedroom. The furnishings were a deep velvety blue that mirrored the richness of space and gave a decidedly masculine feel to the room.

"These are your quarters?" she asked faintly, wondering what she should have expected.

Micah nodded, turning her to face him as he heard the uncertainty in her voice.

"I would prefer you to sleep here with me while you're aboard, my sweet. But if you have an objection, speak it now."

She thought for a moment, then nodded, turning back to the scene unfolding as they pulled away from the planet that had been her adopted home for the last two standard years.

"I'll stay with you, Captain, if that is your wish."

"It is my wish. And my pleasure to have your companionship on our voyage."


"Where are we going?" she finally thought to ask. Only at that moment did she realize how truly naïve she must appear to not have thought of such an important thing before.

"Liata first," he said with a small smile, pulling her close. "Your horses will bring a tidy profit. They are going to a lovely home on an agricultural world where they will be truly appreciated."

She smiled up at him. "They'll like that. May I look up information on your comp systems so I can tell them about it? Some of them have been wondering if there would be grass or woodlands, that sort of thing, where they're going to live."

He gave her a look of wonder. "I've never thought of horses in that way. Until I met you. You are a miracle, Jeri. Do you know that?"

He bent to kiss her and she believed him for that moment, surprising herself with the idea that she really might have something special that a great man like this could admire about her. He released her only so she could watch Pantur grow smaller and smaller against the starscape.

"You're welcome to use the comp, but you can also ask Trini all about Liata. It's her homeworld. I know she is looking forward to seeing her family."

"She's blue," Jeri observed rather simply as he held her against him, watching the stars. "I've never met anyone who was not some shade of cream or brown before. Is everyone on Liata blue-skinned?"

Micah chuckled and squeezed her closer. "Yes, varying shades of blue, but every last one of them is blue. Something to do with their sun, I think. Wait 'til you see the colors of their clothing. They seem to enjoy bright hues that almost hurt the eyes."

"I like blue," she said, indicating the mostly blue furnishings of his compartment.

"I'm glad." His smile warmed her insides as he pulled her toward the console that controlled most of the room's functions. "Let me show you around. There's the bathing and reclamation chamber," he pointed to a small cubicle next to the door. The cubicle next to that was a wardrobe that contained his clothing. She was shocked to realize that he had more clothes in this small wardrobe than she had owned in her entire life.

"You can move my stuff over to make space for your things. I'm not picky." His offhanded acceptance of her presence in his personal space would take some getting used to. She'd always been solitary since her family's murder and it would be hard for her to adjust, but beggars couldn't be choosy, or so she had always thought.

"I have little to disturb your peace," she said softly, her gaze downcast in embarrassment.

But his hand cupped her chin, bringing her flushed cheeks and sad eyes up for his inspection. "You disturb me in many ways, Jeri. All of them good." He kissed her sweetly, doing away with her embarrassment and easily turning her mind to other things. "I know you didn't take much with you. I'll do my best to remedy that, I assure you."

Pride made her chin rise further. "I don't want charity, Micah. I'll make do with what I have and earn what I need."

Micah pushed a button on the console and the bed emerged from the wall, folding down and out, taking up much of the space in the cabin. He plopped down to sit on the edge, regarding her with almost tired eyes.

"I understand your desire to make your own way, Jeri. I even admire you for it. And I'll make this deal with you—you may participate as a member of my crew in whatever way you feel you can contribute. For that you'll earn a wage, like the rest of my crewmembers. It's yours to do with as you wish." He sighed as he leaned back, his eyes serious. "But I'm a wealthy man. I enjoy giving gifts to my friends and companions. Ask anyone on board. They'll tell you the truth of it. If you share my bed—hells, even if you don't—I will no doubt want to give you things. But I never want you to feel as if you must repay me for anything I may give you. I've never had to pay for sex, and I won't start now." His voice grew harsh as he spelled out his thoughts in unequivocal language. "If you stay here in my cabin, you stay of your own will and not out of some kind of perverse sense of obligation."

She realized that she'd somehow insulted him and she wanted to make amends, but at the same time she was relieved to understand more about how he wanted to proceed. It was obvious to her that their relationship, or whatever it was they had, was very uneven. She was a refugee with few possessions and even fewer credits while he was a powerful starship captain with comparatively great wealth. If she'd known this about him before she left Pantur, she wasn't entirely certain she would have been brave enough to do so.

She sat gently on the edge of the bed beside him, meeting his gaze with great seriousness. "Since you have set my mind at ease," she began hesitantly, "let me do the same for you." She folded her hands in her lap demurely to stop their trembling, but he probably saw it. "I have never whored myself, and I never will. Not even for you." Her blunt words surprised him she was glad to see. "I am not always comfortable accepting gifts. I have more than my share of pride and I do not want to be a kept woman. I want to contribute, though I will readily admit I have few skills that might be of use to you. I've only been on one starship before in my life and that time I was a stowaway."

He laughed softly as he took her hands in his. "That is a tale I would like to hear. For now, sweetheart, I am just glad to have the air clear between us. I'll try to comply with your wishes, but I will give you things when it pleases me." He trailed his fingers over the jeweled collar on her throat, tracing it down between her breasts. "Resign yourself to it."

Her body shivered as he used one finger to trace gently along the gossamer strand of sparkling stones set about her neck. He followed the tails of the necklace downward, between her breasts and her gaze shot up to his.

"Do you want this, Jeri? Do you want me?" His deep voice sent shock waves through her system. She nodded mutely as he began to undo the lacings of her shirt. "Be very certain," he said, stopping suddenly, with the loose laces held tightly in both hands. "I want you with me." His eyes held something in their depths she had never encountered before. "I want you to be mine. For now. And perhaps for a long time to come." He pulled her forward, resting his forehead against hers. "Tell me if you do not want me, and I will find the strength to let you go. I'll give you your own cabin and leave you alone. It might kill me, but I'll do it. But tell me now, Jeri. For once I have you in this bed—my bed—I'll want to keep you here for a very long time."

He drew back to look into her eyes. There really was no decision to be made. She'd already made up her mind to take what he offered—transport off Pantur, training for her rogue Talent, and the incredible ecstasy he had shown her last night. They were mixed together in her mind, part of this one amazing man who had stormed into her life and turned it completely upside down. She didn't want to be with him, on his ship, without being his lover. She would never have left Pantur had she not wanted to share and repeat the pleasure she'd known the night before. She wanted him and she dreaded thinking of a time in the future, whether it was a week or a year ahead, that he didn't want her in return.

She would cross that bridge when she came to it. For now, she would enjoy him for as long as she could have him. If there was one thing she had learned, it was to appreciate the good things while they lasted, for something always came along to change things, and not usually for the better.

She hesitantly reached out with one hand and cupped his face, delighting in the tremor that ran through this strong man as she stroked him gently. She held his gaze with her own, knowing that he needed her unequivocal agreement on some basic level.

"I want to be your lover, Micah. For as long as you will have me."

He groaned and swept forward, sealing her words with a long, lingering kiss that rocketed through her. He wasn't the gentle, considerate lover of last night, but rather, a desperate, powerful male who needed his mate on some elemental level she hardly understood. But the fire in his caresses spurred her on and ignited a similar flame within her very soul.

He laid her back on the bed and rose over her, undressing her with record speed until she was naked beneath him. His own clothing was tugged and pulled until it came loose with a tear of ripping fabric. He didn't seem to mind the destruction of his finery, only groaned when he could finally place his skin against her softness.

"I want to be inside you," he whispered as he nuzzled her neck, biting down with enough force to make her yelp. He soothed the love bite with his tongue, sliding her up onto the bed as he straddled her legs and brought his chest to rub against her nipples. "I want to live inside you."

He used one strong knee to separate her thighs, then spread them wide and pushed upwards. His hot, thick sex was pressed against her moist heat. Micah brought most of his weight down to blanket her small body, closeting her within the heat of him, bracketing her head with his arms. His head lowered and he kissed her deeply, stroking her with his whole body.

She felt overwhelmed and incredibly turned-on. Her few experiences with intimacy the night before had not prepared her for this saturation of the senses or the command he had over her responses. He mastered her without any real effort and she let him, reveling in his knowledge and control. She knew she would probably never let another man do what he did to her body or her mind, but she also knew that he was way out of her league.

She could have him for now, or perhaps for as long as their voyage lasted. She would enjoy every minute of it, she decided. She would store the memories of him against the future, for she believed she would never find the ecstasy he brought her with anyone else.

"Come inside me, Micah," she pleaded with him as he

bathed her in kisses, using his tongue in ways she'd never dreamed of. But he didn't move inside.

She opened her eyes to find him smiling above her.

"We have plenty of time, sweetheart. I intend to make the best of it. For both of us."

She raised her gaze in question, but he simply lowered his head, dragging his mouth down her neck and to the swell of her breasts. He nipped and licked and sucked his way to her sensitive nipples, bathing first one and then the other with his swirling tongue. He sucked hard enough to make her cry out in pleasure. Micah knew just how to touch her.

He raised his head to smile at her before he continued his downward journey, and she reached out to stroke her fingers through his hair. He kissed her belly, making a meal of her softness. After an endless, pleasure-filled time, he moved lower, separating the folds of her pussy with his wicked tongue as she gasped and grasped his head with desperate fingers.

He settled on his elbows between her splayed thighs, using his hands to spread them even farther as he feasted his eyes on her wet pussy. His bed was so large, they could both sprawl loosely over its surface. The crushed deep blue velvet of his bedspread stroked their skin erotically with each movement.

"Look at me, baby," he said from his position between her thighs, his hands spreading her wide as his fingers stroked lightly along her folds. They dipped inside briefly to bring her moisture upward to the tight bud of her clit and then shockingly downward to rim the rosette of her ass. "I want you to know whose tongue is licking your sweet cream, whose fingers are buried in your hot channel. I want you to know who brings you pleasure, and I want you to scream my name when you come."

"Micah," she gasped when he lowered his head once more,

licking one long line through her slit. He ended with a languorous circle of her responsive clit, spending long moments swirling his tongue through her soft folds. When she mewled in pleasure, he speared inside her, making her scream as she came hard against his tongue.

He licked at the salty sweetness, lapping up her cream as if it were a rare treat. After a few moments, he brought her to an even higher peak, sucking her clit between his lips and drawing on it with enough force to arch her back off the bed.

"Micah!" she shouted, and then she felt his smile of satisfaction against her softest tissues as he rumbled his approval.

The vibrations against her clit brought her to another peak, this one higher than those that had come before as shudders of completion racked her small body. He didn't let her go. He rode her through the tremors of her climax and brought her still more.

He licked his way up her body, replacing his mouth on her pussy with one of his hands. Skilled fingers stroked deep inside, then down to poke lightly at her ass, making her gasp, increasing her tension.

"I will claim you here one day soon, sweetheart. But not today," he whispered against her breast as his finger pushed slightly inside her opening. The sensations were oddly exciting, and they brought her arousal to a new height.

He kissed her lips and she tasted the odd saltiness of herself on him. She squirmed with pleasure as he lowered his weight onto her, surrounding her, engulfing her in his fiery heat.

"I'm making you mine," he whispered, rising just enough to stare down into her eyes as he positioned his cock at her opening. "Can you feel us joining? Like we were never meant to exist apart." He pushed a few inches inside, resting and pulling out only to push in again, wetter and hotter than before. "I am part of you, Jeri." He stroked out and then in again, seating himself fully in her hot core. "You are mine."

She sobbed as he sheathed himself fully, his body possessing hers as his eyes allowed her no escape. Everything she felt, everything she thought was there for him to see as he held her gaze with an almost hypnotic pull. She saw his desire, his passion and lust, as well as something more tender. She felt his need to possess and claim and was touched by his passionate words. In fact, his words alone were almost enough to bring her to climax yet again.

When he started his slow pulses inside her, she reached a peak so quickly she almost forgot to breathe. Through it all he kept steadily increasing his rhythm and strength, giving her as much as she could handle. Before long, he was pounding into her with a rhythm that made her scream. It was his name that she screamed as she came to the highest climax yet.

She felt him pulsing within her as he groaned heavily, spurting his seed in jetting waves. At length, he relaxed in slow increments, his muscles unclenching one by one as she stroked his skin. He surrendered to her embrace, collapsing onto her for a few glorious moments.

He rolled them to their sides but did not leave her body. He simply pulled her close, positioning one of her legs over his hip and settling her head on his shoulder. Nestled together, they drifted in a daze of completion, gazing into each other's eyes and eventually sleeping softly.

Just before she dozed off, Jeri thought being in this huge bed of his had to be the most comfortable she'd ever felt in her life. It was a happy thought. Almost as happy as the thought of the man who even now rested within her. She smiled as she drifted into sleep.

It was at least two standards later that Micah finally showed Jeri to the bridge of the *Circe*, much to the delight of his grinning crew. Darak went so far as to snicker as he greeted his captain and turned over the command position to him.

Jeri couldn't help the scarlet flush that heated her cheeks. She hadn't ever been in the situation before where everyone obviously knew she'd just been having hot, steamy sex with their captain. She'd avoided just such situations since she'd fled her homeworld and made a cold place for herself within the Hill Tribes' only slightly more reserved culture.

Her own homeworld's customs regarding sex had been much stricter. The priests taught abstinence until marriage and then sex only as duty, not to be discussed except between man and wife and then only quietly. She'd just been coming into her teens when her family had been killed. Reaching puberty had brought about the maturation of her Talent as well as her desire to know more of the opposite sex. The Wizards' arrival and brutal slaughter of her parents had destroyed any semblance of a normal life, and she'd left thoughts of boys behind as she hid and then later fled for her very life.

"If you're through grinning like a fool, may I have your report?" Micah stepped up to Darak and held his hand out for the datapad his XO held. The smirk never left Darak's face as he looked from Micah to the small woman standing uncomfortably behind him.

Micah took the datapad with a lingering look meant to caution the often brash warrior. He scanned the pad, then handed it back.

"I hope you've found everything to your liking so far, milady." Darak leered comically at Jeri over his captain's shoulder. She nodded, blushing once more as he chuckled, and Micah sent him a quelling glance.

"Ignore him, sweetheart. It's what I do when he gets like this." Micah put one hand on the small of her back to guide her around the bridge.

It seemed the entire crew had assembled to meet her. The state-of-the-art ship required only a few people to man her, and they were all there, watching Jeri with varying degrees of amusement and interest.

Micah escorted her to the line of computers along the starboard wall and the tall, sandy-haired man sitting before them. He rose as they approached, leaving his work for a moment to formally greet her. She saw sparkling intellect behind his pale eyes and an otherworldly cast that was somehow as comforting as it was eerie.

"This is Specitar Agnor," Micah said softly though the titles meant little to her. Still, the reverence with which he spoke the honorific indicated this was a man he held in deep respect. She bowed her head briefly as she'd been taught back home but was surprised when the other man smiled widely and reached out to take her hand in his, moving close.

"I look forward to working with you, *dama*," the tall man said with a deceptively gentle voice as he drew closer and kissed her lips once, sweetly. Jeri was overwhelmed by the gesture, which was so different than any custom she had seen on her homeworld or even among the freewheeling Hill Tribes.

"Agnor runs comms for the *Circe* as well as diagnostics and scientific studies. He will be working with you on testing your Talent and to what path it will lead you."

Jeri jerked her attention to Micah as he spoke, questions running through her mind that she didn't dare voice yet, lest she look stupid in front of these sophisticated beings. She was feeling very much the backwater hick at the moment, though the pale man's sparkling eyes made her feel a little better, as did Micah's supportive hand at the small of her back.

"I'm pleased to meet you, sir." She squeezed his hand as he smiled and then released her, letting the captain maneuver her to continue the introductions.

He brought her to a small glowing table on which several displays were layered. A woman stood before them, making some sort of calculations, but she straightened and smiled at them as they neared.

"Seta," he said softly, smiling at the gorgeous woman, "this is Jeri. Jeri, Seta is our navigator."

The woman stepped around the table and took Jeri's hand much as Agnor had. She also leaned close to kiss her lips, but where Agnor's lips had been cool and dry, hers were plump and moist. Jeri had never been kissed this way by a woman, and it was oddly enchanting. But what was more disturbing were the clothes this woman was wearing. Or perhaps *not* wearing would be a better description.

The woman was voluptuous with big breasts, a tiny waist and rounded hips. The skirt she wore was nearly transparent and short enough to perhaps qualify as a wide belt. It barely covered the important parts and the top of the outfit didn't even do that. Her breasts were bare, supported by the top in a way that lifted and showcased her pierced nipples.

She didn't have a chain like the one Micah had given Jeri, but she did wear two jeweled dangles from the piercings in her nipples that swung and swayed as she moved.

"I've been looking forward to meeting you, milady."

Her voice was a seductive purr that made Jeri blink. This woman practically oozed sex appeal in a way Jeri had never before encountered.

"Seta is from Virula, a planet known for pleasures of all kinds." Micah smiled a little too warmly at the beautiful navigator for Jeri's comfort, but his hand stroked the small of her back, as if in silent reassurance.

"I've never heard of your world, but then, I have little knowledge of worlds other than those to which our herds were sold when I was a child." *Great*, she thought, *the country bumpkin rides again.*

But Seta's smile was friendly and just the slightest bit lascivious in a way Jeri was coming to realize was part of her nature, and she was not at all condescending. Jeri returned the woman's smile after subduing her urge to run and hide from the changes swamping her.

"I remember when I first left my homeworld," Seta said kindly. "I knew nothing of other planets, trusting to the man who bought me as a sex slave to see to my safety. I was marooned on one of Othar's moons when the fool crashed his ship. He died in the wreck and I managed to learn cartography and navigation from the one functioning comp left on the ship. I made sure that the next time a freighter came through I could flag them down and hire out as something other than a whore."

Her story scandalized Jeri, but she did her best to just nod and try not to let her shock show too much.

"I was a stowaway," Jeri offered. "I hid among the herd to get off Mithrak, then trekked to the Hills when we landed on Pantur to hide."

"I should like to hear this tale," Seta said with a warm grin. "Perhaps you will join me in the lounge after third shift meal sometime, and we can swap stories."

"Perhaps," Jeri answered noncommittally, not sure what Micah would prefer her to do, but willing to answer the overture of friendship from this strange woman.

"Maybe in a few days I will be willing to let her out of my cabin," Micah said, sliding his hand around her waist and dragging her close. "Don't expect to see her idling in the lounge any time soon." His smacking kiss hit her heat-flooded cheek as she rolled her eyes. She was becoming a little more used to his openly suggestive ways, but to have him come out and say something like that made her flush.

Seta laughed and winked at the captain. "Lucky girl." She reached forward and kissed Jeri again, as Micah pressed his growing arousal into the softness of her backside. "I'm glad to see our captain so happy for a change," Seta said as she moved back to her nav board. "He's been moping around here for ages, interfering with our pleasures and finding none for himself. Maybe now that you're here to pleasure him, we can have some fun for a change." Seta winked at Jeri this time, smiling and nodding as she bent back to her board.

Micah laughed as he moved Jeri forward, keeping her in front of him as they reached a small area where two young men waited patiently, at semi attention. They didn't look as if they had posts here on the bridge, but perhaps they'd come and positioned themselves in the null space by the viewport to be out of the way and still be on hand to meet her.

Micah stopped in front of them. "And these two rascals..." he said with a grin and an indulgent tone in his deep voice, "...are our Yeomen for this run. My nephew Kirt, and our cousin Welan. They work mostly for Trini and manage the hold, the crew areas and the rest of the ship. And they man the top and bottom guns in battle."

"Guns?" Jeri turned her head to look up at Micah as the rest of the crew watched in some concern. "I thought this was a freighter, not a warship."

Micah looked around at his crew, silencing their questions

with a sigh and a resigned look. "This is a freighter, but with a dual nature. Each and every one of my crew has some Talent, and a few are very high ranking. I'm a StarLord, Jeri, and I sit on the Mage Council. I use the *Circe* to accomplish certain missions on their behalf."

"Cousin," Darak broke in. "I think you go too far."

Micah turned on him. "She will know this anyway, Dar. You saw her readings. There is little we can hide from her once she is trained. I would prefer to have as much honesty as possible from the beginning."

Darak backed off, but his face was dark. Clearly he didn't agree, but would hold his own counsel for now.

"I want you to know that you are safe on the *Circe*," he said, taking both of her shoulders in his hands. "We can more than defend ourselves if it comes to open fighting, as we have in the past. I will never let anyone like your Wizards take you from me. Not without a fight. And I will fight to my death to protect you." He stroked her cheek with one long finger. "Do you believe me?"

Jeri could hardly catch her breath. His gaze was so serious and his energies so focused on her, it was hard to doubt him. She looked deep into his eyes and nodded.

"I believe you, Micah."

He smiled as if she had given him a great gift. "Good. Then we will set up a schedule for your training to begin."

He dismissed the Yeomen after they had each given her the ritual greeting kiss, Kirt lingering just a bit longer than anyone else had, which made her wonder. But they left to go to their regular stations and Jeri was led over to the Captain's command station where Micah seated her on his knee while he worked out a very rough schedule of times she could meet with Agnor and Darak.

She felt a little more than conspicuous, sitting on his knee while he massaged her waist and backside with his free hand, but the rest of the crew seemed to think nothing of it, so after a while, she relaxed. She asked him a few questions to which he replied in low murmurs, showing her how to access the comp and giving her access to the one in their cabin by entering the commands into his station.

She felt him hardening against her thigh and didn't object when he finished abruptly and swept her from the bridge. That bed in his cabin needed another session to make certain it was absolutely the most comfortable bed she had ever been in. Maybe more than one, she thought with a devilish grin.

# Chapter Five

Darak checked in once in a while over the shipcomm to give status updates, but he had a knack for interrupting at crucial moments that invariably made Micah groan. Jeri laughed the first few times it happened, but she began to wonder how Darak could possibly know what they were doing to time his calls so perfectly.

Micah had just signed off with his XO and taken up where he'd never quite left off thrusting behind her as she kneeled on the kingly bed. The covers were in a shambles, and Micah and Jeri weren't in much better shape themselves. They'd barely taken a few minutes out over the past two days to use the reclamation chamber and eat a few morsels. But oh, how much pleasure there'd been.

And how much more pleasure Micah had in reserve for her, she thought with relish as he increased his pace. She came with a gentle explosion unlike the heated urgency of their first joinings, but every bit as satisfying. Micah came with her, jetting deep inside her.

Sometime later, he withdrew and set her down easily, spooning her close as he settled on the bed beside her. From his breathing she could tell he wasn't quite asleep yet.

"How does he know?" she asked, curious and a little afraid of the answer. "How does your cousin Darak know when to call?"

Micah sighed and stroked her arm. "It's not anything you're thinking, sweet. There's no surveillance in my quarters. I'm too powerful a Talent not to know. It's just..." He hesitated, and she turned in his arms to look at him.

"What?"

"I think he's picking up on you, Jeri. Your Talent is strong and unpredictable. I can't always contain it. I think it leaks out around your shielding at certain moments." His devilish smile left no question as to what kinds of moments he meant.

"Oh no!" Her face flamed with embarrassment.

"Oh, yes," he grinned. "Darak is a tease. He just likes to poke fun at me by calling when we're in the middle of things, and he senses when your shielding fails a little bit. I admit I've been somewhat lax about shoring up my shields at the critical moments too. You overwhelm me."

She kissed him gently for the tender words, but she was totally embarrassed. "What can I do?"

He tucked her under his chin, holding her. "It's mostly my fault. I haven't wanted to let you go, even to begin your training." He kissed the crown of her head. "Let's get a little sleep, then we'll see when Agnor can test you. I'd like you to start with him to get a base level before we show you anything major."

"You'll teach me?" her voice was small and sleepy against his chest.

He smiled. "Yes, I will. As will Agnor and that bastard Darak." The rude name was spoken with humor and affection. "We are all qualified to take on students, and we'll help you."

"I don't think I can face Darak." She cringed inwardly at the thought of how the other man knew each time they'd made love.

And they'd made love *a lot* over the past two days.

Micah chuckled. "The act of love is not something we hide, Jeri. In our culture, sex is out in the open. We could have sex in the companionway and no one would raise an eyebrow, though a few of my crew would stop to watch or even ask to join in." Jeri was scandalized by the very thought, though it did inexplicably make her squirm closer to his warmth. "I think Darak has been enjoying poking some fun at me, but I don't think he meant to embarrass you. He doesn't realize how reticent your home culture was."

"I'll try to get used to your ways, but bear with me, Micah. I'm not ready to do that in public yet, and I don't think I will be anytime soon."

He snuggled her closer. "I would never ask anything of you that you would not give freely, sweetheart. Rest assured. But I do think you'll learn our ways better once you live with us for a while. I've been selfish keeping you all to myself these past days. It'll be First Shift in two hours. Let's sleep a bit, then we can clean up and get you started on your testing, okay?"


Agnor Dallesander was just coming off shift when the captain and his companion made their way to the bridge. The shifts were loosely designed to allow crew members to sleep in turns so that the ship was never totally unmanned at any particular moment.

Agnor was tall—taller even than his captain and the other members of his extended family that crewed the *Circe*. He bowed his head to Jeri as she stopped before him, the captain standing just behind her. Micah's broad hands were on her shoulders in a show of ownership that was not entirely unconscious, Agnor realized as the captain's hard gaze met his.

Agnor nodded to the man he respected and considered a

friend. He had few. The way of the Specitar was often lonely, but Micah was a special man and made allowances for Agnor's sometimes odd behavior, as did his cousin Darak. Both men were friends and long-time companions since they had come up through the ranks fairly close together. Agnor understood now that Micah was claiming this little backworlder, though she probably didn't realize it, not being familiar enough with their ways yet.

"My friend..." Micah said with warmth that indicated the truth of the appellation, "...we need your assistance. I would like you to work with Jeri a bit and give us a base level for her Talent from which we can work. Do you have the time now?"

Agnor smiled slightly and bowed his head. "It would be my honor. Will you shield and observe?"

"I'll shield, but I'd like you to run the test alone. I don't want to influence the result in any way. I think we all may be surprised by your findings if I'm not mistaken."

Agnor acknowledged the eager grin with a light smile and nod of his head. "As you wish." He refocused his gaze on the petite woman in front of him. "*Dama*, will you come with me and submit to the test?"

He could see her swallow her fear and it predisposed him to like the feisty woman who had brought a sparkle back to his friend's eyes. She nodded and stepped forward, away from the lingering touch of Micah's hands on her shoulders. He let her go with little fuss, though she did not see the look of longing, pride and something more in Micah's eyes as he gazed after her.

Agnor led her off the bridge and into the crew deck companionway. They walked past the captain's quarters to a door two hatches down. It was his quarters and he pressed his hand against the door to open it. He motioned her to precede him and was pleased by her little gasp of pleasure when she saw his domain for the first time. He didn't let many people into this place, lest they leave behind disturbing vibrations, but he sensed he would not regret admitting her to his special place.

"You don't sleep here, do you?" she asked quietly, almost reverently as she took in the bare space that contained few furnishings but many tools of his trade.

Agnor chuckled, allowing the door to shut them inside. He undampened the chimes to allow them to ring softly as he passed them.

"No. This is my meditation chamber. As a Specitar, I have somewhat different needs than most other Talents. Our captain has been kind enough to set aside this space so that I may see to them in private and comfort. Most other starship captains would not be so understanding."

She turned to face him, questions in her wide eyes, and he had to catch his breath. This creature was indeed beautiful, but he had to remind himself sadly she was not for him. She belonged to one of his best friends and with Micah she would remain, probably forever, if Agnor was right about the depth of their feelings. Micah had the look of a man in love—a look he'd never seen in him before. Agnor believed it was a good thing. It made Micah happy for the first time in a very long time, and anything that made his friend that happy was something Agnor would endorse.

"What is a Specitar? I'm sorry I don't know the way your rankings work." She seemed truly embarrassed, so Agnor smiled to put her at ease. He also took a seat on the softly padded floor in the center of the room, facing the large viewport. He had a spectacular window on the stars. Trying to put her at ease, he reclined against a long bolster, hoping his casual body language would comfort her. He motioned her to sit opposite him and waited until she was comfortable before beginning his instruction.

"Do not worry over your lack of knowledge. We understand that our culture and traditions are new to you. There's no shame in asking questions when you do not understand." He leaned back and folded his hands, a position he used when in thought that helped him clear his mind of everything except the subject at hand.

"We rank our Talents based on strength and achievement for the most part. There are specific requirements for each level. The lowest level is that of the Novitar. They can either be newly discovered Talent that is working its way up in skill or a low-level Talent that will remain at that level their whole lives. Not all people start at Novitar, but it is usual for youngsters to pass through several levels until their Talent fully matures." He looked up at her to see if she was following and was glad to see the light of interest in her eyes. "After Novitar there are the intermediate rankings of Apprentar, Acoltar, and Authoritar. After that, the lowest of the advanced rankings is Dominar. Darak is at Dominar strength now, but I believe he is not far from the next level, that of Mage. If and when he reaches Mage level, he will be given a seat on the Council. Mages are very powerful indeed, and there are only several hundred in any given generation. Our captain reached Mage level as a young man and only recently made the unexpected jump to Mage Master. I think he was as surprised as the rest of us when he passed those tests, achieving a Talent level found in perhaps less than fifty people in each generation among our worlds."

"Wow," she breathed. "How did it happen?"

Agnor leaned forward, meeting her curious gaze. "It is a long story and it is not mine to tell. You must ask the captain and he will tell you of it if he so chooses. Suffice to say, he did not intend to kick his power to the next level in quite that way. Rather, it was forced upon him, and it wasn't an entirely pleasant experience." He leaned back, relaxing—or giving the appearance of relaxing at least. "With great strength comes great responsibility, and we do not always find our strength unless and until it is needed. Micah needed great strength, and he found it within himself, pushing the limits of his Talent and elevating himself to a higher level. More than that, I will not say." He nodded once and resumed his teaching pose. "After Mage and Mage Master, there are the highest rankings of Vizier and Sha. Viziers are few and far between. Perhaps there are a handful in each generation and right now there is only one Sha, and she is very old."

"But what about your title? Where do you fit?"

He smiled at her. "Caught that, did you? Well, I said almost all our rankings are based on strength, but there is one ranking based solely on skill. Specitars such as myself usually fit somewhere between Mages and Mage Masters in overall strength, but we excel in specialized areas. For example, my specialty is telepathy. I can reach farther with my mind than most anyone except perhaps the Sha and most of the Viziers. But my other skills are not that strong, except cognition. I have developed my mental processes—influenced by the telepathy, I believe—so that I can solve scientific problems faster than most computers, using human intuition that comps just don't have."

She looked duly impressed so he sat back waiting for questions. They were not long coming.

"So you and Micah are the strongest Talents on board? Do Specitars have seats on the Council too? Do you use your telepathic skill when running comm? And where do the rest of the crew fall in your list?"

He chuckled at her eager questions, but answered them all. "Yes, Micah and I are of comparable level, though he technically outranks me now that he's a Master. Specitars are given seats on the Council but also sit on the Board of Specitars, which is a subsection of the Council devoted to scientific and technological matters. And yes, I do send telepathic messages when required. For one thing, there is no way to intercept them. It is useful when we are on missions for the Council or Board to have totally secure communication." He sighed as she took it in like a sponge. "As for the crew. Darak is a Dominar who, as I said, will probably make Mage in the next few years. The lovely Seta is an Authoritar and that's probably as high as she'll ever go since her Talent is close to fully developed. Then there is Trini, an Acoltar. Kirt is just at Novitar level and young Welan is an Apprentar. Both of them should be moving up shortly as well. The line of Geneth Mar has notoriously strong psi Talent. Only the *Circe* can boast four Talents of that bloodline, two near peak and two just developing."

He could tell she had more questions, but he sat back, centering himself for the work ahead. "Arrange yourself as I am, *dama*. We have some serious work to do, and I would not keep our captain waiting too long for the results of our testing this day." He smiled at her as she crossed her legs and sat in a mirror of his position on the padded floor. He placed a set of crystals in geometric shapes between them and was pleased by the way her sparkling eyes followed each of his deliberate, ceremonial movements.

"Do you feel the captain's presence? Do you feel his protection?"

He watched her close her eyes briefly, then smile. The smile was one of warmth and love that made him catch his breath. A moment later wonder passed over her delicate features as she opened her eyes and stared across at him.

"I hadn't realized," she said in an excited whisper. "I've been so overwhelmed since I met him, I didn't realize the strength of his shields extending to me. I feel it, like a warm caress against my skin. And I've felt it at other times too. I've never felt anything like it before."

"He protects you, *dama*. He spreads his wings around you when you are vulnerable and now, because he will assist with the testing. Since you must lower your shields, he will keep you from detection by replacing them with his."

"Can he really do that? I never knew you could shield someone else."

"He is a Mage Master. He often shields the entire crew of the *Circe* when we go into dangerous situations, though you are right. It is not something very many Talents can do"

He watched her close her eyes once more and bask in the warmth of her lover's shields surrounding her. Agnor could feel the surge in strength as if Micah knew what she was doing and perhaps, he thought, they were so connected that he did. Agnor got back to the task at hand, positioning the tools he would need for the test as he watched her with great interest.

When he was ready, he took a deep breath, centering himself. What would come next would undoubtedly be a singular experience. He'd seen the nearly off-the-chart reading Darak had taken from above Pantur when she'd been unshielded before. It was saying something that Micah trusted only Agnor and himself to be around her when she was fully unshielded. They were the only ones who had even a hope of matching the reading he'd seen.

"Now, I want you to relax as fully as you can, *dama*. When you're ready, I want you to speak the words *selta, passa, sum,* then lower your shields as calmly as you can. Do you understand?" She nodded and he continued his instruction. "When your shields are down, I want you to concentrate on the sphere." He tapped the crystal sphere, the first of the geometric shapes arrayed before her. "Concentrate your thoughts on the sphere and let it fill with your strength. When I call next I want you to move to the cylinder, then the square, then the pyramid and so on up the line. We may not get through all of them, and I want you to tell me when and if you want to stop, all right?"

She nodded, her eyes eager and a little tense. "What will happen?"

Agnor smiled reassuringly at her. "I cannot say. Not because I don't want to..." he was quick to clarify, "...but because with each Talent, the response of the crystals is somewhat different. I will watch and evaluate, and based on the crystals' response to your energies I will be able to formulate a base-level ranking for you. That is the point we will work from as we train your specific strengths and weaknesses. It is how we train all Talents, whether they are known from birth or are found later in life, such as yourself."

She smiled, but he could see she was nervous. "All right," she said finally, closing her eyes and taking a few deep breaths. "I'm ready when you are."

He smiled at her quick grasp of the task before her. "Give me the warning count of *selta, passa, sum*, then lower your shields and begin."

She nodded and breathed deeply once more, beginning almost before he was ready. He'd switched on the recorders unobtrusively when they entered, since he didn't want her to know they were there. Undoubtedly the Mage Council would be interested in what transpired here, during her first test, if the reading taken above Pantur proved to be anywhere near accurate.

Agnor watched carefully as she called out the ritual warning count then tried to prepare himself for what was coming. A second later when she lowered her shields in his presence for the first time, he realized there was no way he could have prepared himself to feel that surge of raw power. It was amazing. It was exhilarating. And it was damned powerful.

She focused her energies on the sphere and immediately it developed a pale purple glow from within, indicating a strong but latent healing Talent. He called for the next shape once the patterns in the sphere were fully developed. The cylinder brought forth a pulsing golden light that shot out both ends to swirl around the room and form double arcs around himself and Jeri. Agnor had never seen the like, but was pleased by the indication of a kind heart that sought to unite rather than destroy. He called for the next shape, and she moved on to the pyramid.

Agnor knew he shouldn't have been all that surprised when a bright white light concentrated in the point of the pyramid to shower out and down around them as they sat in his sealed mediation chamber, bathing them both in the pureness of her spirit. It was the strongest he'd ever seen in a new testing Talent, and it humbled him. Tears were in his eyes as she moved on to the cube, generating a bright and deep cobalt blue of conviction and power to protect her friends and those weaker than herself.

As they moved through the progressively more complex shapes some were weaker than others, but all gave some indication of either mature or latent strength that they could develop further. She didn't hesitate, didn't tire and worked her way steadily through all the shapes he had on hand, proving her worth in this first test. Agnor was nearly overwhelmed. Never had he encountered such a strong, pure, raw Talent, and he doubted he ever would again.

When she finished with the last crystal shape she looked to him for guidance and Agnor caught his breath at the dancing power behind her eyes.

"You may call your energies back to you now, *dama*, then raise your shields as gently as you can. The test is almost complete." He watched carefully as she harnessed that which she'd loosed in the room, not missing any stray telltale trickles of her energy, but calling it all back neatly and under her complete control. It was something even Dominars had trouble with. She then simply winked out of psi existence as she raised her incredibly tight shields.

They not only hid her strength but disguised it completely. That was a rarity. Not even Mages could so completely hide their Talent when among other Mages. But, if she'd been in hiding from the Wizards of Mithrak since childhood, then perhaps the skill was born out of dire necessity. Perhaps, Agnor thought grimly, it was the only thing that had saved her from being forced to join with their enemy and give up her very soul.

Agnor breathed a quick sigh as he felt the captain's shields holding strong. They'd gotten through the tough first test, and she was so much more than even he'd expected. Micah would be pleased, Agnor knew, as Agnor was pleased at the thought of helping develop such a strong and vital Talent. Micah would of course be her primary teacher, but there were skills peculiar to a Specitar that could be of use to her and Darak's particular talents would come in handy during the training as well. And wouldn't Darak be miffed when he found out this little slip of a girl had tested out at a base level he'd worked many years to attain? Agnor looked forward to sharing the news with him.

"It is my honor to award you the rank of Dominar."

"You're kidding," she said softly, apparently remembering how high on the rank scale that would put her.

Agnor smiled broadly. "Indeed I am not. You are at Dominar strength in most areas. Above in some, but you do require quite a bit of training. Your Talent is raw in many places and could be greatly improved with steady work. I would not be surprised if you end up with your own seat on the Council eventually."

Jeri looked shocked, though a pleased smile lit her eyes. "I can hardly believe it," she breathed. "Have you told Micah?"

He tilted his head. "Good of you to realize that as a telepath I could have done so already, but no, I will let you share the news with him yourself. Though he was shielding you the whole time. I would not be surprised if he did not guess already from the amount of power you were putting out."

He rose, and she followed suit. "I go to my rest period now, *dama*. But perhaps we can begin your training later. I will look forward to it. Training new Talent is a favorite occupation of mine. It is one of the things Specitars excel at in general."

"I will look forward to it," she said formally, moving toward the door with him. "Enjoy your rest."

She slid out the door and practically bounced down the corridor as she left him, eager to tell her lover of her success.

Micah was waiting for her when she walked up the companionway to their door. She flung herself into his arms, the residual energy flowing through her making her giddy.

"So what's the verdict?" he asked after kissing her deeply. "What did Agnor think of your Talent?"

She pulled slightly away to smile up at him. "You're looking at a Dominar," she said with just a hint of shy pride, rewarded when Micah picked her up and spun her around.

"I knew it."

She laughed with him. "I was surprised after he explained the rankings. I figured because I'd had no training I'd be very

91

low on the scale."

He set her down and kissed her. "It doesn't work that way. It goes by your level of power. And you are one of the strongest raw Talents I've ever encountered, even among my own family, and we're pretty Talented. I'm duly impressed. But then, everything about you impresses me, sweet, sweet Jeri."

"Well, I'm just glad I didn't embarrass myself." *Or you*, she thought.

She couldn't quite get past the fact that they were totally mismatched on the social scale, and she wondered what his people must think of their lopsided relationship. At least now that she had some rank to speak of, maybe some of the questions would be answered, allowing her to take some pride in herself and her relationship with this powerful man. But the fact remained that he was way out of her league. She'd resolved with some sadness to enjoy this time with him because it was almost certain to come to an end once they reached any sort of civilization.

Oh, he could have her as his lover in his cabin and in the small confines his ship, but she would never be a suitable companion to stand by his side in society. He was a Master Mage from an old and powerful family. She was strong but untrained, and the daughter of a comparatively poor horse tamer. There was no future for them, only the present, and she intended to enjoy every last moment with him while she had him. For this time would never come again.


The lift doors opened in time to showcase Trini's bare blue ass as she jumped up to wrap her legs around Darak's waist and seat herself firmly on his thick erection. Jeri was shocked to her core, even more so when Trini laughed and started to gasp as Darak began pumping into her wet folds.

There was little she could do but enter the lift. She had summoned it, wanting to go to the cargo deck. She was dreadfully embarrassed but Darak's bold gaze, holding hers over Trini's shoulder as his thick cock slid in and out of the woman's pussy, dared her to run.

Jeri decided she was through running. She was part of this crew and needed to get used to their ways. Micah had told her how out in the open their culture was about sex, and she secretly worried that he would grow dissatisfied with her inhibitions. She had to start getting used to these people and their scandalous ways.

Firming her chin, she entered the lift, pushing the right pad on the control unit to signal her destination, trying for a calm she wasn't even close to feeling.

"Mmm, harder, Darak," Trini moaned.

Darak chuckled low and sexy, the sound rubbing along Jeri's stressed-out nerves. "We have company, Trini."

Trini's dazed gaze met hers as her supple neck swiveled around. "Oh, hi, Jer." She turned her head back to Darak and caught his lips in a biting kiss. "Move, Darak. Harder!"

The lusty XO complied with a wink in Jeri's direction, which she studiously ignored. He laughed as he tugged the woman in his arms higher, using his hips to piston in and out faster and harder as Trini moaned.

When the lift doors opened, Jeri shot through quickly, ignoring the masculine laughter that drifted after as the doors shut the two lovers within the lift once more.

Jeri spent a productive few hours with her friends in the herd of horses, making sure the lift was totally empty before she headed back to the cabin.

But as she passed the open archway to the crew's common room, she saw a sight that made her stop in her tracks. The gentle Specitar who had tested her with such patience was seated on the couch while Trini knelt between his legs, sucking on his rod, and Seta knelt at his side on the couch, one of her nipples in his mouth, the other pinched in his fingers. He shuddered and groaned as Trini moved to take his thick cock into her pussy.

Jeri stood in the hall, shocked and somewhat amazed by what she was witnessing. With all the hot action on the couch, the two young yeomen playing at some kind of air propulsion table on the far side of the room seemed oblivious. But then she noticed Seta's glances at the two young men, and as she rose, leaving Trini and Agnor to their pleasure, the two muscular young men moved to join Seta on another of the long couches. Both quickly disrobed as she wrapped herself around both of the virile youngsters.

Jeri felt her own temperature rising as the young men's bodies were exposed, one blond with sun-kissed skin and kind eyes, the other with cinnamon-colored hair and an engaging smile. Jeri almost forgot to breathe as the blond one seated his hard cock in Seta's pussy, watching as his cinnamon friend lubed her ass and slid gently inside with her loud encouragement. They began to pump in counterpoint as she moaned and spurred them on with her words and hands

When Jeri felt a hand slide around her waist, she nearly screamed. Within a breath she realized it was Micah. She'd been so engrossed in the scene unfolding before her, she hadn't heard him come up behind. Now she was embarrassed to be caught peeking at the archway like some kind of voyeur.

Micah's breath was hot at her ear as he leaned down and pulled her back tight against his chest. "Like what you see?"

She tried to move away from the doorway, but his large body kept her in place, watching.

"I didn't know that was even possible," she admitted finally, her face heating once more as both young yeomen fucked Seta's squirming body at the same time.

"Two men at once?" he seemed to ponder the idea. "It can be very pleasurable, or so I'm told."

"Have you ever...?" she couldn't quite finish her question.

"Taken part in a threesome? You bet I have." He brushed her neck with his lips. "Would you like to get some of what Seta's getting?" He licked over her sensitive skin with a hot swipe of his tongue, making her shiver. "I can arrange it."

She turned in his arms, pushing until he allowed her to move them away from the opening to the common room.

"I don't think so. I'm barely used to you yet, Micah."

He let her drag him down the hall, but he didn't let her go. Instead, he backed her into their cabin, undressing her as they went until they were both naked and on the wide bed, hot, hard, wet, and ready for each other.

# Chapter Six

Hours later, Jeri and Micah lazed in his wide, luxurious bed after making love again. He sifted his fingers through her hair as they faced the viewport, watching the stars go by. The *Circe* sped through space and time, cocooning her crew safely inside. Micah reflected on the peace he felt at that moment, Jeri's cheek pressed lightly to his chest as she lay next to him, her arms wrapped loosely around him, and he realized he'd never felt more at one with another being, more at ease in his own skin or more right in sharing this moment and all the moments since he'd first encountered Jeri, at her side.

She was fast becoming more than just a pleasant fuck. She was becoming important to him in ways that he didn't dare examine too closely. She was his equal in many ways, though he enjoyed teaching her the things he could. She certainly was a good student. She'd applied herself to learning the ways of pleasure and each time he made love to her, she surprised him with new and more amazing heights of passion.

"It's beautiful," she said softly, gazing at the distortion of light that indicated stars as they sped through space toward their destination.

He moved his hand to cup her cheek and turn her eyes upward. "You're beautiful." He kissed her lips softly, impressing his words on her skin. She smiled against his lips, and he was happy. When he released her moments later she moved one hand to stroke his chest more firmly, making him even happier.

"I never got to see the stars the last time I was in a spacecraft. I was stuck in the hold, hiding the whole time. Scared." He smoothed the small frown that creased her brow with a soft stroke of his big finger.

"You're a woman of power now, Jeri. You will have little to fear in the future."

"How can that be, though?" She leaned up on one elbow, facing him with questions in her eyes. "I've lived most of my life in fear, Micah. Even in your world, though I have some Talent, I'm still a nobody. I own nothing more than the clothes on my back, and most of those you gave me."

"Is this any way for a base-level Dominar to talk?" he asked with a smile, scooting up and back on the bed to rest against the padded headboard, bringing her with him. "We don't even know what you'll be once your Talent is trained, but even a Dominar has certain rights and privileges in our society. Ask Darak, if you don't believe me. He's been a Dominar since First Test."

"Like me?"

"No," he shook his head, tucking her head over his heart as he tried to put her fears at ease. "You've not had First Test yet."

"Then what was that testing I did with Agnor called?"

"I forget you are new to everything about our ways. Forgive me." Micah sighed as he stroked her hair. "The testing you underwent with Agnor is just a base-level test we give all Talents that manifest when they hit puberty, usually. It gives us some indication of how to train them, though they are not told of their results until after they have been trained and have had First Test around age twenty or so. With very strong Talents, it can be more obvious that one youngster is more powerful than another. We use the base-level testing to help keep like-level students together so they can train with and challenge each other." He continued to stroke her hair in a way that made him want to do more, but he would answer her questions first. There was so much she had to learn about her power and where she would fit in his world.

"Since you are well past puberty and have never been tested or trained in our tradition, I asked Agnor to give you the base-level test first so we knew where we should start. We will train you in the things you would have learned as a teenager, had you lived on a Council world and then, when you've acquired some of the basic skills, we'll First Test you."

"Sort of a sped-up program just for me?" she asked.

He nodded, sighing with pleasure as she nuzzled his chest. "Designed just for you, sweetheart. Keep doing that," he whispered as she nipped his pectoral muscle and laved his nipple with her tongue. He stopped talking altogether when her hand moved downward to stroke his growing erection. They didn't speak again for long, passion-filled moments, and Micah thought his life couldn't get any better than this.

Jeri was in the hold the next day with the horses, wearing one of the loose cotton shirts Micah had given her, when Trini called her name from across the wide expanse. Turning quickly, she caught a button on a sharp crate edge and heard a ripping sound as Trini came over to her.

"Oh dear," Trini said, looking at the ruined shirt that had ripped down the center, exposing Jeri's chest. The woman touched her skin lightly where the edge had scraped just over her heart, and Jeri turned away, uncomfortable with the intimate touch.

"Darn it," she said, concentrating on the edges of the

ragged shirt, dabbing at the small line of blood that marred her chest from the scrape. The cotton soaked it up until all that was a left was an angry red line where the skin was abraded, but no longer bleeding.

"That shirt's ruined, but not to worry, the ship's synthesizer can whip up something for you in no time." Trini seemed to want to atone for the discomfort she had so innocently caused her new friend. Jeri tried to remember these people were much freer with their bodies than those in her own culture, but it was hard when faced with new intimacies.

Jeri was intrigued by the idea of the synthesizer as she turned to the other woman. "Really?"

Trini smiled as Jeri clutched the ragged edges of the shirt together and motioned her over to the control panel at the rear of the large hold.

"Sure thing. The captain lets us all use this in a pinch. I've uploaded some great patterns into the memory banks in addition to the standard designs. Let me show you."

Over the next few minutes Trini showed an amazed Jeri the standard patterns for shipsuits, pants, tunics and tops in all kinds of styles, in addition to her own more risqué collection of what looked like undergarments with strategic portions either highlighted or totally missing. Jeri settled on a plain top in a pretty shade of green that popped out of the dispenser in just moments.

Trini watched as she took off the ruined cotton shirt and pulled on the snug top, embarrassing her a bit, but she'd come to realize that among these people nudity was nothing to be ashamed of. Still, she would never have so easily taken her shirt off in front of Darak—had she known he was there.

A long whistle from a few yards away had more than the horses' heads turning as Darak strolled into view. Jeri pulled the new top over her head. Hastily, she pulled it down, uncomfortably aware of how tightly the synthetic material hugged her generous breasts.

"Too bad I didn't get here just a few moments earlier." Darak grinned, putting a companionable arm around Trini. "We three could've had some fun."

The other woman pushed him away playfully. "Come on, Dar, you know the captain's orders." Trini turned to Jeri with a smile. "Ignore him, Jer. He's just teasing."

"You have gorgeous nipples, Jeri," he said, looking at her chest and the points clearly outlined by the snug fabric. "I can see why my cousin wants to keep you to himself."

Without saying a word, she turned to leave but was stopped short by Darak's pull on the ruined cotton shirt she clutched in her hands.

"Whose blood is this?" he asked with a snapping demand in his voice that startled her.

"Jeri was scratched by that crate over there, and her shirt was ruined."

"Let me see." Darak spoke softly, tugging on the cotton until Jeri released it and turned slowly to face him. She was scared by the firmness of his voice. Now, she realized, he was more than just the fun-loving playboy she'd seen so far. He was truly the second in command of this ship, and he expected to be obeyed.

"It's just a scratch," Jeri said softly, backing up a step as he moved toward her. "It's already stopped bleeding." Her hand went to her chest, just above her heart, where the long scratch still stung.

She was shocked when Darak stepped right in front of her, holding her gaze. His dark eyes were exotic and penetrating as he placed his own big hand over hers, pressing against her

100

breast firmly. She felt a warm pulse of his energy and then opened her mouth on a gasp as the stinging of the scratch in her flesh disappeared. He'd healed her with his psi power, and she was amazed both by his gentle touch and the look of true care in his dark eyes.

"There is no need for you to suffer, pretty one," he said softly. "Not when it is a simple thing to ease your discomfort." He winked at her. "My cousin Micah would expect no less."

Jeri caught her breath, once again on familiar footing as the roguish light reentered his eyes. Still, he'd done her a real service and she knew her manners.

"Thank you," she said softly, seeing an echo of caring in his eyes that dumbfounded her. She spun and left them, heading for the lift.

Micah met her in the hall, having felt her moment of hurt surprise when she'd snagged herself on that crate. He'd left the discussion of navigation he'd been having with Seta and headed for the hold, but Jeri was already in the lift before he could get there.

"What happened?" he asked immediately when he saw her.

Jeri shrugged with an embarrassed smile, telling him about the crate and her small injury. When he would have tugged off her shirt to inspect the wound right there in the companionway where anyone could see, she stayed his hand.

"Darak healed it, I think," she said softly. "At least, it doesn't hurt anymore."

"Darak put his hands on you? When I specifically told him to keep his distance until you were more comfortable with our ways?" He was getting upset, and she rushed to stave off his anger.

"He only touched my hand. I was already clothed when I saw him."

At least that was technically true, though she had no idea how much of her little strip show he'd actually seen. Micah's anger was defused, but he took her hand gently and walked with her to their cabin.

"I'm glad he was there to ease your pain." He palmed the hatch and ushered her inside their cabin. "But that top has to go."

She looked down at the little green top that was prettier than anything she'd ever owned. "But why?"

"It's synthetic," he said simply, as if that explained it all. But she had no idea what he could be referring to. He evidently saw the confusion on her face and explained. "Synthetic fibers could be dangerous to you, Jeri. They don't react well to psi Talent above Dominar level. They can fuse, melt, burn or even combust. It's better to wear only natural fibers and substances. Which is why I gave you cotton. You'll notice that Agnor's favorite robes are mostly woolen, and most of my pants are leathers. Until we can get planetside and get you some natural fibers, I'm afraid you'll have to wear my shirts, as you've been doing."

"Because you're a Mage Master, right?"

He nodded. "Because of me, but also because you have quite a bit of power in your own right, sweetheart."

"I'm only a Dominar."

"Base-level Dominar, Jeri. I have no doubt you will First Test at Mage, maybe even above."

"No way."

"Way." He kissed her, unable to resist the wonder in her eyes.

She pushed on his chest after a moment, unwilling to be totally sidetracked just yet. "So how did Darak do that healing thing?" she asked. "I didn't know you could heal with psi energy."

Micah allowed her some space in his embrace, though he didn't let her go completely. "Some people can. Most Dominars, in fact, are taught the simple healings, along with most Mages. It takes a great deal of power, so it's a skill reserved for those with the higher levels of ability in that direction. It's something few people truly master. The greatest psi healers are Specitars, of course, and healing is just about all they do. I have a little more skill than most Mages, but Darak is truly gifted for a Dominar. What he did is rare. Most Talents would have to be in physical contact with the injury, not just touching your hand. But Darak's got a soft heart that he tries hard to hide, and he put out the extra energy to heal you without looking at the injury because he knew it would be easier for you."

"He knows he makes me uncomfortable?" She seemed both amazed and embarrassed at the thought.

Micah smiled ruefully. "He makes a joke out of it, but I think it almost hurts his feelings that you're so afraid of him."

"Oh, Micah, I didn't mean—"

"I know, my love, I know." He soothed her, but he knew she needed to hear only the truth from him if she was to grow comfortable with his family and crew.

"I'm not really afraid of him." She spoke softly, allowing him to cuddle her into his chest. "He's just so...big...and male."

Micah laughed outright at that. "And I'm not?"

She swatted him playfully. "You know you are, but I'm not his lover so it makes him intimidating and sort of scary."

"What does it make me then, I wonder?"

She looked up at him, emotion welling in her eyes. "It makes you perfect, Micah. Just perfect."

She was getting into dangerous territory, revealing too much of her inner feelings to this man who was far out of her league. She reached up and kissed him, distracting him, following eagerly when he led them to the large bed and laid her upon it.

"You know..." he looked at her, spread out before him on the bed, "...Darak told me about you walking in on him and Trini in the lift." Her face flushed with remembered embarrassment.

"I couldn't believe they were doing it there, even stopping to say hello when they were in the middle of...of that."

"We're a tight family here on the *Circe*. In such close quarters, it's almost inevitable that we've caught each other in intimate moments over the years. We're used to it." He shrugged his shoulders.

"So if you'd walked into that lift, you would have what? Joined in?"

Micah shook his head. "At one time, probably. But not now. Not for a long time, actually."

She leaned up on one elbow, seeing a sadness in his gaze that she hadn't seen since those first moments back on Pantur.

"Why? It's not just me being here, is it?"

Micah moved to her side and sat on the edge of the bed. "Your being here is heaven to me, Jeri. Never doubt that. But you're right, I haven't been able to join with anyone, even my crew, in a very long time. Not since I became a Mage Master."

"But why? You were always more powerful than the rest, even when you were just a Mage, so what changed?"

Micah sighed. "I changed, Jeri. It's more than just rising a level in power, though that did make it more difficult than ever to interact with any Talent below Mage level. It's also a feeling that was growing in me for a long time. I was dissatisfied with meaningless pleasure shared among friends. That was okay for a long time, but I started to understand what Agnor had been talking about after his longtime partner left him. I began to understand his loneliness, his isolation, and to feel something like it myself. There are precious few Specitars and even fewer Mage Masters. It is hard to interact on intimate levels with others when you command so much concentrated power. I would never want to hurt any of my crew, or anyone else for that matter, in seeking to fulfill my own physical needs."

"But you've never hurt me." She thought back over the time they'd been together. "You knew I had a high level power, right? Is that why? Is it that you don't have to worry about possibly hurting me?"

Micah took her in his arms and hugged her close. "That's only part of it, but yes, it's a relief to know that I won't unintentionally hurt you with my Talent, Jeri. The rest is something I'm having a hard time understanding. There's something about you—about us—that just feels more right than anything I've ever experienced before. We click. And your presence helps ease the loneliness I've been feeling. You fill a place inside my soul that was empty, Jeri. You're good for me, and I want to keep you."

She smiled as his impassioned words touched her heart. "That's good, because I want to keep you too, Micah." She paused, gathering courage. "You're very special to me."

He pulled off the rest of her clothes with a growl and pressed her down into the soft bed.

"Show me how special," he growled, moving to kneel over her mouth. She didn't disappoint, swallowing his long cock eagerly. He grabbed the headboard for balance and his eyes shut in ecstasy as she used her teeth gently to stimulate his hard shaft. She sucked and licked, making him groan, making him feel how special he was to her, just as he'd demanded. He was on the knife's edge of arousal, his muscles straining as he sought for elusive control.

"Suck me, Jeri. Make me come."

She moaned deep in her throat, sending the vibrations up his sensitive shaft as her hollowed cheeks bore down gently on his straining length. He groaned and pushed deeper, nearly choking her, but she took it. She took him deep, deeper than he'd even gone before, his passion reaching higher.

"I'm coming," he warned, tugging upward to leave her mouth but she followed, wanting everything he had to give. "I'll come in your mouth, Jeri. Is that what you want?"

She moaned again, her eyes pleading for his come as he finally let go, his seed spurting from the heated tip, deep within her mouth. He watched her with blurred vision as she drank from him, his groans of completion mixing with her moans of delight as she swallowed all he had to give.

She licked him clean for long moments as he fought for some sense of equilibrium, but he was wrecked. She had drained him utterly and it was some time before he could find the strength of will to move from her willing mouth. He collapsed on the bed next to her, turning to meet her smile.

"You're a dangerous woman, Jeri. Very dangerous." One of his large hands rose lethargically to stroke her hair as he smiled, quite obviously satiated.

She pretended to consider his words. "I think I like the sound of that."

He laughed and tugged her closer, folding her into his arms and hugging her tight. "I think I've created a monster." He rolled on top of her and pressed her into the mattress.

"Can you teach me about healing?"

"Now? But you haven't come for me yet, sweetheart." His eyes turned devilish as his head lowered to her breast, finding the nipple and sucking it deep into his mouth. She shivered as his hands roamed her body, moving one in front and one behind, cupping her ass and her pussy at the same time and squeezing.

She lost track of what she'd been about to say as his fingers delved deeper on both sides, two entering her pussy from the front while one played with the tight rosebud of her ass. Tremors down her spine made her squirm as he moved to kiss her, plunging in deep with his tongue in the same rhythm as his fingers in her pussy. She was already near the edge, the mere act of sucking him to completion firing her senses and priming her for his touch.

"Micah," she squealed as the finger at her rear plunged inside, the way made easier by the juices flowing from her stimulated core. "I'm close. So close."

"Come for me, Jeri. Come for me now," he ordered on a low growl, his teeth grazing her breast, then nipping in a way that made her scream. Her body spasmed in delight as he pressed her into the mattress, blanketing her with his heavy body and whispering how beautiful he thought she was as she came apart in his arms.

Long moments later, she remembered what she'd asked him before he distracted her so wonderfully. She rested her chin on one hand over his heart as she looked at him.

"When will you teach me about healing?"

"I suppose you won't let me rest until I do, huh?"

She grinned at him. "Something like that."

"All right." He sat up against the headboard, taking her with him. "Just a quick lesson for now. Darak's the man who can really show you a thing or two about healing, but I can at least explain the basics."

"What do I do?"

He loved the eager light in her eyes and couldn't resist kissing her gently. He pulled back before he could get too distracted.

"No more of that," he muttered. "Not if you seriously want to do this."

"I seriously want to do this," she said faithfully, her eyes twinkling at him. "But I want to do *you* too. Just hold that thought until after you explain a little about healing, okay? I promise I'll make it good for you." The purr in her voice had him hardening again.

"All right. Crash course." He pulled her closer, stroking her breast with one hand, unable to resist touching her. "You have to send your thoughts outside yourself, seeking into the other person."

"How?"

"Well, it's not easy. First you ground and center, the way you've been learning, then ideally, you touch the target area with your fingertips, sending just a pulse of your energy at first to make contact and take stock of what you need to do." He shifted her to her side and lowered his head to kiss her neck, moving slowly as he alternately talked and placed light kisses along her collarbone and down onto the slopes of her breasts.

"Different kinds of injuries require different flavors of power. The easiest is the open flesh wound caused by a knife or projectile or the like. Pour in hot energy, it will sort of cauterize the bleeding, then begin knitting the torn places back together. The most complex are internal diseases. Only a real healing

Talent can tackle a complex disease and hope to cure it, though a rough application of high level Talent can prolong the person's life, perhaps long enough to get them to a real healer. Sometimes, very rarely, we can sort of pool our Talents and let them be directed by the higher level healers, but it's rarely done because it can be dangerous to everyone involved."

He sucked her nipple into his mouth and the lesson was postponed for a few hours while they slaked their passions. Eventually Jeri got her first rudimentary lesson in healing and both of them got off...repeatedly.


"I'm excited about seeing home again." Trini's deep violet eyes sparkled as she stroked one of the horse's long necks in the hold the next day. Jeri carefully groomed a pregnant mare that would give birth shortly after arrival on their new homeworld, Trini's native planet of Liata. Jeri was as eager as her equine friends to see the planet, intrigued by the idea that the people who lived there were all varying shades of blue, like her new friend, the effervescent Trini.

"Do you have family there?" Jeri asked softly, thinking about the family that was lost to her with longing.

Trini smiled broadly. "The Clan will turn out to meet our ship, I'm sure. I have a large extended family, headed by my great-grandmother. Both sets of grandparents are alive and my parents gave me five siblings. Plus there are loads of cousins. They usually throw a big *sancha* when I come back, and the whole crew is invited."

Jeri would learn in subsequent conversations that a *sancha* was a Liatan gathering of the Clan where the extended family would converge to tell stories, play games with the younglings and eat for about three days straight. In the long summer of the planet, such gatherings were almost always held outdoors and all but the oldest family members would sleep outside, under the stars if possible.

Jeri told the herd about the people they would join on their new planet, and they seemed content. Eliciting information that would be important to the horses through some pointed questioning of Trini, she realized that the new world they were going to would be a wonderful place for them, and they seemed to agree.

So it was with some excitement that Jeri stood on the bridge a few days later. She watched Liata wink into view in the distance as the supra-light drive was disengaged. At first, the shining blue-green planet was nothing except a tiny ball revolving around a bright binary star. It grew steadily larger as Seta navigated, using the forward momentum left from the supra-light drive and the application of steering thrusters and braking thrusters to get closer and closer. Within a few moments they were in communications range and the cacophony of transmissions that reached them didn't make sense at first.

"We're picking up transmissions on and around Liata, Captain. Something big happened not too long ago by the sound of it." Agnor's face was grim as he tried to sort through the varying signals. This far out, the signals were delayed by as much as a few hours. He was trying to distinguish ambient signals from blaring emergency channels that crossed the *Circe*'s path, which was not the usual course of business when approaching a peaceful ag world at all.

Jeri saw Micah's face take on a stern hardness as he waited for more information. He turned to her with a decisive motion.

"How can I help?" She was relieved to note that had apparently been the right thing to say as relief shone for a brief moment in his dark eyes.

"Go to Trini. If there's trouble on Liata, she'll need our support. But first I have to find out exactly what's going on and she shouldn't be alone."

Jeri nodded, purpose lighting her eyes as she left the bridge. She felt his gaze on her back as she headed for the hold. Jeri knew Trini had wanted to be on the bridge for the down-jump to Liata, but as loadmaster, her place was with the cargo, making sure the horses came through the transition safely. Jeri realized it might've been a good thing that Trini hadn't been on the bridge and didn't know yet that there was some kind of trouble on her homeworld. Jeri would break the news, if Trini didn't comm the bridge before she got to her, and would stay with her while she worried over the fate of her loved ones.

As it turned out, the closer they came to Liata, the worse the picture got. Burnt out hulks of planetary defense ships greeted them in high orbit and a large amount of debris indicated that a horrific battle had taken place a short time ago. What was perhaps worse were the deep brown gouges in the green surface of the planet where space-based energy weapons had scorched the pristine land and crops of the Liatans, killing indiscriminately and marring the surface of the peaceful planet.

Trini broke down and started to cry when she arrived at the bridge after Micah's summons. Darak's hard arms came around her, surprising Jeri, who supported her at the blue woman's side, and the XO and Jeri shared a concerned look before Jeri stepped back allowing him to take Trini and comfort her in his strong embrace. Jeri watched them for a moment before turning to where Micah sat, alone and hurting at his command post. Silently, she moved to him, sliding up under his shoulder and placing an arm around his shoulders.

"What can we do to help them?" She was glad he accepted her presence and the little comfort she could bring him.

"As soon as we stabilize our orbit, I'm going down," he said softly. "I'd rather Trini didn't come, but there's no way I can keep her from her family. She needs to see who's left, if anyone."

Agnor appeared silently at Micah's other side. "*Dama* Jeri can look after the herd for a bit, and I will keep vigilant on the *Circe* in case the raiders return."

Micah smiled, though it didn't reach his eyes. "Am I that transparent, old friend, that you know my orders before I even give them?"

Agnor shrugged. "Darak is better at offering comfort than I. He will help Trini while you assess damage and formulate plans. You might want to take young Kirt and Welan with you to act as runners. I doubt planetside comms are working normally with all the damage."

"I don't know what I'd do without you, Ag." Micah sighed as he rubbed the stubble on his jaw. He looked as if he had the weight of several worlds on his shoulders, and Jeri resisted the urge to squeeze closer. He knew she was there, supporting him. It would be up to him to lean, if he needed to, on her.

In short order, Jeri was ensconced in the hold with the herd, Agnor was running the bridge with Seta's help and the rest of the crew was translocated to the surface to see what could be seen. At first updates came in regularly, letting those left on the ship know that the non-Council troops who had tried to invade were long gone, though the price of resistance had been high.

Agnor began collecting evidence and clearing what orbital debris he could, to help make their path safer as well clear a path for those who would come later. He also used his special Talent to send word to the Council of the happenings on Liata. Though it drained him somewhat, his presence and special abilities paid off when word was received that several nearby Council ships would be there by the following planetary rotation to help defend and rebuild the ravaged planet.

Jeri took a moment away from the herd to clean up and prepare meals for Agnor and Seta, which she brought to the bridge. Agnor was taking only short combat naps while Seta stood watch. He was also depleting his energy with long-range communications delivered using his Specitar Talent.

"You must rest more, Agnor." Jeri worried, noting the tight set of his compressed lips and the hollows under his eyes.

"I'll rest when we are safe with Council ships all around and aid delivered to those suffering people." His words were tough, but his tone mild as he took the plate of food she offered him with a nod of thanks.

She sat with Agnor and Seta on the bridge to partake of the meal together. As they ate, she talked to them, hoping to relieve some of their stress in a small way.

"I've tried to communicate to the horses what's happened." She munched on a carrot as she spoke. "They are eager to begin working. They feel they can help."

Agnor looked surprised for a moment, then a smile dawned. "They can at that." He shook his head with what looked like wonder. "As can you, by communicating with them. I assume you can communicate with other horses, not just the ones from Pantur, right?"

Jeri tilted her head and nodded, not sure where this was going. "I have always been able to communicate with horses, whether my father's herd on Mithrak or the herds of Pantur. Their minds are alike though the breeding is slightly different."

"One of the problems they're encountering planetside is that the herds have scattered and those animals they have are traumatized and spook easily." Jeri knew Seta had been monitoring the transmissions to analyze ways they could help as well as to catalog information for evidentiary purposes.

"I can call the horses together. Most of them should answer, I think, if they're like the horses I knew on Mithrak and Pantur. The herd we have on board could be helpful in calming the others."

"Agreed." Agnor slapped his hand on the comm panel. "I'm going to tell the captain what we've cooked up. It's time some of the planetside crew rotated up here for rest anyway."

Agnor worked with Micah over the comm for the next few minutes to set up the rest of the plan. Jeri would transport and do what she could to interface with the horses of Liata, hopefully solving one of the more pressing problems. Since horses were relied upon for transport and their load-carrying capability on the tech-limited agricultural world, getting the herds settled was of primary importance.

When Jeri translocated about an hour later with part of the herd they had on board, Micah was there to meet her. He gathered her into his arms, hugging her close before even speaking. He kissed her, not with passion, but with an incredible caring that nearly swept her off her feet.

"I thought of bringing you here as soon as I saw the fear in the horses' eyes, but I didn't want to expose you to this, sweetheart." His gaze was anguished as he looked at her. "I would protect you from it if I could."

She kissed him, then smiled up at him. "I have seen much in my life, Micah. I want to help these people, this world, if I can."

He nodded once, grimly, and turned her in his arms, leading her toward the command area he'd set up on arrival. She had to meet the elders whom he'd been dealing with. He didn't let go of her, keeping her hand firmly in his, even when he introduced her to the Liatans.

Briskly, they arrived at the crux of the matter. The Liatan herds were scattered, and the few horses they had recaptured were terrified. As they spoke, the rest of the sale herd was transported down from the *Circe* and seemed content to mill around in the pasture. The Liatans seemed amazed that they didn't wander off without some sort of hobble or fence.

"Mage Denik," Micah called out as he guided Jeri toward a distinguished-looking older man who seemed the only calm center of a rather large storm in the makeshift command center. "Allow me to introduce my lady." He squeezed her hand and spared her a smile, even as he communicated the seriousness of the situation to all present. Talk ceased so everyone could hear what the Mage Master would say to their leader. "Jeri is a base-level Dominar from a non-Council world. There has been little time to initiate her in our ways, but she has some innate abilities that I believe will be useful to you and your people."

The old man looked at her with assessing eyes and she fought not to squirm. Micah's strong hand squeezing hers gave her courage. She had never liked being the center of attention and had run from it all her life, but it was unavoidable in this moment. She knew this broad declaration of her Talent was just one way Micah used to try to make her aware of her place in his world.

"It's my honor to meet you, *dama*. As you can see, we are in disarray and can use all the helpful hands and Talents we can get. How is it that you may help us?"

She stood shoulder to shoulder with Micah, his deliberate placing of her on equal footing much appreciated. She spoke softly, but it was obvious that everyone within the makeshift command center was listening carefully.

"I may be able to gather your horses," she said timidly, clearing her throat in order to try to put some more confidence in her tone. "Perhaps I can calm them as well."

The older Mage looked surprised, then pleased. His gaze rose briefly to Micah as if for confirmation and the Master's short nod brought a sigh of relief from the older man.

"As you may realize, our herds are an important part of our world. We need them for work and transport. What do you need in the way of assistance?"

She thought quickly, throwing her mind into the problem of what to do with the horses once she called them.

"At first, I will need space to work. Preferably a large paddock that can be secured. Once they gather, experienced hands would be of help to separate the stallions. If there's a trainer or two to direct the hands, that would also be welcome as I can devote my attention to calming the worst of the lot." She thought of the injuries some of the more excitable animals may have suffered as they escaped and ran from the devastation visited on the planet from space. "Healers familiar with treating equine injuries should be standing by."

Denik looked at her, a small nod indicating that he was impressed with her thoughts on the matter.

"Jaril..." he spoke to one of his aides, "...take the *dama* to the South pasture. That should be big enough. Send runners before you to gather the hands and trainers." He turned back to address Micah. "Will you accompany your lady, Master?"

Micah didn't answer immediately, instead turning to look at Jeri. "Shall I go with you this first time, my lady?"

She squeezed his hand and smiled gratefully. "I would welcome your presence and support, Captain."

He smiled at her and it was as if they were the only two people on the planet for that short space of time. If they'd been alone she would have reached up to kiss him. She'd been lonely in his bed without him on the ship while he was working so hard here on the planet. But they were together now, and she realized dimly that she felt more alive in his presence—more complete, more powerful—than she did when he wasn't near. He was quickly becoming as necessary to her as breathing, though she dare not think of the future time when they would not be together.

For now, there was no sign yet that he was tiring of her. She made herself put the thought from her mind and concentrate on the present. She would deal with that dark day when it came, just as she had dealt with the devastating things that had happened in her life since her power had come alive. For now, she would revel in his presence and enjoy each and every moment. For now, she would love him with all her heart and all her soul, even if he could never return the favor.

A discrete cough behind them brought Jeri back to the task at hand and she blushed as they followed the aide, Jaril, outside. They walked through what was left of the village to a large green pasture with a sturdy fence and several gates. Men and women were already gathering, some following from the village, some coming from the farmhouses and half-ruined stables in the distance, in response to the runners Denik had sent ahead.

Jeri looked carefully at the fence line. "This is good. But we'll need those gates opened wide so the horses can get in."

Micah nodded to Jaril, and he sent off a runner to have some of the farmers man each of the far gates. He also had

117

some of the villagers man the gates near the village. Soon the gates were wide open with people sitting on the top rung of the fence, waiting for further instructions.

# Chapter Seven

Jeri strode out to the center of the large field with only Micah trailing her steps. He motioned everyone else to stay back and take positions on the fence. He feared that some of the horses might still be skittish and perhaps violent. He didn't want anyone getting trampled or kicked, and he silently vowed to keep Jeri from harm with his own body if necessary.

Jeri closed her eyes briefly, no doubt assessing the power she would need to send her call as he'd been instructing her to do with any expenditure of her Talent. He was pleased as a teacher that already her Talent was becoming more refined and controlled as compared to when he'd seen her do this on Pantur. She'd been totally untrained then, and he'd felt her power usage in a somewhat ragged way that was quite different from the strong, sure, potent surge of psi energy that went forth from her now. She was not only a quick study, but a Talent to be reckoned with. Just as he'd thought she'd be. And he couldn't be happier. His Jeri was quite a woman, in so many ways.

She sent her silent call and it was only moments before the small herd newly arrived from the *Circe* strode peacefully into the pasture. The horses came to her for a quick pat on the nose, rump or flank as she walked among them. Micah noted quiet murmurs from the people sitting on the fence, but these were the horses she'd brought with her from the ship, so the Liatans were reserving judgment. Still, this trick certainly was something out of the ordinary.

When the first of the half-wild survivors of the attack started to come nervously into the pasture, even the most skeptical watched in surprise and interest. Micah moved to Jeri's side, ready to defend her should it become necessary. But as he'd witnessed on Pantur, even the fearful horses were powerless against her call. She crooned to them, touching them and stroking them, communicating silently and working wonders on the damaged psyches of the terrorized beasts.

One by one she quieted the horses, sorting them as she met with each one. She either directed them over to the group she'd brought from the *Circe*, or sent them to a nearby human to either doctor or segregate from the rest of the group. As time wore on, more and more horses came to her call, entering the pasture from every entrance. They walked to her in the center of the large space, waiting for her attention. Some were injured, some frightened, some were fine physically but in need of direction and she gave to each need, caring for her four-legged friends as she would her human counterparts.

Micah watched throughout, staying silent and monitoring her power levels. He also watched the horses and humans alike, alert to any danger to his lady. The sky was turning lavender and then deeper purple by the time the last of the horses straggled in. Some limped badly, and most of the last ones were injured and more than half-wild with pain and shock. These were the hardest for her to deal with. Several times Micah saw tears on Jeri's face, though she hid them as best she could against the strong necks of her charges as she communed with them.

He marveled again at this small woman he was beginning to love. She was so strong, yet so feminine and small, he was

120

afraid a strong gust of wind would steal her away. He felt like a giant standing next to her, but he was glad of his strength to support her when she started to tire. She leaned against him as she silently accepted his strength and support, dealing with the last few of the horses to answer her call.

He was about to suggest they call it a night when a strangled horse's scream was heard in the night, far out beyond the farthest gate. Jeri immediately stood to attention, along with the other villagers, to see where the sound of distress had come from. Soundlessly, she called two sturdy mares out from the herd and mounted one bareback, looking back only once to see that Micah had mounted the other just behind her.

He realized then that even without conscious thought, she wanted him with her. It was a good sign of how far their relationship had progressed and how much she had come to trust him in the short time they'd been together. With an odd sort of lift to his spirits, he followed her out beyond the fence to see what was going on.

"What is it?" Micah asked as they finally slowed. A magnificent, but ragged-looking stallion was down in the tall grass, a blood trail showing where he'd dragged himself, trying desperately to answer her call.

"Can you do anything with his wounds?" She turned to him, desperation in her eyes. "If we can stop the bleeding, he might have a chance."

Micah's face showed his determination as he jumped from the mare's back and walked calmly toward the great beast. The stallion accepted Jeri's gentle stroking, but Micah was a stranger—one without the gift of communication with the huge animal—and he approached carefully.

Jeri crooned to the stallion, calming him though his sides

were quivering in agony. His powerful hooves churned helplessly against the grass as he listed on his side, a huge gash running the length of one flank. He'd lost a lot of blood and older wounds that were half-healed marred the beauty of his black coat, gleaming startling red or dull brown against the black. The whites of his eyes showed as Micah came to his side, following Jeri's lead and laying his hands gently on the worst of the bleeders.

"He was trapped in a ravine with several of his mares and a few young foals. Human children too." She spoke softly, watching both the horse and the man as Micah applied his potent healing touch to the stallion's ravaged flesh. "He was protecting them, but when I called, he fought his way clear of the ravine. He knew he had to get help for the trapped mares and foals, as well as the children. They have water and grass, but no food. The children are not doing well."

Micah looked up at her, determination in his eyes. He also saw that more of the villagers had followed after them to see what was going on. He was thankful for their curiosity and the lanterns they brought with them as night was falling in earnest. He let loose the pulse of healing power along the stallion's side, a little surprised himself at how neatly the flesh began to knit together, free of infection and clean of dirt and grime. He'd never been so strong before, and he guessed it must be due to his elevation to Mage Master. He hadn't had occasion to need his healing skills since moving up in power, and he was pleasantly surprised at the increase.

"Can he tell you how to get to this ravine?" Micah asked, noting the way the stallion's ears perked around to the sound of his voice.

"I see the spot." Jeri nodded. "Micah, we have to help them."

"Let's get him settled with the villagers, and we'll go after them in a hopper. The governor has one that he was using to ferry wounded, but they gave up the search a few days back. They thought they'd gotten to everyone they could get to and assumed anyone they hadn't yet found was dead."

Micah did all he could do for the stallion while Jeri continued to commune with him, assuring him they would rescue the children and his mares. Micah took a moment to comm the ship. He would use the ship's translocator to move himself and Jeri to the local governor's house and take the hopper from there. Since all they had to go on in finding the right ravine was an image in Jeri's mind, they didn't have grid coordinates. That meant they couldn't translocate to the ravine. They had to find it the old-fashioned way.

It was dark when they finally found the spot. Even with the bright landing lights of the hopper, it was impossible to find a place to set down within the ravine.

"This is no good," Micah shook his head as he hovered, looking for a way.

"Those kids don't look good, Micah. The horses are in better shape, but they're scared and confused."

"We can lower supplies, but I doubt those children are in any shape to utilize them."

She looked at him, a plan formulating behind her eyes. "Can you lower me with the supplies? I'll go and do what I can for them and the horses until sunrise. Maybe then you can find a way to land in the ravine safely."

"If one of us has to go down, I'd rather it be me." Micah met her gaze with grave sincerity.

She shrugged, trying to make light of the moment. "I can't fly this thing, but I can help those kids with the supplies and calm the horses."

"Damn," he shook his head. "I don't like this, but you're right." He reached out to touch her cheek, drawing her close for a quick, hard kiss. "Go aft and see if there's a harness you can use to secure yourself to the supply pallet."

With him talking her through attaching the winch cable, securing the load and herself to it, they managed to make everything as safe as possible for a hopper drop in the dead of night with only the landing lights as a guide. The horses milled around beneath, but when she sent out her call to them, they moved back, giving her room as Micah activated the winch from the cockpit, lowering her slowly toward the rocky ground far below.

She hit the ground with a jarring thud, but made it safely. The horses stayed back at her command until she managed to unhook the winch cable and jump into the hopper's hover path to signal Micah she was safe. She began setting up three emergency floodlights. Self-erecting stands made them easy to get going. Soon the area was flooded with light and Micah moved the hopper back up to the rim of the ravine and landed.

He'd given her a short-range comm so they were able to stay in touch as she set up the work area, then went about finding the children who were too weak to walk and began basic med care for them. Most of the first-aid packs they'd brought with them were automated so thankfully they didn't require a great deal of skill to use. She attached the sensors where indicated and let the units do the rest.

Before long she had a row of children of varying ages being treated by the first-aid units. A few others were eating ravenously from the supplies she'd unpacked. The horses were standing respectfully back, watching all and waiting their turn as she promised them. She kept up a silent dialogue with them, letting them know their leader was safe and had accomplished his mission to get help. She was pleased by their warm feelings of pride in their stallion and was interested to note the memories they shared of his leadership. He'd led them away as a devastating path of destruction rained down on them from the heavens, bringing them to this ravine. The energy weapons from above had sealed off the entrance, trapping them, but there was water and grass, so the equines were reasonably happy for the moment.

It was the children, mostly the offspring of field workers, who were suffering in their captivity. There was little in the canyon that the human children could eat, though the water was plentiful.

As soon as Jeri was sure she'd found and helped all the kids, she moved to the horses, touching each one and reassuring them when necessary. Most were injured in some way and she worked through the night doctoring their wounds with what skill she had. She talked frequently with Micah over the comm, giving him updates and just wanting to hear his voice. Before she knew it, the shorter-than-standard night of Liata was ending and dawn was turning the horizon lavender and gold. She had worked through the night and was truly exhausted, but there was still more to do.

The horses were finally cared for and the children were slowly improving with real food in their stomachs and medications in their systems. Micah alerted her on the comm that he was going to look for a landing site, so she stood to survey what she could of the ravine in the early dawn light to try to assist.

It was easier than she expected to land beside the small lake at the center of the ravine. Within minutes Micah was out of the hopper and dragging her into his strong arms, holding her close.

"I'm glad that's over." He kissed her soundly. "I don't like it when we're apart, Jeri. I spent all night worrying about you."

His tone melted her heart, and she relished the feel of his strong arms pulling her tight against his hard chest. She was bone tired, but his presence buoyed her up, giving her strength and making her feel warm deep inside. With his help, they got the survivors out of the ravine.

Micah hadn't been idle during the night. He'd been organizing rescue. On the rim of the ravine, many vehicles waited to transport the children. Earth-moving machines went to work at first light to reopen the entrance so the horses could climb out on their own.

The children were taken to the nearest med facility that was still standing and the small herd was reunited with their stallion. He was recovering from his wounds, but the wild herd would require more of her special communication before they found their way in the human society. Jeri promised herself that she would find a good place for the herd where they could stay together, working with their human counterparts in a mutually beneficial arrangement.

The Board of Governors was waiting for them upon their return late that day—or at least, what was left of the Board. Final tallies were being completed and the Governors were all accounted for in one way or another. An emergency meeting had been called to help organize the relief and rescue efforts around the planet. After seeing what Jeri could do, they asked that she spend the next days traveling the surface of the planet, sending out her call to the native horses and rounding them up.

Micah went with her as she greeted the equine survivors and calmed them with quiet word-pictures in their minds. Everywhere they went, he stayed by her side, often holding her by the hand or supporting her with an arm around her shoulders. It became clear to the Liatans that they were a couple. Accommodations offered them were those that would be given to couples, and they never declined a moment together as they traveled the surface of the planet using the ship's translocation system to transport them from place to place with a minimum of fuss.

Everywhere they went, Jeri chose members of the herd from Pantur that would fit in well with the people and circumstances they met. Micah never accepted any payment for the expensive horses, gifting them to the hard-hit people of Liata, who needed them now more than ever. Everywhere the Mage Master and his lady went, peace and order soon followed.

After the first few planetary rotations, the Council warship *Valiant* made orbit to help defend Liata from further attack and join in the work of clearing the immediate space around Liata of debris and bodies that would be honored with rites of death as soon as they could be identified and hopefully returned to their families. After the *Valiant*, two more Council ships arrived with supplies and experts to help rebuild and replant, salvaging what could be salvaged of the scorched landscape.

None but the Mage Master's lady could calm the herds, and word spread of her amazing Talent and the incredibly powerful man who guarded her day and night.

So too did word of the Mage Master who had amazing skill with healing Talent. Both Micah and Darak used their Talent to heal those people who they came into contact with, while teaching some of the skills to Jeri. She was proficient, if not truly gifted with healing Talent, and was able to heal simple hurts as long as she was in contact with them. Micah used whatever opportunity he had to teach her more control of her Talent because the attack on Liata had driven home to him, as nothing else could, how vulnerable she would be until she learned to control her Talent and use it to defend herself.

127

Luckily for him, she was an able student. Much of the control exercise came as second nature to her. Jeri's hard-won and nearly impenetrable shielding had taught her the basics and been a skill that impacted many of their lessons in a positive way. She was already half-taught, though she had no terminology for the things she had made herself do in order to survive and hide her incredible power from those who would enslave it.

She had no need to hide on Liata, and she was expending a great deal of her power daily in order to help them rebuild. Each night as they lay together, Micah and Jeri's powers replenished themselves, feeding off the passion that never dimmed and only seemed to glow brighter the more they were together. Part of the reason sex was so open among the Council worlds, Micah admitted one night while he held her and they talked idly of their backgrounds, was due to the fact that the energies created and released during the sex act so readily replenished those with Talent.

With each passing day, Jeri began to understand more about her abilities, more about her lover and more about his culture. With each passing day, more of the ravaged world of Liata was put back to rights—or at least as close as could be after such devastation. With each passing day, Jeri found herself a little more in love with Micah, though she realized more than ever she was living a fantasy. Everywhere they went he was treated with the respect due someone of almost royal lineage. People would look askance at her rough appearance at his side, and she realized their time together was a fantastic idyll that would never last beyond the here and now.

She feared that her heart would be well and truly smashed to smithereens when the time came that they had to part. Until that day though, she would memorize his face, his touch and his smile, revel in his rare laughter and bask in his attention.

She would give him a memory or two along the way, she vowed, and store her memories against the time when she was no longer with him. Though she knew already that she would miss him forever.

The work was never ending and the pace was grueling, but Jeri and Micah spared little time for themselves except to eat and sleep. Of course, they managed to fit in making love sometime in the planetside night. Still, when Darak commed to tell them the *Valiant* had made orbit, Micah nearly groaned with relief. The warship's presence would take a lot of pressure off his crew. The *Circe* had been watching the space around Liata in case of renewed attack.

After speaking with Darak, the next comm was from Jened, captain of the *Valiant*. Jeri was nearby and was surprised when the voice over Micah's comm was that of a woman. Micah's eyes twinkled as she moved into his embrace while he wrapped up the courtesy call with the other captain.

"Mmm, you feel good in my arms, Jeri." He breathed deeply, inhaling her unique scent.

"I like being in your arms, Captain."

"Then we are in agreement," he said playfully, squeezing her bottom as she snuggled closer. She was tired, he could tell, but holding up like a trooper. "Captain Jened will be coming to meet with the Planetary Council and wants to hear what we've found. She'll probably transport to wherever we are sometime tomorrow. Jened and I were at school together. You'll like her."

Jeri nodded tiredly against his chest. "The *Valiant* is a warcruiser, right? And a woman is in charge? I think I like her already."

Micah laughed as he led her to the bed they'd been given for the night, removing her clothing as he guided her. She was so sleepy he gave a moment's thought to letting her sink into sleep. But he wasn't strong enough to deny himself—to deny them both the pleasure and the renewal of their energies that would come with the act of making love.

He undressed her and stretched her out on the long bed, coming to rest beside her. He swept his clothing out of the way and onto the floor. One good thing about coming planetside was that they'd finally been able to get some decent clothes for her, the kind that fit well and came off easily. His favorite.

When he had them both naked, he moved with languorous slowness, starting at her ear and working his way down her body with his mouth, leaving no portion untouched, or unkissed. She closed her eyes and simply enjoyed his efforts, sighing when he hit particularly sensitive spots along his journey.

When he reached her thighs, all he had to do was tug and she eagerly spread her legs for him, her pussy almost crying for him to take her. But he wanted to taste her first. He wanted to sweep his tongue through the soft folds that belonged to him, bringing his woman the pleasure only he could bring her.

He realized distantly that with each moment he spent with Jeri he was becoming more possessive of her, but he dismissed the thought before it could take root. He would enjoy her for as long as he had her, and he was beginning to realize that if he could convince her to stay forever, he would be a very happy man.

He pushed thoughts of the future away as he leaned in to swirl his strong tongue through her folds, using his fingers to spread her lips wide while his tongue lapped at her cream. He settled himself on the bed between her thighs, knowing he would not stop until he'd brought her to fulfillment at least once with his mouth. It was one of his favorite pastimes.

He'd also learned over their time together that sometimes he could excite her with just his words. She was so responsive to anything he wanted to try, but he didn't want to push her too far or too fast. After all, she'd come to him a virgin. She'd still been virgin at an age when most of his people had long since discovered the pleasures of the flesh. He enjoyed bringing her new experiences and discovering with her the secrets of her own sexuality. She was more adventurous than he had imagined a virgin would be, and it set him on fire when she responded in such an uninhibited way.

"Remember that day in the game room?" He tongued her clit between words. "Remember when the men were doing Seta at the same time?" He felt the clenching of her little hole around his tongue as he took a moment to delve deep. He knew she remembered the hot scene and how it turned her on. He smiled against her pussy as he moved his hand around behind her to finger the tight rosebud of her anus.

"Do you imagine that sometimes, Jeri? Do you wonder what it would be like to have me and another man take you together?" He smiled when her breath caught and her pussy creamed so close to his lips. He couldn't help but lean in to lap up her sweet juices. "Maybe Agnor? He could take your pussy while I take your ass. He likes hot pussy, and I know he's thought about yours. He told me so."

She whimpered as she pushed her hips up at him, but he refused to lick the tempting bud presented to him, pushing instead on his finger, embedding it in her ass as she cried out. She was so slick with her own juices, his finger slid in easily as he watched, transfixed by the sight.

"Or maybe Darak. I know you saw his cock in the elevator when he was with Trini. Just imagine it moving in your ass. Darak likes your butt. He watches you walk when he doesn't think anyone's looking. The poor guy practically pants when

131

you walk by."

"Micah," she cried out as he added another finger and began moving them rhythmically, opening her up.

"You like that?" He chuckled as he watched her ride closer and closer to the edge. "I'll give you anything you want, Jeri. Anyone you want. As long as I can be there too. Always."

She flew apart in his arms and he stayed with her through the crisis, kissing her skin with tender lips, heightening her pleasure as he sucked on her clit, making her rise higher. He didn't think too long or too hard about what he might have just admitted in a roundabout way, but deep inside he realized he couldn't picture a time when they weren't together.

She calmed after long moments, and he began to drive her back towards a new completion, but this time he planned to go over the edge with her. She was still primed and he was hotter for her than he'd ever been for any other woman. She was special in so many ways, but especially in this way, she was his match and more.

He stalked upward, over her body, allowing her to pull him in close for a deep kiss. He knew she liked the taste of herself on his lips. She'd shared that with him weeks ago, and he never missed a chance to let her taste him in whatever way she wanted. She surprised him by grasping him around the neck and tugging just enough to indicate that she wanted to roll over. She wanted to be on top this time, and he didn't object at all. In fact, he chuckled as he moved to settle her over him, positioning her long legs on either side of his hips, just as he liked.

"You'll be the death of me, woman. But what a way to go."

He woke her later in the planetside night with a deep stroking in her pussy that she could not ignore.

"Did you like what we did before? Did you like my fingers up your ass?"

He felt her squirm and knew she was embarrassed. She was so cute when she was embarrassed.

"Tell me true, baby. Do you ever think about taking my cock up your ass?"

He knew she found his whispered words scandalous. He could tell by the clenching of her pussy around his fingers as he teased her.

"I've been thinking about it," he admitted with a chuckle. "Probably more than I should be."

He turned on his side, moving away from her. Now would come the decision. He wouldn't pressure her, but if she wanted him the way he wanted her, she'd come to him. He left the choice up to her.

Moments later, he sighed with relief as she found her way back into his arms. She snuggled against his chest in the way he'd come to treasure as he kissed the top of her head in grateful appreciation.

"I've thought about it, Micah. But I don't know. It seems like it would be painful."

Her whispers in the dark touched him, and he pulled her closer reassuringly. She was so precious to him.

"I won't lie. It can be painful if the man rushes his partner or doesn't know what he's doing. Or if he just doesn't care. But I would never hurt you, baby. And I've done it before. Many times. I know how to make it good for you."

"I don't like hearing about how many women you've had, Micah."

Her grousing endeared her to him though he'd never felt the possessive pride when other women had felt jealousy over him. This little Mithrakian horse tamer was something altogether new and different in his realm of experience. She was incredibly special.

"Just be glad I know what I'm doing. You're going to love this, baby. I promise."

He reached for the tube of lubricating oil he'd left on the bedside table and moved quickly and efficiently. Warming a generous amount in his hands, he reached down, stroking over her sensitive flesh, enticing her with his caresses until he'd reached his objective. Parting her sumptuous cheeks, he zeroed in on her ass, spreading the special oil and dipping it inside.

She squirmed and gasped at the uncommon invasion, but she was with him. He could tell by the gushing of her pussy and the response she could no longer hide from him. He knew her body too well. She was enjoying every move he made, and he vowed to keep it that way.

She shuddered around his fingers in a tiny completion, and he moved her further into passion, adding another finger to stretch her ass. She was tight, but eager and he would prepare her fully before he took her.

"So you do like that?" He pushed deeper and was satisfied with her gasp of delight. "I knew you'd be hot like this, Jeri. I've dreamed of this."

She was nearly ready, so he took a few extra moments to enjoy her little gasps and whimpers as she grew used to his possession and prepared for more. Eventually he couldn't hold out any longer. He moved her around, positioning her with pillows and his hands so that she was open and ready to accept him. Sliding forward on the bed, he came to his knees behind her. It was a sight he would never forget, nor would he forget the look of his thick cock, sliding home within her virgin ass.

He pushed gently, letting her get used to him a little at a

time, but she was taking him eagerly and with little pain since he'd prepared her so thoroughly.

"Push down, baby. Let me in."

# Chapter Eight

Jeri did as he asked, knowing enough by now to trust him and follow where he led in pleasure. He'd never led her wrong. She gritted her teeth and pushed back into him, feeling a muted pop when the head of his cock pushed past the tight ring of muscle guarding her rear. The sensation was indescribable. Nerve endings she never knew she had were screaming in pleasure and the small pain was heightening her senses in a way she never would have expected.

Micah thrust lightly, letting her acclimate to his size, but it was easier than she had thought it would be. And much more pleasurable. She felt him push steadily into her, moving slowly and letting her get used to him, and her passions flamed. Just the thought of what he was doing to her made her pussy wet. And Micah knew it, since he had one of his long fingers in her pussy, rubbing until she squirmed.

"You're tight, baby. You're burning me alive."

"Micah," she cried as he hit the bundle of nerves inside her with knowing fingers. He stroked over and over as he began thrusting in earnest. The combination of the two sensations was earth-shattering and she started to come multiple times, with little space between the orgasms until it seemed she rode one incredibly long, hard wave of pleasure that threatened her consciousness. She'd never passed out from pleasure, though

Micah knew how to bring her close to the edge. This time, she feared she'd tumble over it, but Micah would be there to catch her. She trusted him.

She felt Micah moving hard and fast inside her as she keened her pleasure, then the tightening and the warm squirt of his come as he came deep inside her. At length, he collapsed on her, pushing her into the mattress, still digging into her ass with short strokes as he possessed her as completely as a man could possibly possess a woman.

She felt claimed. Staked out and possessed utterly. It was an oddly reassuring feeling that she never would have imagined. But she liked belonging to this man, this StarLord who was so far out of her reach. She liked being his, and she hoped he realized it just the tiniest bit.

Micah stopped shuddering after long moments, and her own amazing tidal wave of pleasure left her drained and nearly unconscious.

"Is this any way for a StarLord to greet a member of the Fleet?"

The laughing female voice sounded through the small room, waking Jeri immediately. She gasped and pulled the thin sheet over her nakedness. Micah was slower to react as he opened one eye to glare at the woman standing over their bed in full uniform.

"It's good to see you, Jened. I think."

She laughed and sat next to him on the wide bed, apparently untroubled by his nakedness. Jeri felt her face flaming with embarrassment and a bit of righteous anger. This woman was acting all too familiar with *her* lover's body.

"I couldn't resist, Micah. How've you been? And who's your little friend?"

Jeri couldn't seem to stifle the squeak of indignation as Micah hauled her close with one strong arm wrapped around her waist. He kissed her with a smooching sound on the cheek before nuzzling into her hair in a display of affection.

"Jeri, my heart, this insane woman is Captain Jened of the *Valiant*. You'll learn to ignore her bossy ways eventually."

Jeri was at a loss as to how to greet a warship captain while wearing nothing but a thin sheet. And the sheet wasn't very effective as an article of clothing at that.

"The poor girl looks mortified, Micah. She's not from a Council world, is she?"

"Jened, Jeri base-tested at Dominar, so show a little respect." His words were laced with familiar sarcasm. Jeri could tell these two were old friends and she found herself a little jealous of their easy banter while two of the three people in the room were stark naked. Micah ruffled her hair, stroking it back from her face as he pulled her up to sit on his lap.

"Forgive me, *dama*." Jeri was somewhat gratified when the other woman's attitude toward her changed a bit. She thought she saw a wary sort of respect flare in her eyes, though Jeri couldn't be absolutely certain.

"To answer your question," Micah continued, "Jeri was born and raised on Mithrak."

Jened's face grew stern. "Wizards give you trouble, *dama*?"

"They killed my parents, scattered our herds, and took my sister. I was hunted for many years before I escaped." Jeri was surprised by the other woman's apparent knowledge of the situation on her homeworld.

Captain Jened bowed her head. "I'm sorry. I've heard things about their practices. I'm glad you got away from them."

Jeri considered the woman, touched by her very real show

of compassion. Maybe they could be friends after all. If Jeri could ever get beyond her embarrassment.

Captain Jened transported out a short time later, after discussing plans for the various ships in orbit and those that had been dispatched but wouldn't make it to the planet for some time yet. Jeri watched with new respect as Micah and the woman captain made detailed plans for the defense of Liata, should it become necessary, even though their two lonely ships couldn't do much against a large-scale attack. She listened with interest as they planned and strategized for all contingencies, learning a little about the way military commanders worked in the process.

A week or so after they'd arrived, Liata was well on the way to recovery. Many had died in the scorching of the land and more had died in orbit, defending the planet from the raiders. Trini had lost a sibling as well as a set of grandparents and an assortment of cousins, but her extended family were accounted for in one way or another by the time Micah, Darak and Jeri returned to the original transport site.

Jeri sought her friend Trini while Micah and Darak went to interface with the planetary governors, as was their duty. Jeri found Trini, her deep violet eyes wet with tears as she sat by the bedside of her youngest brother, Tendil.

"What's wrong, Trini? Isn't he recovering?" Jeri asked as she took in the pale face of the young man and Trini's sad expression.

"He isn't responding to the treatment, they say." She hiccupped and threw herself into Jeri's arms.

Jeri held her close and soothed her, already using her new skills to send a telepathic message to Micah and perhaps Darak, if her range proved to be that broad. Communicating telepathically was something Agnor had been teaching her, though she hadn't seen him for more than a few moments in the days she'd been traveling all over Liata with Micah.

Still, she had been learning steadily as she used her skills and maybe she shouldn't have been so surprised when both Darak and Micah acknowledged her summons and arrived only moments later. Darak brushed a large palm over Trini's head in a comforting gesture, then went directly to the bed where her young brother lay, unmoving. Micah joined him and motioned Jeri to take up a position at the foot of the bed as Trini watched with hope in her dark eyes.

Darak took the boy's hand in his. Jeri knew he was sending out his energy to mesh with the boy's fading life force, taking stock of what might be done.

"He's weak, but he's a fighter." Darak smiled gently toward Trini. He turned to Micah and his eyes were shadowed, Jeri could see. "I may need your assistance, cousin."

Micah moved closer and motioned Jeri to stand with him. "We can both help."

Darak looked sharply at Jeri for a moment but then nodded. "I'll have to go deep," he turned back to his young patient, his eyes narrowing. "The infection has moved fast and lies deep within. Once I start, do not interfere. Just feed me power slowly and steadily when I start to fail. I'll only have one shot at this."

Micah nodded grimly and set one hand on Darak's shoulder, taking Jeri's hand with his free hand, completing the link. She could feel him touching the energy link they'd formed over the days of training and loving together. She didn't resist, interested to see how one Talent could aid another in such a way. The idea was somewhat foreign to her, but it made sense that if it could be done, someone with as much power and skill as Micah would be able to do it.

She remembered his warning that such things were never done lightly because it could harm all parties involved, but from the dire condition the boy was in, there seemed to be no alternative. She sat and watched, feeding power at Micah's direction, letting him lead the way in this tricky maneuver. He was the most skilled and most powerful among them, and he would feed and watch over Darak's specialized Talent in healing the boy if at all possible. It was dicey, but it was necessary if they wanted to save him.

It took a lot of work and great skill, but Darak was able to make the connection with Tendil's flagging spirit and remove the worst of the infection from the boy's system. By the end of the long treatment, Darak couldn't even stand. Micah helped him with one hand around his shoulders to another room that had a large bed and deposited him on it before helping Jeri to the same bed and collapsing himself in utter fatigue. Within seconds all three were heavily asleep.

In the other room, Trini kept watch over her weak little brother, but his cheeks were flushed with returning health and his fever was almost completely gone. He was drained from the fight, but she felt his spirit glow strong and knew her friends had worked a miracle. They'd saved her little brother. She wept with joy and relief as she bathed his brow and kissed him, unwilling to let him out of her sight until he woke. She would keep watch over him, and over the truest friends she had ever known while they slept and renewed themselves.

Warm hands woke Jeri from the deep, dreamless sleep she'd stumbled into after feeding so much of her power to Darak through her link with Micah. She was still half asleep, her mind fuzzy, but she felt the warm presence at her back with familiar happiness as two large hands reached around to stroke her breasts and warm her blood.

Warm lips nuzzled her neck, the rasp of male skin making her shiver as strong teeth bit down gently. She was on fire. The heat was all around, behind her and...in front of her?

Jeri's eyes shot open and met the questioning gaze of her lover. Micah was less than a foot away from her, on his side, watching her carefully, banked heat in his eyes.

But then, whose strong fingers even now massaged her naked breasts, pulling at her nipples? And when had she lost her clothing?

It could only be one man. Darak.

And Micah didn't look mad. He looked cautious and...excited?

"You are so beautiful, Jeri." The lips at her neck spoke softly against her skin and she shivered, holding Micah's gaze as Darak continued, "Will you share yourself with us? Will you let me in?"

Jeri sought some direction from Micah. She didn't know what to do. But her body cried out for more of Darak's skilled touches as he continued to excite her senses. She knew Micah well enough by now to know that he was enjoying this, but he wouldn't push her to do anything she didn't want to do.

"Micah?" Her voice was a whimper as Darak shifted one big hand to trail down her stomach and play with the curls above her pussy. He lifted her top leg up and back, over his own, curling one knee between her legs and spreading her wide as he moved his hand to toy with her clit. His hands were so hot. They made her squirm as her pussy spasmed and she creamed for him.

"She's wet, Micah. She likes me." Darak's chuckle sounded

against the soft skin where her shoulder met her neck as he nuzzled, licked and bit softly, heightening her confused passions.

"Only if you want it, Jeri. You don't have to do this. Only if you're ready." Micah raised one long-fingered hand to gently touch her cheek. "I didn't plan this when I dumped us in here last night, but we've expended too much energy. This will renew us. But only if you want it. Such a thing cannot be forced." He traced her lips with one fingertip, making her shiver. "Do you want this? Do you want to share yourself with us both?"

Her mind was a flurry of confusion. She loved the sensations Darak was creating in her body with his knowing hands, his fingers blunter and thicker than Micah's. She had only ever known Micah and though the idea of having two men at once was a titillating fantasy, it was quite a different thing when faced with it in reality. She didn't know what to do. Her body craved the pleasure these two men could give her, but her heart and soul belonged to Micah alone.

Still, she'd come to respect and even like Darak. She'd learned by watching him with the others that he wasn't the total bad boy he liked to portray. He had a good heart and he truly cared for others before himself. She also knew she'd hurt him by her fear of him, though he would never admit it, and perhaps she could prove to him in this way, without saying the words, that she really did care for him, and wasn't afraid anymore. He was a good man, but he wasn't easy speaking of emotions or the things he'd done to safeguard his people and his small family aboard the *Circe*.

"Don't be afraid," Darak whispered softly in her ear. "I would never hurt you, *dama*, only worship you as you deserve." His soft breath made hers catch. His use of the formal title and his tone made her think he really did care for her and didn't want her to be afraid of him. That, more than anything, decided her. She didn't want him to think that she still feared him. She could tell how much that hurt him, and she never wanted to hurt such a valiant and brave warrior, a protector of the weak and a man every bit as deserving of respect as her lover, Micah.

"Do you want this, truly?" she asked Micah, who watched carefully. She noted the flare of heat in his eyes as she smiled, placing one of her hands over Darak's where it played with her nipple and holding one out to her lover.

Micah took her hand and brought it to his lips, kissing her palm as he held her gaze. "I want you to know the pleasures we can bring you. I only want your happiness, Jeri. And I want to share in your pleasures. Always."

Darak's head came up from her shoulder and she could tell he was watching his cousin intently, but Micah only had eyes for her as he turned her hand and sucked her fingers deep into his mouth, laving them with his tongue. After thoroughly sucking them, he moved her hand down his chest, trailing the residual wetness, until he wrapped them around his aroused cock. She took over from there, squeezing the way he'd shown her and smiling into his gaze, which had never left hers.

"I want you. Both. I want to know what it's like."

Darak lowered his head, growling against her skin as he sucked the sensitive flesh of her neck. His hand delved deep into her pussy, setting up a rhythm that had her squirming.

"Be at ease, sweet Jeri, and have no fear. Micah will oversee the joining of our energies and he and I both will direct your pleasures. Just relax and let us do the work." He rolled her onto her back so that he could meet her gaze. "I have wanted to kiss you for so long." He placed an almost chaste kiss on her lips, making her want more while he toyed with the ends of the chain she wore around her neck, his eyes darkening with desire. "I want to see this beautiful adornment upon your

144

nipples, even though it's not my mark. I've wanted to show you how much I appreciate the light and laughter you've brought to Micah. He is part of my family, and I love him as my own brother. You've been good for him, Jeri. It makes my heart happy."

She saw the truth of his words as this normally reticent man spoke of his feelings for her and for his cousin. She knew Micah heard every word and she could feel his surprise and deep love for his cousin through their shared link. This would be a joining of hearts as well as bodies, she realized. It wasn't the tawdry display she'd been taught to expect by the more restrictive morals of her homeworld. Among psi Talented people, this act of pleasure could join hearts and souls.

"I'm sorry I was afraid of you at first, Darak." She reached upward to cup his cheek in her hand, pleased when he moved into her caress. "And I'm sorry if you think I'm still afraid of you. I'm not. I've come to see how much Micah relies on you. How much he loves you. And I've admired the way you care for him and for the crew, even though you try so hard to hide it."

Darak gave his cousin a rueful smile. "The wench sees too much, Micah. Does she lay bare your soul as well with so few words?"

Micah leaned on his elbow, just as Darak was doing, on her other side. He smiled slowly, moving one hand up to cup her breast and excite her nipple.

"She sees straight to the heart, Dar. Straight and true."

"A rare Talent, indeed. I've never joined with a woman with as much power as you, Jeri. I felt the flavor of your Talent when you were helping me heal and it was heady. As is the scent of your skin." He bent his head to bury his nose between her breasts, inhaling deeply while she giggled. Meeting Micah's gaze, a serious light entered his eyes. "I will be careful. But you'll be guiding us, right? I don't want to hurt her."

Micah actually laughed at his cousin's worried look. "Don't worry too much about her, my friend. It's more likely she'll singe your senses than the other way around."

"Really?" Darak looked from Micah to the woman between them with wonder.

"Truly." The look on Micah's face was one of pride. "The energy we fed you in the healing was only a small fraction of the brightness of her flame. It's a beautiful thing to behold, Dar. Almost as beautiful as she is." Micah placed a kiss on her lips, gentle and reverent, and she was nearly overwhelmed. "I will watch over you, Jeri, always. Don't worry." His words were whispered against her lips as he met her gaze with pride, reverence and something more that she couldn't quite identify, but it warmed a place in her heart she thought long dead.

Micah moved back then, making himself comfortable at her side, propping his head on one hand as he watched them. He occasionally reached out to fondle her as Darak went to work arousing her senses.

"First a kiss, sweet Jeri. I've wanted to taste your lips for a very long time." Darak's dark eyes were serious as he watched her reactions. He gave her plenty of time to object, but in the end, she moved her head up fractionally to meet his lips. They were warm, firm and demanding, and his taste was like fire and strong Edian wine. It was a pleasant sensation and she fell headfirst into his expert kiss, following gladly where he led.

His hands roamed her body and he unfastened the chain from around her neck expertly. Darak took one nipple while Micah assisted with the other, tugging until they were hard, then laving them with their mouths until her nipples were long and pointed. The two men tightened the loops over her nipples working in tandem while she gasped at the twin sensations.

When they were secure, Darak leaned up and back, tugging the chain with expert pressure, making her moan at the sensation. He was gentle, but firm as he spread her legs wide.

"Let me see your pussy, sweet Jeri. I've dreamed of this moment so many times." Easing the pressure on her nipple chain, he moved down the bed, concentrating on the V between her legs, spread wide for him. "You're beautiful," he praised her, touching lightly, then with firmer strokes as he explored the folds and dips revealed to him. "And so wet for me. Do you like this?" He plunged two big fingers into her, gratified by the immediate increase in wetness and the easy glide of his fingers into her innermost core. "Answer me, wench. Do you like it?"

"Yes." Her answer was dragged from gasping lips as he set up a rhythm with his fingers that was different from Micah's usual touches, and oh-so-exciting. She'd only ever been intimate with Micah and having a different man's hands on her was new. Everything he did was titillating. And Micah watched with proud, approving eyes as she climbed higher and higher, occasionally reaching out a hand to stroke her soft skin as if he couldn't quite help himself.

At the same time, she felt her Talent rising, reaching out as it sometimes did with Micah. This time, it reached for Darak. She knew enough now to sense Darak's own strong Talent reaching towards her. It was a warm, enveloping sort of feeling that made her feel cherished and respected in an odd way. She knew Micah was watching closely to make sure their Talents were compatible and that no clash of energies would be unleashed. He would call a halt at the first sign of incompatibility, but she felt the rightness of Darak's energies meshing with hers and by Micah's calm demeanor, she could tell there would be little problem unless perhaps one of them lost control. She hoped it wasn't her. As the novice Talent here, she knew that of the three of them, she had the least amount of real control over her energies. If anybody got hurt here, it would most likely be her fault.

She could barely focus on such things when Darak leaned down to stroke her clit with his long, wet tongue. He ate her like she was a tasty treat, smiling and humming against her clit in a way that made her reach a small climax, flooding his hand with more of her moisture as he continued to piston inside her with his fingers. He added a third finger, smiling when she began the rise to ecstasy once more.

His touch was a little rougher than Micah's, but it was exciting all the same. He moved to kneel between her legs, never removing his mouth from her clit as she felt herself approaching that peak once more, this time a little higher than the last. The wave broke, hard and fast as he kept her primed, ready and gushing.

"Open your eyes, Jeri. I want you to know who possesses you." The words were low and gruff and oddly stirring. Jeri looked up into the bottomless pools of Darak's dark eyes and felt for the slightest moment that she could see the bright shining energy that was this special man's soul. It was a beautiful sight.

"Take me, Darak. Let me feel you inside me."

She felt the joining of their energies first, a stark meshing that was different from the seamless way she joined without thought with Micah. It was a little jarring, but it felt good when their Talents merged and fed off one another while Darak's long, strong body began to possess her fully. He moved between her legs, making her feel pressure then an unfamiliar fullness. Micah was a big man, as was Darak, but Darak's cock was a little longer than her lover's. Longer and curved slightly, making her feel things in a whole new way as he brushed the sensitive nerves inside her sheath.

Micah was an extraordinary lover and Darak seemed his match in almost every way. Both of these men were able to stir her senses to such heights, she didn't ever want to come down.

Darak began moving inside her, starting slowly, then picking up his pace as he felt her readiness. His gaze held hers with hidden messages of love, respect and honor that made her insides quake. His soul was completely open to her for the first time since they'd met. The wall he usually hid behind was well and truly down, she realized with some awe, and the soul behind it was every bit as sensitive, caring and loving as she'd imagined. She saw it all in his eyes, so dark and deep, though no longer as mysterious to her. He was a special man indeed. As special as Micah, in his way.

"Darak," she cried out at the small explosion in her core. His low chuckle only fired her senses further. He was keeping her on edge, letting her have multiple little explosions, but building up to a crescendo that might very likely kill her with pleasure.

"All in good time, sweet Jeri. I want you to remember this."

"You're killing me."

Both men laughed at her tone and she turned her eyes to Micah, noting how excited he was to witness his lover being taken by his best friend.

"Don't let her off easy, Dar. Make her scream for it."

Her growl made Darak laugh loud and long, stirring his dick inside her in a way that made her whimper. She was so close. She felt another minor explosion go off inside her, building toward who knew what as Darak sped up, his force increasing until he was pounding into her, hard and rougher than Micah had ever been. She loved every minute of it.

Darak was in heaven. It was just that simple. This small

Mithrakian woman was sweeter than the finest wine he'd ever tasted, more responsive than any woman he'd ever had and more exciting than anything he'd ever known. He'd felt attraction from the moment he'd seen her, and his heart had plummeted as he felt her fear of him. But nothing could prepare him for the deep, scary feelings she brought out of the deepest recesses of his soul.

There was a reason he was the way he was, never staying with one woman for very long, playing the field and spreading his attentions around. He'd been hurt badly and he feared he would be hurt at the end of this affair, though he'd known going in that this small woman was his cousin's mate in every way. Even if Micah and Jeri didn't realize it yet, they were mated, well and truly. Neither would be complete without the other now and the entire crew of the *Circe* was beginning to realize it.

Still, he couldn't help his uncontrollable desire for the little spitfire his cousin had brought back from Pantur. She was delectable. She was intelligent and gentle, and hotter than hell. She was scorching him with her tight pussy and even hotter Talent, meshing with and firing his own. He didn't know how Micah could stand it, but then, his dear cousin was much more Talented than he was, a Mage Master to his Dominar. Still, she was inflaming his senses in raw power and zesty pleasure the likes of which he had never known. He would be forever changed after this, he knew, but it would be worth every single moment.

He let go, pounding into her, trusting in Micah to guard them both and alert him if he went too far. He trusted Micah as he trusted no man in the universe. He was his soul brother, in every way that mattered. And his woman was just as important. Darak would care for her and watch over them both for as long as he lived. They were his family, more so than any of his siblings. They were his chosen family, and he loved them deeply.

He couldn't help the truth he knew was shining in his eyes as he made love to Jeri, reveling in her sweetness and light. He knew he could trust her with his innermost soul as he was being trusted in turn by both Jeri and Micah.

"I'm so close, Darak." Jeri's whispered words pushed him higher. His name repeated on a scream, and he knew he was ready to let go.

He grabbed the nipple chain and tugged, sending her over. "That's it, sweet. Scream for me."

She did, and he came in a blinding rush that caused every muscle in his body to seize momentarily in the greatest pleasure he'd ever known. He felt her coming and coming against and around him, sobbing and crying out as she reached the highest pinnacle yet. He opened his eyes to enjoy the sight. She squirmed under him, draining his dick with her inner contractions, milking him of his seed and begging for more.

He felt too the building of their psi energies and the strengthening they underwent as they both exploded. He'd never been so easily recharged by pleasure as with this small, Talented woman. His eyes swiveled to Micah, still at their sides, grinning broadly.

"Is everything okay?" Darak couldn't be totally sure this was normal. His senses were almost overwhelmed.

Micah chuckled, stroking Jeri's cheek with the back of a finger. "Singed you a bit, did she?" When Darak nodded mutely, Micah's smile widened. "You're both fine. Your energies mesh beautifully. There was never any danger in this joining. Rest easy."

Darak let the last of his worries leave him, collapsing down to his forearms, still held within the cradle of Jeri's warm, soft body.

"Thank you, my sweet." He leaned in to kiss her softly on the mouth. "This was the most beautiful joining I have ever experienced."

Jeri seemed shy, incredibly, now that she was coming down from her peak. A gentle blush came to her cheeks, and she seemed to find it hard to meet his eyes. Darak pulsed into her, reminding her that they were still joined as close as man and woman could be and her blush increased, though her gaze shot to his. He grinned and winked as she laughed, finally a little back at ease with him.

"I bet you say that to all the girls."

He could see the genuine regret in her eyes as she thought of the women he'd joined with and perversely, he found himself wanting to put her mind at ease. She was truly special—if she only knew how different this experience was from the others that had preceded it.

He used his big hands to cup her cheeks, directing her face and attention to him. His eyes were serious and his lips met hers in a kiss of respect, longing and love that she could not mistake.

"I say this to you alone, Jeri. I have never had a joining like this one, and perhaps never will again. You are special, and I treasure your gift to me." He kissed her, more deeply this time, sensing the rise of her passions, just beginning to stir to life once more as his dick was beginning to stir in interest, still within her tight sheath. She gasped, feeling him rise and he pulled back and smiled at her. "This next time, you will get what you've wished for—both of us at once. Would you like that, sweet Jeri?"

She blushed again and both men chuckled as Darak rolled away from her to his side of the bed. He and Micah took up mirror positions on either side of her, using their hands to gently bring her back to the fire of her passion. Darak was pulsing with the energy of their first joining, ready for more. Truly this joining was unique in many surprising ways.

# Chapter Nine

Micah watched Jeri's responses, knowing her body and mind well after these past weeks together. He would lead this next foray into the realm of pleasure. Darak's explosive joining with her proved there was no further danger of their Talents colliding. They knew each other's taste and would be safe to explore deeper.

Micah had every intention of exploring every facet of pleasure with his Jeri. He liked the sound of that—*his* Jeri. For she was truly his in a way no other woman had ever been. He'd been her first, and up until a few moments ago, her only lover. He had taught her the ways of pleasure and shown her how to please him. She was new to pleasure, yet had much to learn. And he was just the man to teach her. In all things.

He loved the way her eyes would light when she discovered some new facet of their lovemaking or some new use for her Talent. He enjoyed teaching her both of her power and of love. She was an able student in both, and he found himself enjoying the lessons as much as she.

"Ready for more, baby?" He stroked her breast, pulling gently on the jeweled chain that bore his mark and connected her nipples. She shivered in response, and he smiled at her. "I'd say she's more than ready. What do you think, Dar?"

Darak was ready to go again, Micah knew. He had the

same reaction to their powerful joinings. Jeri renewed him like no other woman and joining with her was a more potent experience than he had ever known. He could tell Darak was feeling a little of the same by his renewed energy and eager expression.

Darak started to pet her, down to her pussy and deep inside, swirling their combined wetness around, deeper in her cleft, to the dark pucker of her anus.

"She's ready all right, but how well does she take it up the ass, I wonder?" Jeri's breath caught at the sudden invasion of her ass by Darak's finger. "Hmm, judging by that, I'd say she likes it."

Micah smiled and kissed her deeply before replying. "She likes it, Dar, just go easy at first. You're a little longer than I am, and it's a very tight fit."

"Mmm, sounds like heaven." Darak nibbled his way down her abdomen, tickling her belly button with his tongue.

Micah put one arm under her shoulders and raised her body gently in his arms, motioning to Darak to change position while he moved her onto his lap.

"It *is* heaven, Dar. *She* is heaven, right here on Liata." He hummed with pleasure as he seated himself in her tight pussy, slick with his cousin's release and Jeri's strong desire. "There's some oil in my kit," he said urgently, nodding to Darak. "Prepare her well, then join with us. She's waited for this a long time."

Darak reached over the side of the bed for Micah's kit bag and quickly located the bottle of lubricant while Micah settled her more comfortably against himself, being sure to leave room for Darak at her back. The two men had done this before many times in the past, but not since Micah had been elevated to Master and become so morose. It was good to have his cousin back in his life and he would thank Jeri forever for sharing her beautiful soul as well as her body with him. She'd brought him back to life. She'd shown him hope once more. Everything he did now, he did for her.

"I've been dreaming of this since I first saw you, Jeri," Darak whispered into her ear, coming up behind her. His fingers were well lubricated as he slipped two of them back into her anus, massaging and stretching, making her ready.

Micah felt his cousin's fingers through the thin membrane that separated them and enjoyed the once-familiar phantom touch. It had been too long since they'd shared a woman, but Jeri would call the shots from here on out. If she wanted a threesome, he'd be more than happy to oblige, but he knew he would never need to seek it out on his own. She was more than enough for him and would be for many, many years to come. If only he could keep her.

Jeri squirmed as Darak worked her ass, making way for his invasion while Micah stroked inside her pussy.

"Do you know how beautiful you are?" Micah asked her, shocking her dazed gaze to his as he wrapped his arms around her, settling her more tightly against him as he leaned against the headboard. "Do you know how much I'm enjoying giving you this pleasure, watching you come for him, knowing that you've never felt this before? Knowing that I'm the one giving it to you? Knowing that you trust us enough—trust *me* enough—to let me?"

She leaned up to kiss him. "I do trust you, Micah, with everything. With my life."

He groaned as a wave of pleasure hit him with her words. "Your trust is a gift I will never take for granted, baby. It's a treasure beyond value." He stroked faster, her words and energies meshing together to bring him so close. But Darak was taking his sweet time. Micah didn't want to come without him.

"Get a move on back there, Dar. We're more than ready for you." He could feel the ease with which Darak was moving his fingers in and out of her ass and knew she was fully prepared for his larger invasion.

Darak looked the tiniest bit sheepish when he moved up behind her, his eyes meeting his cousin's with a roguish light.

"Sorry, Micah, I got a little carried away." He placed a smacking kiss on her neck, tickling her with his tongue. "You have the sweetest ass, Jeri. I've watched you, you know. I love the way your hips sway when you walk."

Jeri laughed, surprising him as she leaned her head back to look at him. "Micah said something to that effect once, but I hardly believed him." Secrets danced in her eyes.

"Believe him, sweetness. I've never considered myself an ass man, but yours has me fascinated."

"What did I tell you?" Micah laughed as he strove for calm while Darak positioned himself at her rear.

He just knew this was going to be the wildest threesome he'd ever had—would ever have. He loved Dar like a brother, and Jeri was fast becoming the brightest light in his life. Between the two of them, he felt more for these two people than he did for almost anyone in the universe. If he hadn't learned the lesson before now, there was no way he could live through this and not know that true and honest feelings made sex so much better, it was immeasurable. The exchange of energy and sex was so much more powerful when you actually cared for the person you shared yourself with. He could never go back. Never have sex just for the sake of having sex. Not after this. Not after having Jeri in his life for even these short weeks. She'd ruined him for all other women.

"Almost there, sweet. Almost home," Dar whispered as he

worked his long cock into her ass. Micah held still, gritting his teeth as he felt each inch of the penetration, seated fully as he was in her pussy.

Micah soothed her shudders when the pleasure and pain mixed reached new levels, but she was eager, he could see it in her eyes. Eager and still somewhat scandalized at the idea of having two men in her at once. He kissed her to reassure her.

"You doing okay, baby?" He thought he could tell she was doing way more than okay, but he wanted her focused on him while Darak seated himself fully. Just in case she felt any real pain, he wanted to know about it quickly.

"I'm fine." Her voice was breathy with desire, and her senses were spinning. Having two men at once was like nothing she ever would have imagined. No fantasy could have prepared her for this amazingly shocking reality. She moaned as the pleasure/pain peaked in her ass as Darak slid home within her. She was stuffed full, almost completely overwhelmed by the pleasure.

"Good goddess, she's tight." Darak groaned as his hands tightened on her hips, guiding his shallow thrusts as she became acclimated to his possession. Micah was still for now, his eyes watching her closely.

"Feels good?" Micah asked with knowing eyes.

She smiled at him. "Better than I imagined." She could barely speak, but the throaty whisper of her voice seemed to excite both men.

"It gets better," Darak promised, meeting Micah's gaze over her shoulder.

She had no doubt these two rascals had perfected this technique with many other women but she couldn't work up a good head of steam over it. After all, she was the beneficiary of

Hidden Talent

those experiences. These men knew what they were doing, and she trusted them completely. Letting go, she let them lead her in this pleasure. She knew they'd treat her well.

"Show me."

Her simple command seemed to spur them into action. Micah held her upper body in his strong arms, supporting her while he thrust into her pussy. Darak held her hips, thrusting behind, both men working together, thrusting lightly in counterpoint to each other until she began to pant hard, unable to catch her breath.

They began to move faster and harder as she became used to the double penetration. Micah set the pace, and Darak seemed content to follow, grunting every once in a while as he bit her neck or licked her skin. Micah leaned forward, plunging his tongue deep into her mouth, nipping her lips and sucking on her tongue in a way that made her insides clench. Both men groaned when her inner muscles tightened.

"Do that again, baby. Show us how much you like this." Micah's plea made her clench once more and their pace increased until she could barely comprehend the pleasure rushing through her veins.

"I'm close, Micah."

"I know. I can feel it. Let go, baby. Let it all go and take us with you."

His voice panted in her ear as she felt the world explode around her and within her. She spasmed over the cliff, clenching over and over again on the two thick cocks buried deeply in her body. She felt them tighten and begin to erupt in the haze of her own pleasure as she leapt from one amazingly intense orgasm to the next with barely a flicker of thought. The pleasure kept building and building as the men shot their warmth into her body in unison, groaning against her skin, worshiping her femininity.

"Jeri, you're incredible." Micah's shoulders were tense as he came, his warm sperm coating her insides and leaking out her pussy still stuffed full of his cock. She felt Darak reaching the wall of his pleasure behind her, his slippery come coating her ass inside and out as he continued to thrust, though more shallowly as he finished in pleasure.

He pulled with steady pressure from her ass, reaching to take her in his arms as Micah left her pussy, hugging her tight, her back to his front. He turned her head toward him, kissing her lips sweetly as Micah stroked her hair.

"Thank you, sweet Jeri. I will never forget that for as long as I live."

His dark eyes tempted her, windows to his soul.

"Neither will I," she admitted.

He kissed her again, deeply, taking his time. He seemed reluctant to let her go, but eventually he released her into Micah's waiting arms. He went to the small bathroom, and she heard the water running as Micah stroked her from head to toe.

"You're so beautiful." She settled into his arms, still coming down from the highest high she'd ever experienced.

"You make me feel that way."

"Never doubt your beauty. Inside and out. You have a gorgeous soul, Jeri." His words were whispered against her temple.

"That's quite possibly the sweetest thing anyone's ever said to me." She smiled at him, leaning up for a quick kiss that he took further, delving into her mouth with his talented tongue. She felt the bed dip as Darak came back, but Micah was kissing her so divinely, she barely noticed until she felt herself being moved, her ass cheeks spread once more. She gasped as a wet washcloth teased her ass, stroking along the inflamed tissues, cleaning her. Darak was caring for her, to her great surprise. She hadn't expected such gentle treatment from him. Oh, Micah had treated her with this caring attention several times, but she never would have guessed Darak capable of such gentleness.

He was such a devil—or at least he played the part to most of the world. But underneath there was a core of sensitivity that she hadn't really seen before tonight. She'd guessed at it, from the way Micah spoke of his cousin and the little things he'd done for her and for the rest of the crew on the *Circe*. He'd even expended great amounts of his Talent for the people of Liata, but always with that roguish grin and outwardly brusque manner. It was as if he didn't want anyone to really see the gentle soul beneath his exterior. But she knew it now, and she would never forget it. She would never forget the care and passion he'd shown her tonight, though she didn't know what the future would hold for her and these beautiful men.

She would stay with Micah until he threw her out, or it otherwise became impossible to continue together. That much she knew. But she also dreaded the return to his homeworld since their great differences in social position would most probably be insurmountable once back in his society. She would cling to him until then, but when the time came to part, she would leave with her head held high. She wouldn't hurt him with her tears, though she would be crying hard on the inside.

She refused to think more about that now. Not when she had two of the most handsome men in the universe at her beck and call. She might never have this experience again and she wanted to enjoy it to the fullest, now that she knew a little more of what to expect.

She reached both hands downward and found the objects of her desires. Both men started when she took hold of their cocks, already beginning to regain their former stiffness. She'd known how potent Micah was and it was good to know that Darak could match him. She wanted them again, though she didn't question the quick rise of her desire. It was as natural to her as breathing. As natural as her Talent. And she had Micah to thank for that. He'd taught her so much.

She knew just how to begin repaying him. Scooting back on the bed, she licked her way down his chest, toying with him until she reached his glistening cock. He was still slick with his own come and her juices and she relished each long lick along the sides of his thick cock as she cleaned him. She was aware of Darak watching every move and of Micah's accelerated breathing.

"Take her from behind, Dar. She's more than ready."

"You sure? She's barely had time to recover from the last round."

Darak positioned himself behind her, helping her to her knees as she moved swiftly to accommodate him. He loved the view. Her pussy was pouting open and slightly swollen from the hard pounding both he and Micah had given her. Her ass also showed titillating signs of his recent use. And she was dripping. Eager for more.

"She bounces back fast," Micah told him. "There's something about the way our Talents mesh. Don't you feel it?"

"Now that you mention it," he said with wonder as he took stock of his amazingly renewed energy levels, "I do feel better than I've ever felt after this kind of thing. Does she have this effect on you every time?"

Micah nodded, in heaven. "Every single fucking time. She's amazing." He groaned as she sucked extra hard, smiling around his cock as she appreciated his compliment.

"You ready for me, sweet?" Darak stroked the cheeks of her

ass as he bent down to whisper in her ear.

She pushed back against him in answer, clearly eager for more. Darak didn't disappoint, entering her pussy easily from behind as she sucked hard on Micah's straining cock. He watched her work Micah's dick with relish, his heat rising steadily as he stroked in and out of her hot core, the angle deeper from behind, just the way he liked.

He also liked watching her ass from this position. All it needed was a little color.

He slapped her ass lightly, testing to see how she took it, and was rewarded with a small yelp of surprise and a clenching around his cock, followed by a gush of moisture. She liked it. A lot.

He looked up to see Micah's reaction, but he figured Micah had already introduced her to such erotic play. He knew from past experience that Micah liked a pink ass as much as he did. Micah winked at him, and Darak knew all was well.

He slapped her again.

"Man, she has the prettiest ass I've ever fucked. I knew it would pink up beautifully."

Darak spoke almost conversationally to Micah. He knew the rough words were exciting to her. Micah had told him how sheltered she'd been as a youngster. He knew she'd never heard any kind of sex talk before Micah, and he knew he had a much dirtier mouth than his gentler cousin. If nothing else, the stream of her moisture around his dick told him his words and actions were making her hot.

"Yeah, she likes to be spanked." Micah reached one hand up to tug on the nipple chain hanging down from her luscious breasts as she got to her hands and knees, her head buried in his crotch.

"You should try a paddle or a lash. It might make her even

hotter."

"She likes the paddle," Micah agreed. "And the crop. Just about as much as I like to be ridden. And she likes being tied up too."

"Man, cuz, why didn't you tell me that before?" Darak chuckled evilly.

"Sorry, Dar. Maybe next time?" They both watched her reaction carefully on that point. Only she would decide if there was ever to be a next time.

"If the *dama* so desires." Darak's words were gracious, but his pace increased as he watched her bring Micah to orgasm with her succulent lips. Micah came hard and sudden, and she swallowed every last drop like a pro. Hard to believe she'd come to his cousin a virgin, but then he knew his cousin was a good master and if he didn't miss his guess, she more than enjoyed being his pupil.

"That's so hot," he mused as he moved more swiftly inside her. She was licking up the last of Micah's come, cleaning his rod as Darak watched. He swatted her at unexpected moments until she came around his cock, triggering his own release. It was long and hard and more pleasurable than the two that had come before. He hadn't believed it possible, but each time with this special woman got better and better.

His cousin Micah was a lucky man.


The three of them loved through the night, taking various positions and many different pleasures. She sucked Darak off with Micah's encouragement, then learned just how expert Darak was with a rope as he tied her up and made her come no less than five times before the men had her once more together.

By the next morning, they were completely reenergized. When Trini came in to wake them with a hearty breakfast on a tray, she sent them a knowing smile that made Jeri blush to the roots of her hair. Trini thanked them all for what they'd done for her brother, reminding them of just why they'd been so drained the day before.

Trini herself was looking ragged, having kept vigil all night by her brother's bedside. Micah ordered her to seek her own bed and Darak promised he'd check on her brother throughout the day. The three of them enjoyed the impromptu breakfast in bed, then rose to greet the day and the various tasks ahead of them.

The Board of Governors cornered Micah not long after he'd left the house where Trini and her brother had taken refuge. They wanted an update on the help that would be forthcoming from the Mage Council, and Micah was glad to inform them that Specitar Agnor would be transporting down to deal with them. Tendil was well enough to transport, though he would require a great deal of rest to finish healing and Trini and her family had asked Micah to take the boy aboard the *Circe*. There was no way he could refuse. The boy had Talent, though he was young, and the healing worked on him could have very well kicked his Talent up a notch before its time. He would need to be closely monitored, and where better than on his ship?

Plus, Trini was devastated by the losses in her family and having her baby brother with her might help ease the pain. They were close, those two, and they needed each other for the time being. So when Trini and Tendil translocated up, Agnor came down planetside.

Agnor's arrival made quite a splash since the only other Specitar on the planet had been killed early in the fighting. They'd thought all long-range communication was gone, but Agnor was like the magician's white rabbit being pulled out of a top hat. Micah hadn't gone into detail about his crew, but even he was surprised by the Board of Governors' reaction to Agnor's appearance on planet.

They treated him like royalty and the survivors planned a small feast in honor of the crew of the *Circe*, making Agnor and Jeri the honored guests. They thanked Jeri for her work with their all-important herds and Agnor for getting out the word so quickly to the Mage Council. Darak and Micah were honored for their work but it was clear Agnor and Jeri were the stars of the show.

All through the ordeal and the work they did to help these people, Darak, Micah and Agnor used every opportunity to teach important lessons to the yeomen and Jeri about their use of Talent. Real world training was invaluable to the youngsters and Jeri's already accelerated learning was progressing by leaps and bounds as she got to use her Talent in real situations. All three students were learning more in this short layover on a war-ravaged planet than they would have learned in a year of simulated practice onboard the *Circe*.

On a purely mercenary note, Micah knew the goodwill they were earning from the people of this planet would more than make up for the lost profits from giving them the sale herd. Though their profit from this trip would be drastically diminished, the reputation of the *Circe* and those aboard would be greatly enhanced, not only on this planet, but in many star systems around. The *Circe* was cementing its reputation as a good merchant ship that was willing to help those in need rather than only seeking profits. In some quarters, such humanitarian acts would garner Micah and his crew great favor. As a merchant ship with the hidden task of routing out spies working to bring down the Council, such favor could be immensely helpful.

Liata was on the edges of Council space, but not in a very strategic position, which was probably what had kept it safe so far. But things were changing—drastically, if the enemies of the

Council were willing to attack a peaceful agricultural world that was firmly decided on being under Council protection. The Liatans had a representative government and way back when the Council had first come and offered membership for the small ag world, the people had voted and decided overwhelmingly to join. The vote had been renewed periodically since, and each time the Liatans had decided to stay with the Council.

But the Council's benevolence and democratic system was not employed by other powers in the sector. Micah and Agnor had monitored certain information and rumors about the Wizards of Mithrak and their new alliances with other worlds that used Talent as a weapon and forced those with it into virtual slavery. The Wizards were by far the worst, taking small children when their power first came to them and subjugating them from the very start, but other worlds also used those with Talent as unwilling tools, not letting them live free among the mostly un-Talented population.

There was fear of those with Talent, but the Mage Council had formed to band Talents together and give them standards by which to act, to protect and serve those without. Not so on many other worlds. And just lately the Mithrakians had been rumored to be seeking allies of like minds in an effort to expand that made Micah understandably nervous. The prospect of war did not sit well with him, and he feared Jeri's reaction when she learned just who he suspected was behind this attack on Liata.

There was no way to protect her from the knowledge. A few prisoners had been caught. Some were soldiers left behind when the invaders ran off without them. One prisoner was proving a valuable source of information to the Board of Governors, for the broken soul had gone mad and was speaking openly to all who would listen. The Board had asked Micah to see the man, to use his Master's abilities to see what was truth in the man's scrambled mind and he reluctantly agreed. Sorting through someone's thoughts was not something he felt comfortable doing at the best of times, but when that person was mentally injured and captive, it was even more distasteful.

Still, he knew it must be done. If for no other reason than to see if this poor soul could be helped back to sanity in some way. It was with a heavy heart that Micah went to see the prisoner.

He'd been warned, but he was still surprised by the level of unfocused Talent the man displayed. He was like a child, just manifesting his Talent, unable to harness and use it. He had Talent in plenty and it could be dangerous to others when uncontrolled at these levels. Micah immediately reinforced Mage Denik's shielding around the man in order to protect others. It was only a temporary measure. Something more permanent would have to be done.

With a sane prisoner, Micah would have suggested the use of a reflective field. This prisoner, however would probably not know how to turn off his Talent in his excited state, and might suffer horribly when his flailing Talent was reflected back at him.

"She's coming!" The man ran up to the bars and pounded with his fists when he saw Micah enter. "She's coming back to finish it. She'll kill you all!"

"Who is she?" Micah asked calmly, searching with his Talent to see the images brought forth in the man's injured mind. He saw a woman in a red robe—a woman who looked eerily like Jeri. So much so that at first, he thought it *was* Jeri, and he caught his breath in shock. But then he saw the fine lines around her eyes. This woman was older than his lover, and she carried a jeweled scepter with a blue stone at its heart. The mark of the Wizards of Mithrak.

"Jana!" The man sank to his knees and sobbed. "Mistress Jana will come and kill us all. I failed her."

Micah couldn't take much more of the man's raw Talent flashing harshly against his shields. He questioned the prisoner carefully, sifting through his thoughts to find the truth of what he knew. What he learned didn't please him. Liata wasn't out of danger if this poor soul was to be believed.

He also saw a little of what this man had once been, and he laid a gentle psi balm over the torn patches in his soul that had once been part of the Wizard collective. He was cast adrift, a survivor who should not have survived when his ship crashed on the surface of Liata. The Wizards had cast him out, torn the connection to his power as they fled and left him half-insane with the loss of their voices. It was probably the first time in his adult life that this poor man had heard nothing but the silence of his own thoughts, and he simply couldn't deal with it.

Micah pitied him, and he did the best he could to begin the healing that only the most skilled of mind healers could complete. Hopefully, if they survived the second wave of attacks, the Council would see fit to help this poor raving man. First Micah had to warn the Board of Governors and the ships in orbit. If this lunatic was to be believed, there was already a second wave of attack planned and underway. They had little time.

Mage Denik was waiting for him when he left the prisoner, so he informed him of the renewed threat. Denik would alert the rest of the Board of Governors. That taken care of, Micah commed the *Circe* and the *Valiant* as he strode forcefully to the barn where Jeri was working with some of the injured horses. If she could be persuaded, Jeri might just be their ace in the hole.

But it might not need any persuasion. Jeri often told Micah

about the pain losing her family had caused and she wondered what had happened to her older sister. Now that he knew what Jana had become, he feared his lover's reaction. But he also knew her heart well enough to know that if there was any hope of freeing Jana from the Wizards' collective, Jeri would seek it. No matter the cost.

Micah only hoped he could protect his woman while he helped her free the sister she'd lost so many years ago. At the same time, they had a planet to defend. It all hinged on two small, powerful women, and he would stand with Jeri, whatever she chose to do.

He found her in the big barn that had escaped most of the damage done to the other buildings. She was just finished helping with one of the more seriously injured horses, calming her while the healer tended her wounds. Jeri wiped her hands as she stepped out of the wide stall, looking up with a welcoming smile as she saw him coming toward her.

Micah couldn't help himself. He pulled her into his arms and hugged her close. So much would change when he told her what he'd learned.

"What is it?" She knew him so well, he marveled. She could read his moods easily.

"I've just come from questioning a prisoner. There's a second wave of attacks planned, and it's coming soon. We have to prepare."

"Oh no. What can we do?" She pushed out of his arms but he wasn't letting her go.

"There's more, baby." His eyes bore down into hers and he couldn't resist placing a quick kiss of reassurance on her lips. "The Wizards of Mithrak lead the attack on behalf of a new alliance they've made with the Mendinians." Her face paled in fear, but he had to tell her all of it. "Your sister Jana leads the

Wizard force."

"What?" She swayed in his arms and would have fallen if he hadn't been holding her so tight. "Jana? How do you know? Is it true? Jana's alive? And coming here?"

"The prisoner they found was half-mad. He has a strong Talent, but wild now that he's been cut off brutally from the Wizards' collective. The Board of Governors asked me to read him and I agreed. I saw the truth of his ravings in his mind. The attack on Liata was a two-pronged plan all along. They're coming back and your older sister is leading them into battle."

She clung to him, needing the security of his arms. She shook like a leaf in the wind at the news and he wished silently he could take the pain and shock from her. But she was strong and she soon began to calm as he stroked her back, willing his own strength into her. At times like these it was second nature for them to mesh their energies and help each other, though he had never done so with any other being.

"Jeri, there might be a way to separate her from the collective. We might be able to free her."

"And without their leader, the armada might be thrown enough to disrupt their attack plan."

He kissed her brow. "That's my Jeri. Always thinking ahead. Yes, there is a chance we could help the Liatans and our own chances of survival at the same time. I know you care about your sister. I'll help you free her if I can. I think together, you and I might have just enough power to be able to do it. Though there is considerable risk."

She pulled back to look up into his eyes, tears rolling unashamedly down her face. "For myself, I'll take any risk to help save her, but I can't ask you to put yourself in danger for my sister."

He held one finger to her lips, stilling her words. "I'd risk anything for you, Jeri. You are my world."

The tears fell freely as she stared at him. He hoped it was a good sign, but they didn't have time to talk further as the alarms started sounding around the city. The second wave of attack was starting.

# Chapter Ten

They were ready, but barely. Two ships were a poor defense against the ten that had jumped insystem to threaten them. The *Valiant* was fighting well and the *Circe* had some tricks up her sleeve. Jeri and Micah transported up with the rest of the crew since the *Circe* needed everyone aboard in battle and they could do more good defending the planet from orbit than down on the ground.

"They've seen us," Agnor reported from his comm station. "Three enemy vessels breaking off to intercept."

"Kirt, Welan, are you in position?" Micah used the shipcomm to check on his two young yeomen in the hidden gunnery positions. They'd barely had time to run to their stations and power up. In this fight, every second would count.

The two young men answered in the affirmative, keeping a line of communication open between themselves and Seta, who would make snap navigation computations to help them stay out of the kill zone while getting their enemies well in their sights.

Trini manned another set of guns on the back of the ship, near the main hatches to the loadbay. She checked in with Darak, who manned a bridge console of missiles Jeri had never noticed before. Together they would watch the fore and aft of the ship. She wondered what she could do, but she knew from a brief conversation with Micah that she would be used as a special weapon, when the time was right. He wanted to use the surprise of her appearance on the comms to confuse Jana, if at all possible. But he wanted to wait until the right moment. Timing in this very unequal battle would be everything.

"Jeri, stay by me," Micah ordered, watching the display carefully. "I want you nearby when we get through to the command ship."

Proximity would help, she knew, if their hastily devised plan had any chance of success. But they had to get past the three warships that were already closing on them first.

"I've pegged the command ship, Captain." Seta's voice had an edge to it Jeri had never heard. The voluptuous woman was all business as she plotted the complex trajectories of all the ships now converging on Liata.

"Can you microjump us closer to it?"

Seta looked back at him with narrowed eyes. "This close to the atmosphere it'll be tricky, but I think I can get us right up in the middle of that swarm, dead in front of the command ship."

"Do it."

Jeri said a quick prayer as Seta returned to her furious calculations. This was an all-or-nothing maneuver. He was microjumping them into the lion's den. If Jeri's attempt to contact her sister had no effect, they would have no chance to escape before all those ships fired on them.

"Make it fast, Seta. They're on us."

Darak's low voice warned the navigator of the approaching warships just as the first shots were fired by Kirt on the starboard side. The whole ship shuddered as the energy cannons let loose on the approaching enemy. Darak fired his first missile as another of the enemy came into range, at the

174

same time initiating evasive maneuvers.

A split second later, they were in the unique realm of microspace. Not quite here and not quite there, they were jumping between two very close points—a dangerous and tricky maneuver. An eyeblink later, their gamble paid off as they reappeared in the path of the enemy command ship.

"Jeri, you're up." Micah moved her to stand before the vid pickup that would transmit her image to the command ship while he joined his hand with hers. Together they would direct their considerable energy to separating the commander of the enemy fleet from the collective.

Agnor sent the feed live as Darak prepared to defend. The timing was quick and the enemy hadn't had a moment to figure out quite what the tricky little cargo ship had done.

"Jana, this is your sister, Jeri. Please stop this. The people of Liata have done nothing to you. I've done nothing to you. I've been looking for you since they took you away from Ma and Dad. I've missed you so much, Jana."

"Enemy ship, power down your weapons." The booming voice of a man came back over the comm, cut off a moment later as a vid signal was sent from the commander's station directly. An older, harsher version of Jeri looked back at her.

"Jeri?" The voice was faint, faraway, as was the look in the woman's eyes. She wore fancy red robes and there was a scepter with a blue stone at her side. Jeri knew the blue stone was the focal point that connected the collective that faced them. Shatter that, and they would all be disconnected from the collective.

She tightened her fingers against Micah's as she sought his power, meshing so tightly with her own. He let her direct the power, not quite knowing what she was planning, but willing to follow her lead. After all, she knew more about the Wizards of her home planet than anyone on the Council.

"Jana, my sister, I've been searching for you everywhere."

Jeri directed her thoughts and their combined energies at the stone in the scepter, so close but yet so far away on the neighboring ship. She felt it resist her first pushes and she knew she needed to focus more, her thoughts a tight laser of energy with one intent.

"Jeri? Little Jeri? Where are you?" The voice of the woman was confused and lost as she fought against the collective control in her mind. Familial love was the one thing the collective could not completely destroy, it seemed.

"I'm here for you, Jana. I've come to free you. I need my big sister." All the while Jeri concentrated, sweat breaking out on her brow as she felt the stone begin to tremble in the scepter at her sister's side.

Blindly she saw Jana reach for it and the moment she made contact with the scepter the stone settled down. Jeri redoubled her efforts.

"I need you, Jana. I'm so alone. I want my sister back."

Micah watched what she was doing with interest. Once he realized the focus of the fight—the shiny blue stone—he joined his energy to hers, silently pulling Darak into their alliance against the enormous power seated in that stone.

With Darak's added power and the way he could mesh his energies with Jeri's and his own, they were stronger than the protections around the stone. He just knew it. Analyzing the problem with one part of his mind, Micah shaped the energies they sent, guiding Jeri's raw Talent silently, communing with her on a soul-deep level.

With a last effort he threw every bit of his power into the

stone, battering at it, keeping nothing in reserve. Either they would stand or fall in the next few moments. He pushed and pushed until the blood pounded in his ears and then finally, he felt the stone crack with a decisive shiver.

Once started, it crumbled quickly, exploding outward and releasing a wave of pent-up energy that rocked every person on the *Circe* and every Talent on the ships all around.

"She's hurt. Jana's down." Micah was hardly aware of Jeri's hand slipping from his grasp as she ran to the ion transport console.

Under normal circumstances the enemy ship would have countermanded any translocation order sent from his ship to theirs, but nothing was normal now among the enemy fleet. Every commander of every one of their ships had been connected through that scepter and was now adrift, left to their own devices. Without the collective will of the Wizards to direct them, most of them turned and ran for sectors unknown. Micah watched the retreat unfold with glee.

But he was transfixed when the ion transport rematerialized Jana, still in her resplendent red robes splotched with her own blood, directly in front of his chair. Darak moved swiftly from behind his console, down but not out apparently, while Micah felt his own head spinning from the huge wave of energy that had poured over them when the stone had shattered.

Darak cradled the woman in his arms as gently as a child, using a pulse of his power that Micah could feel in his unshielded state to send her to sleep, his hand over her eyes, closing them peacefully. He then wasted little time in shredding her robes, looking for the injuries that caused so much blood to pool beneath her on the deck. Jeri helped, silently praying as she moved with disjointed coordination. They were all suffering the effects of that enormous wave of psi energy released when the stone shattered.

"Will she live?" Jeri's voice was parched, croaking as her energies pulsed unsteadily.

Darak spared a moment to look at her. "I will ensure it. Leave her to me, sweet Jeri. I won't let her leave you again."

Jeri leaned forward to place a kiss of thanks on Darak's lips, comfortable enough with him now that they'd joined to show her appreciation in a way he would readily understand. Micah smiled to himself as he watched the surprise on his cousin's face, but his thoughts grew speculative when Dar returned his full attention to the enemy commander. Jana was no doubt cast adrift without her collective, a strong Talent with no direction.

Sending her to sleep had been the smartest thing he could do. They were in less danger from her unfocused Talent. Micah thought he would set Agnor to training Jana how to shield at the first opportunity. But first he had his woman to comfort. He stumbled to Jeri and took her in his arms, kneeling behind her on the decking.

"You saved her, Jeri." He kissed the top of her head as she relaxed against him. "Seta, how goes the battle?" Micah spared a glance to his shaken navigator. She was recovering her station after the psi wave had knocked her nearly unconscious.

"The enemy fleet is disbanding." Her voice was weak as she checked her readouts. "Even the command ship has turned tail and run. They're running, but a few of the others seem to be running at random."

"Freed of the collective control, I'd bet a few of those ship captains are making a break for freedom. Mark their positions. Agnor, when you feel up to it, maybe you could try comming them? Some might be willing to seek shelter with the Council."

Agnor was already using his gift of communication to seek out some of the Talented captains now freed from the collective's control on the ships that were fleeing in all directions. He felt a change in his power that he couldn't quite believe. Sure, they'd been hit by a dangerous wave of psi energy and lived to tell the tale, but never had he been able to so easily contact multiple unknown minds in such short order.

"Three of them are returning. They will seek refugee status with the Council. Or so they say. I've already commed the *Valiant*. They'll see to the disarmament of the enemy ships in short order. All three are smaller than *Valiant* and shouldn't pose a threat, even if they're lying, which I sincerely doubt."

Micah tilted his head in question, but Agnor had no real answers for the incredible increase in his already strong Talent. It was a matter for study—something Specitars truly relished doing—and he would study this odd circumstance thoroughly as soon as he had a moment to spare.

"Comm from planetside, Captain. They want to know what's going on. They see the ships scattering on their remaining satellites. Shall I fill them in or would you rather?" He raised an eyebrow at his friend Micah, a small smile on his face as he realized how deeply that massive psi wave had affected everyone on the ship. He'd touched the youngsters' minds without their knowledge, just to make sure they were okay. It was something he did from time to time in his role as teacher and guide. But what met his newly expanded senses was surprising. Both Kirt and Welan had been knocked unconscious as the wave passed over them, but they were waking, shaky and with expanded senses.

Agnor also sensed Trini feeling her way through the darkness of the hold on rubbery legs, fear in her heart as she felt her Talent pulsing in a way she'd never before experienced. Agnor spared a thought to communicate directly with her mind. He didn't do it often, but she needed to know she wasn't alone.

*"Trini,"* he sent gently, a whisper of comfort in her mind. *"You're all right. Come up to the bridge. The danger is past."*

*"Agnor?"*

He nearly jumped in his seat as the loadmaster used a skill she'd never manifested before, speaking directly into his mind. Her voice was soft and sweet, much like the woman herself.

*"Bright stars! Can you hear me, Agnor?"*

He shook his head to clear it a bit. *"I hear you, Trini. Come to the bridge, sweetheart. We're all feeling the effects of the psi wave."*

*"Sweet goddess in heaven. I'm 'pathing to you."* The flavor of her thoughts was tinged with awe. *"I've never been this telepathic before. I tried and tried in training, but I couldn't do it with any real power."*

*"It's always been inside you, Trini. It took this trauma to bring it out, perhaps. Don't be afraid. It's a natural part of you."* He could feel her fear and uncertainty, and it touched his heart. This small woman was such a good friend to him in times of need, he was glad to be here for her when she felt doubt.

*"I'm out of the bay now. I see Kirt and Welan stumbling into the hall. They don't look too good."*

*"I don't doubt it. The poor boys passed out when the wave hit. Can you help guide them to the bridge?"*

*"I'll take care of them."* She chuckled in his mind, tickling his senses. She had a beautiful mindvoice. *"We'll be with you in about five minutes. I'm going to stop in and check Tendil. He probably slept through the whole thing. Kirt and Welan are moving kind of slow, and I'm still shaky as hell."*

*"So is everyone else. Including me."*

Darak reached out with his hands, now covered in Jana's blood, and sent his power seeking outside himself. It flowed more freely than it ever had before, but he took little notice of it at first. After a while though, when he healed wound after wound on the badly cut woman with no diminishing of his own power, he began to wonder.

"Micah?" His voice was uncertain, his eyes questioning as he raised them briefly to his cousin, continuing to treat the woman in his arms. "Are you noticing anything strange about your Talent right about now?"

But Micah was too involved in holding his woman to answer. It was Agnor who turned to meet Darak's questioning gaze.

"I'm noticing something, Dar. I'm comming ships and foreign minds well out of my normal range with no strain. And Trini is 'pathing with no effort."

Darak's eyes widened as he sought the rest of Jana's wounds. The shards of stone were embedded in her body, in some cases the shiny blue crystals were fused directly into her skin in a way he had never seen. He didn't know what to do for those odd wounds. His primary focus was to stop the bleeding. She'd lost too much blood and was still bleeding from a dozen different points. He worked methodically as he stopped one bleeder after another, ignoring the glints of sparkling blue stone fused to her flesh. He'd figure out what to do about that after he saved her life.

"Trini's 'pathing? No way."

"Way," Trini answered from the hatchway, the two young yeomen following shakily behind her as she entered the bridge. She was somewhat steadier on her feet than she had been just moments before.

"Kirt? Welan? Are you two okay?" Darak felt his healing gift swell and nearly spill over, but it wasn't draining him like it usually did.

Both young men nodded, making way for another young man who no one had seen on his feet yet.

"Your brother?" Agnor asked, clearly surprised by the young man's remarkable recovery.

Trini beamed as she put her arm around her little brother's shoulders. "The wave woke him, he said." She prodded him forward. "Tell them, Tendil."

He ducked his head a bit, but faced them all squarely. "The psi wave broke over me and filled me. At least it felt that way. I was mostly fine physically, thanks to your healing, sir." He nodded his head respectfully at Darak. "I remember that. But my energy was so low. When the psi wave hit, I was suddenly renewed and now I feel stronger than I ever have."

"Amazing." Agnor shook his head, deep in thought.

Micah straightened with Jeri in his arms, sitting in his chair and depositing her on his lap.

"How is she, Dar?" Micah nodded toward the unconscious, nearly naked woman on the deck. She was covered in blood, but she was looking better than she had just moments before.

"She'll live." Darak continued to work on her, less urgently now, but still with great care. "I'm going to seal up these last few bleeders and then we can move her to a bed."

Jeri sobbed, turning her cheek into Micah's neck, wrapping her arms around him for support. She was falling apart now that the battle was over. Micah stood, lifting her in his arms and headed for the hatch.

"We'll be in my quarters. Agnor, you have the bridge."

Agnor nodded then looked over at each member of the crew in turn, taking stock. "Trini, it wouldn't surprise me if you were now at Authoritar level, at least. The way you were 'pathing back there was nearly flawless." He liked the open-mouthed surprise on her face, and he smiled at her reaction. "I'm going to retest everyone once things settle down. I want to know if this is a temporary thing or if we'll all be...elevated a bit after this experience."

"It has been known to happen," Darak speculated as he worked on Jana. "I know I'm doing stuff that I would've had to really struggle to do just a few hours ago."

Agnor nodded sagely. "I wonder what the Council will make of you, Dar?"

"The Council? Why should they care?"

"Well, when you take your seat as a Mage, I imagine there'll be quite a stir."

Darak sat back on his heels, his patient stable for the moment. "You've got to be kidding."

"'Fraid not, my friend. I know a Mage when I see one, and you're it. Possibly even a Master. You were close enough to Mage level before that wave hit us." Agnor enjoyed the look of dismay on his roguish friend's face, but he wasn't through with his speculations yet. "And if I'm not much mistaken, we've just witnessed the birth of a Vizier. Maybe two."

"Good goddess in heaven." Trini couldn't hold in her surprise. Viziers were few and very far between. To even see one in your lifetime was a big deal, but to know and work with one—or maybe two—was an honor that was nearly unheard of.

"What do we do?" Darak was all business as he lifted the unconscious woman into his arms. "Viziers are precious. We have to protect him—them—at all costs."

Agnor nodded. "With your agreement, I'm going to contact

Vizier Brandon. He should be able to hear me, even across this distance, and he'll probably have sound advice for us."

"They'll order us back, Ag. You know that."

Agnor sighed. "Yes, I think you're right. Micah won't like it, but, Dar, we really have no choice. You said it yourself. We have to protect him. Even from himself."

In the dimness of the Captain's cabin, Micah laid Jeri on his soft bed. The past moments had frightened him badly, and he wasn't a man who took fear well. He'd been so afraid they would lose the battle, and that he would lose this precious woman in the process. Hell, the battle didn't even matter next to the possibility of losing Jeri. She was that important to him. And that scared him as well.

He knew now beyond the shadow of a doubt, that he loved her and he wanted her in his life for all time. But he wasn't sure of her heart. She was so innocent, so new to the delights the Council worlds would hold for her as a woman of immense power. He feared he alone would not be enough to keep her interest.

"Do you want me to invite Darak to join us?" He was practically snarling as he thought she might want another man on a permanent basis.

Jeri looked at him and the confusion in her eyes made him feel slightly better. She was embarrassed. He could tell by the blush staining her soft cheeks.

"Well, that was a nice experiment, but it's not something I'd like to do all the time, if you don't mind." Her voice was shy, but it reassured him enough to expose a little part of his own soul.

"Are you sure, baby? Am I enough for you?" The answer to that question mattered too much.

"Are you kidding?" She entangled her arms around his neck, drawing him close for a leisurely kiss. "You're almost too much for me, Micah. I don't think I'll ever get enough of you." Her words were whispered against his lips as she pulled him down for a long, deep, hot kiss.

He loved it. He loved the fact that she would initiate this intimacy and felt comfortable enough with him now to tell him these things. But he wanted more. He wanted it all.

"I know I'll never have enough of you, Jeri. I realized something that I should probably have known all along." He sat back and she tracked him with her eyes, smiling but intrigued by the change in him.

"What's that?"

He held her eyes with his, laying it all on the line.

"That I love you."

She was silent a moment, her little mouth opening in shock as tears gathered in her eyes. He took it as a good sign.

"You love me?" Her voice was breathy, her emotions running high as the tears started to spill over. He hoped they were tears of joy as he nodded, taking her hands in his.

"I love you for all time, Jeri, and if you'll have me, I want you to be my bride, my life-bonded mate."

"Oh Micah." She threw herself into his arms, placing little, joyful kisses on any part of his face and neck that she could reach. "I love you so much. I love you too."

She dissolved into incoherence as he captured her words with his lips, worshiping her and sharing the joy in his heart. He felt a lightness in his soul he never would have imagined, a completion as their energies started rising and joining together, as their passions increased.

She was panting, her hands everywhere as he undressed

her with equal haste. She freed his cock, bending low to take him in her mouth even as he rid her of the last of her clothing. She didn't bother removing his pants, he thought with a last trace of humor. She was apparently in too much of a hurry.

Well, so was he. He had to get inside her before he exploded. The pressure built between them, demanding completion. He lifted her by her shoulders, gentle but firm as she struggled to return her mouth to his cock, but he wanted an even better pleasure. He *needed* to come in her luscious body, joining them together in body as they would be in soul.

He stretched her out on the bed, not bothering with preliminaries as he covered her, staking his claim, filling her channel with his hard cock. He slid home easily, her wet excitement welcoming him into her body as her precious love welcomed him into her heart.

He stilled just for a moment, enjoying the feeling of knowing the one he made love to loved him in return. It was something he'd never quite experienced. Something he'd always wanted that had been just out of his reach.

He cherished this time and this woman. This love that they shared. It fulfilled him and brought joy to his existence, and he vowed in his heart to prove his love to her every single day for the rest of their lives and beyond.

"I love you so much." He breathed the words he never thought to speak and reveled in the feelings that swelled in his heart.

His deep voice stirred her senses. She'd loved him for so long, not daring to hope that he would return her feelings. But she saw the truth in his eyes, felt it in the way he worshiped her body with his own. He did love her. She could hardly believe it!

"I love you more than life, Micah. I want to make you

happy." Her words were whispered against his lips as he began to pulse softly within her, picking up the pace rapidly as the desire overcame them once more.

"You make me happy just by breathing." He moved in her with relentless passion as she sighed, then whimpered, then moaned as the pleasure increased fast and hard. "My happiness is in your arms. In your life. In *you*." He pounded into her, emphasizing each of his words so that she would never forget them or forget this moment. "You can't ever leave me, baby. It would destroy me."

That last whispered admission sent her spiraling over the edge, her body clenching hard on his, spasming in the throes of the hardest, hottest, fastest orgasm she'd ever experienced. He came with her, shooting deep inside, warming her from within with his come as he continued to pulse.

She held him close as his crisis continued, wrapping her legs around his ass, just barely revealed by the pants they hadn't taken time to remove completely. They'd never been so explosive before. She smiled as the aftershocks continued, her bliss rising.

"I will never, ever leave you, Micah." She licked his ear, whispering her vow close as she held him tight in her arms and in her body. "To part from you would destroy me."

He pulled back, moving slowly within her, feeling the echoes of the pleasure they'd shared. His eyes were wet, their skin heated from the amazing passion that flared between them.

"We are a part of each other. Whatever comes from this day on, we face it together."

She broke into tears, so happy she couldn't form words. She clutched at his shoulders, rolling with him as he turned them so he could snuggle her close while she rode the emotional storm. He kissed her softly, stroking her hair and her skin, comforting her as the emotions overwhelmed her. He seemed to understand, and she marveled anew at the fate that would bring such a man as this into her life. He was the most special man she had ever known and she loved him with all her heart.

She whispered that last thought to him as she drifted into sleep, exhausted from the day's events and the emotional storm, the relief, the joy, and most of all the love. The love is what would make her life sparkle like the most precious of jewels from this day forth.

"What in hell was that?" Darak asked when he could breathe again. He was on the bridge, and he'd just come in his pants. Judging by the expression on the faces of the other crewmembers they'd had similar experiences. Seta was panting, and Agnor was grinning like a fool.

"If I'm not much mistaken, our new Vizier doesn't quite have a handle on the higher level of shielding he and his lady require yet." Agnor shook his head in wonder. "Damn, that felt good—and that was just an echo. What must she be like in the flesh?" Agnor stretched, a wide, satisfied grin on his mouth as he picked at his own wet clothing.

Darak had the nerve to laugh. "She is heaven itself, Ag. She blew my mind and then some."

"You mean he actually let you join with her? I thought he was too possessive to share her with anyone. Even you."

"I'm pretty sure it was a one-time thing." Darak was abnormally uncomfortable speaking about such intimate details where Jeri was concerned, but these people were closer than family. If he couldn't trust them, there was no one else in the universe he could trust. "Did you know she came to him a virgin? She never had a man before him. I think he just wanted to give her the experience of two men at once. She was so responsive. She singed my senses."

"That one has a fire deep in her soul. Her Talent is just beginning to bloom, and it could well be the strongest I have ever tested." Agnor's eyes took on a faraway look.

"She's that powerful?" Seta was recovered enough to ask, eyeing the two men from her console.

Agnor nodded. "After the way that psi wave affected all of us, she's either Mage or Mage Master material right now. Perhaps Vizier like I believe Micah is. It wouldn't surprise me. They are well matched in all other ways."

"Good goddess in heaven," Seta whispered. She seemed shocked that such power could reside in anyone she knew. "And I teased her."

Darak laughed outright. "She likes you, Seta, even if you made her uncomfortable at first. You have to admit, you come from a much more permissive culture than she is used to. A Mithrakian virgin was bound to be stymied by a sexy Virulan wench like you."

Seta tilted her head, as if considering his words. "You think?"

"Don't worry over it, Seta. She has a kind heart, and she's been good for Micah. Haven't you noticed how much he's changed since she's come into his life?" Agnor's calm words had both Darak and Seta nodding.

"I, for one, am glad he found her. He was falling into a pit of despair and there was little we could do to help him out." Darak stood and headed for the door. "I'm going to go clean up. Ag, you have the bridge until I get back. I'll make it quick so you can change too." He grinned devilishly. "And maybe I'll knock on our captain's hatch and tell him to shield a bit more carefully so we don't run out of dry clothing." With a wink he was gone, whistling a jaunty tune as he left.

Agnor used the shipcomm to check on the rest of the crew. Trini's brother had fallen into a deep healing sleep, so he was oblivious to the phenomenon. The two young yeomen were chuckling like fools when Agnor explained what he thought had happened. Yes, indeed, they'd felt the orgasmic power as well. And enjoyed it.

Trini's response was more practical. She told him she'd had a nice orgasm, thank you very much, then went on to speculate that she was glad the horses were already off the ship.


"Micah..." Jeri turned to him as he came out of the bathing chamber, "...what you said before, about inviting Darak to join us?"

He came over and wrapped her in his arms loosely, placing a kiss on her forehead.

"I was a jealous idiot. I didn't really want him here."

Jeri sighed in relief. "That's good." She seemed nervous, so he stroked her soft hair, encouraging her.

"What is it, sweetheart?"

"It's just that, well... I was wondering if that was something that you would want. I mean, I know you've had other women, but will you still want other women after we're formally bonded? I don't know what bonding really means on your world." Her words came out in a nervous rush and he pulled her closer, understanding dawning on him. She was jealous and he felt like the cat who swallowed the cream. He liked that she was possessive of him.

"It means faithfulness to each other, for all time. And I haven't wanted another woman since the moment I laid eyes on you, Jeri. I don't need multiple partners to get off, as you well know. All I need is you." He kissed her, smiling against her lips.

"Are you sure, Micah? I know your culture is different from mine."

"And you'll come to enjoy the freedoms of Geneth Mar society, I promise. But you won't ever have to share me with another woman. I grew up on Geneth Mar. I've had multiple partners and done wild things when I was younger, but that pales next to the love I have with you. You're all I need to be happy, Jeri." He kissed her lightly on the brow, then tickled her. "Of course, that doesn't mean we won't both enjoy watching."

She blushed rose red at his words, just as he'd known she would. He chuckled and continued to tease her.

"And I know you were virgin until you met me. There's lots you've never tried. As long as I'm with you, directing your pleasure, you can have just about anything you want." His eyes grew devilish. "You can even have Darak again, if you want him. But only when I say." He noted the way her flush and breathing increased. The thought excited her. Damn, she was beautiful. Everything was so new to her. It made him feel like a teenager again.

"So you want to be in charge?" She was comfortable enough with him to challenge him, teasing in return. He liked that too. It showed she was coming into her own, learning her place in his life, becoming his equal, beloved partner.

He grasped her around the waist, lifting her bodily into his kiss. "I definitely want to be in charge in the bedroom—or wherever we make love."

She eyed him for a moment. "I can agree to that. I like it when you're masterful. And I love it when you're making me come." She let all pretense of teasing drop. "But I don't need other men. Only you. Forever you."

He kissed her long and hard before ending the embrace with great reluctance. He would keep her in bed for the next week if he could, but he had a ship to run. He'd already neglected his duty enough as it was. Still, he couldn't resist making everything clear for her, heightening her anticipation. He wanted to leave her with something to think about.

"And you'll have me," he agreed. "You'll also have the benefit of my knowledge and the things I'll enjoy doing to you. I may bring Darak back one of these days to show you something special, and maybe even others, but trust in that it will always be to expand your pleasure, my love. Whatever I bring you—whoever I bring you—will be brought in love. And it won't be often. Just sometimes."

She shivered at the look in his eyes and he knew in that moment that she had truly surrendered the power over her pleasure to him. It was a heady feeling and a trust that he would never abuse. This was *his* woman. He would cherish her and teach her things about pleasure that she never would have imagined. And he would love every minute of it, just as he loved every inch of her.

# Chapter Eleven

Micah and Jeri reappeared on the bridge with broad smiles and accepted the crew's teasing with good humor after they'd learned what had happened. As soon as they'd settled down— Micah in his command chair with Jeri on his lap—he hit the button to broadcast through the whole ship so everyone could hear what he had to say.

"We have a little announcement." He stared into Jeri's eyes with a smile meant just for her. "Jeri has made me the happiest of men. She's agreed to be my bride." He leaned forward and punctuated his announcement with a smoldering kiss to the accompanying cheers and congratulations from his crew.

"So that's what that little firestorm was all about." Agnor clapped Micah on the back and kissed Jeri in congratulations. "I'm very happy for you both."

The look in his eyes told the truth of his deep feelings. Along with roguish Darak, Agnor was one of Micah's oldest and truest friends. He was glad to feel the genuine warmth his friends had toward his intended mate. He knew she felt uncomfortable about his social position and her supposedly inferior origins, but with friends like Ag and Dar to welcome her into his circle of friends and family, he hoped things would be a little easier for her.

"Thank you, Agnor." Jeri was shy about being kissed by

other men, as well as being embarrassed about their earlier passion spilling over to the crew, but Micah held her firmly, bathing her in the warmth of his love. She was a strong woman. She would be a strong and loving life partner. The goddess of all had smiled on him, indeed.

"Ag, will you comm the Council? They'll want to know about my intended change in status and maybe you could explain about finding Jeri and the fact that she'll probably need a seat on the Council as soon as we get back home?"

Agnor nodded sagely. "I've already thought about it and with all that's happened and my apparently expanded abilities, with your permission, I'm going to address my comm to Vizier Brandon himself."

Micah chuckled, as did Darak. "Want to make a splash with your new power, hey, Ag?" Micah shook his head as he smiled. "Then I say go for it. The Grand Vizier will be able to sense your increase in power even over this distance. You're right. He's probably the best person to start this ball rolling."

"Who is Vizier Brandon?" Jeri asked quietly, still sitting on his lap.

"At last count, there were seven Viziers on the Vizier Council. It's an offshoot of the Mage Council that has certain powers assigned to it in our constitution. Not all of them participate all the time, but when higher-level consultation is needed, it's Brandon that ties them all together. He's the Grand Vizier, head of that Council, and he's a good, solid man. Taught us as children, as a matter of fact."

"It also doesn't hurt that he's our uncle," Darak put in with a chuckle.

"Micah said your fathers are brothers, right? So then Vizier Brandon is another brother?" Jeri asked Darak since Micah was rolling his eyes.

"Got it right in one, sweet. Uncle Brandon swatted our hides when we were just little tykes, getting into trouble, then he was one of our teachers after we started manifesting our Talent. He was tough, but fair."

"This coming from Darak the Dreaded," Micah accused, laughing heartily. "That's what Uncle Brandon calls him."

She laughed with them, leaning close to whisper in Micah's ear. "Does that make you Micah the Magnificent?" She wasn't as quiet as she'd thought because Darak picked up on her words and howled in laughter.

"It must be love that blinds her, truly." Darak pounded Micah once on the back as he headed to his console.

Micah was stilled by his words and by the look in Jeri's smiling eyes. Her face was red with embarrassment at being overheard, but she was looking at him as if he held the stars in his grasp.

"I do love you, Micah. With all my heart."

She leaned forward to kiss him and the rest of the crew no doubt felt the fire of their passion light.

"None of that, you two." Darak stomped over to them, lifting Jeri out of Micah's lap. "We have work to do. And until you two learn to clamp down on your new power, you'll have to keep your hands off each other unless you want us all to stop what we're doing to enjoy it with you. Okay?"

Micah laughed uproariously at the pained embarrassment on Jeri's face. She looked around at the bridge, settling on Seta's smiling face.

"I'm sorry." Her whisper was met with a smile and a nod as Seta motioned her over to sit with her.

"You sit with me for a while, Jer, okay? Just until we get the business of running this ship squared away. Then we can all have some fun."

"I am so embarrassed." Jeri's voice was low but Seta heard it as she made room for the other woman at her station.

"Nothing to be embarrassed about, Jeri." Seta cleared a screen in preparation for showing Jeri how to help her track the former enemy ships. They were keeping a close eye on them, just in case. "Where I come from, sex is even more out in the open than on Geneth Mar. Some folks with Talent even train to give orgasms using our psi Talent alone, or to make others experience our orgasms, much the way you did with the Captain a few hours ago. It's considered an art form. One that I studied for a few years."

"Really?" Jeri seemed scandalized and intrigued at the same time.

"Truly." Seta nodded, setting her breasts bouncing under their minimal covering. "I told you once before that I was a sex slave for a while. It was not one of my better moments, but necessary at the time. Part of the reason I was enslaved was the way my Talent was trained early on to give pleasure. It's a highly prized and rare skill among sex slaves, since so few people with Talent ever find themselves in that predicament." She sensed Jeri was going to ask how it had happened to her, but Seta wasn't quite ready to relate the sordid story of her life. The others knew where she'd come from, of course, but it was hard to think back on the past and the rough times. Even worse would be to tell this young woman, raised in the strict culture of Mithrak, who had come to Micah a *virgin* for heaven's sake. Better to change the subject, Seta thought, turning quickly to the screens before them.

A few moments later she had Jeri engrossed in the task of tracking the former enemy ships. Seta marveled at how quickly the little horse tamer learned. She hadn't really expected much, since she knew a little of Jeri's background and the lack of any kind of technical training, but Jeri was not only a fast study, she had a quick, sharp mind. If she hadn't thought so before, Seta began to realize just how good a match this woman was for Micah, whose own keen intelligence had saved them many times in the past.

Seta watched Jeri soak up knowledge, feeling Darak's dark eyes upon her. She looked up, and he nodded knowingly. She knew Darak had approved of Jeri long before this moment, but she'd thought his feelings based only on sex and the basic attraction of male to female. She was starting to realize for herself that this little horse tamer was a whole lot more than just a pretty female with strong Talent.

Seta was glad. She was truly happy that Micah had found a mate worthy of him in every way. He deserved the best and if she hadn't been fully convinced before, she was now. Jeri was a complex woman who would keep Micah guessing and happy for years to come. She smiled at Darak while Jeri worked, oblivious to the silent approval she'd just gotten.

Agnor had been quiet for nearly an hour when suddenly he expelled a deep breath and opened his eyes, blinking several times. He had news to impart—some that would be welcome and some that would give pause—but it was his task to relay it, no matter the content.

"Vizier Brandon sends his best regards to the crew of the *Circe*."

Micah started, then held up one hand. "Should you get on the shipcomm so everyone can hear the general stuff first?"

Still a little fuzzy from the long telepathic communication, Agnor nodded. "Good thinking." He hit a few buttons and repeated his first statement so that everyone could hear it no matter where they were on the ship. "At our captain's request, I've been in contact with the Grand Vizier and apprised him of our situation. He sends his compliments and congratulations, and he's ordered all of us to report directly to him for retesting as soon as we get back home. He's also authorizing reimbursement for the horses we gave to the Liatans, so our profits from this trip will not be lost."

"Good man," Seta murmured from her seat next to Jeri, smiling happily as Agnor continued.

"We've also been recommended for commendations and special recognition for rendering humanitarian assistance to the people of Liata in their hour of need and getting the word out to the Council. The tacticians want copies of our engagement records, so please gather whatever you have from each station on the ship and forward them to me at comm. We've been ordered to set course for home, but not right away. We are to leave only after the reinforcements arrive, so we'll have a few days here before we head home."

Agnor cut off the shipcomm and turned to address Micah directly. "Your uncle also had a few words to say about your bonding." Micah grew uneasy, and Agnor decided not to tease him. "He congratulates both you and Jeri and is eager to meet the new addition to the family." The broad grin that lit Micah's face warmed his heart.

"On a more serious note, he warns that the remnants of the enemy fleet might regroup. He was interested in the wave that hit us when you shattered that stone and wants us to stay alert until help arrives." He turned his attention to Darak. "If you have any splinters of the stone, he wants you to keep them in a psi-shielded vessel and preserve them for him."

"I have a few, but most of them are still welded into Jana's skin. I don't know what to do for her. It's beyond my healing ability."

Agnor nodded calmly. "I described it to him and he's most interested. He's having the highest level healers meet us when we dock to see if they can help her." Jeri breathed an audible sigh of relief as Agnor turned his reassuring gaze on her. "The Grand Vizier wanted me to tell you, Jeri, that every attention will be paid to healing your sister. On her own account and for your sake as well. You are, after all, part of the family now."

"That was a lot of communication over a very long distance, Ag. Are you feeling all right?" Micah was, as ever, conscious of the needs of his friends and crewmembers.

"I'm fine, actually. No strain at all. Which surprised your uncle as well. He's going to talk to the Specitar Council about me and the huge leap in power this psi wave seems to have given us. He warned that it might be a temporary effect, but odds are in favor of it being permanent. He tried to follow the energy pathways in my communication but we're too far away to do a good job of it, he said. Still, what little he did see gave him pause. My pathways were blown open in a way he's never seen, even in another high-level Specitar." Agnor felt a little lost for a moment, but Micah stood, putting his hand on his shoulder in a reassuring move that really did put him at ease.

"Whatever the changes, Ag, we're in this together. We'll get through this. Okay, my friend?"

Agnor nodded, glad once again to count this special man among his closest friends. A Specitar's life wasn't often filled with such camaraderie, mostly because most Specitars were solitary, insular people by the very nature of their power. They were specialists—their Talent lying in only one or perhaps two areas while the majority of people with Talent had it in broad-ranging fields. It was often hard for them to relate to Specitars and their special needs and vice versa.

But Micah and then Darak had bridged the gap with Agnor and the rest of the crew slowly followed. These people were closer to him than he had ever been with another Talent who was not a fellow Specitar. They were closer even than his own family, who did not quite understand their oddball son. And he loved them.

"I'm okay, Micah. It's just going to be an adjustment getting used to this."

Micah looked sheepish as he glanced at Jeri, heat flaring noticeably in his eyes. "You're telling me."

Vizier Brandon's admonition to stay sharp came to bear not ten standards later when a small group of enemy ships regrouped to try to overtake the *Circe* and reclaim their lost leader. How they knew she was still on their ship, Micah didn't care to speculate. When the enemy reappeared, Micah asked Darak to send Jana into an even deeper level of sleep and switch on a reflective field in her cabin, just in case they tried to harm her in some way.

It turned out to be a good move because as Darak opened the door to the small room they were keeping Jana in, he felt the first wave of energy hit her small form. She started convulsing and the blue shards still embedded in her skin started to smoke as she screamed in pain.

He threw himself against her and ordered her troubled body to sleep, taking a jolt of his own power as he switched on the reflective field. But it was worth the momentary pain to end her torment. As soon as the field came up, all connection with the psi attack was severed, the energy thrown back at those who had sent it.

Darak dropped his own shields and sat quietly for a

moment on the side of Jana's bunk, stroking her hair. She'd reopened one of the larger wounds and was bleeding just a tiny bit, but with the field up he couldn't use his Talent to heal her. Instead he fumbled in the bedside compartment for the med kit, using old-fashioned bandages and some healing cream to stop the trickle of her blood and kill any organisms that might infect the wound to make her sick.

He found himself stroking her skin just a moment longer than strictly necessary, but he couldn't help himself. She was every bit as beautiful as her sister, if not more so. He felt a little disloyal even thinking that, but Jeri was Micah's woman. Darak had no right to feel the least bit possessive of her.

This woman was another story entirely. Close enough in looks to be thought Jeri's twin rather than her older sister, Jana had a lost look to her face now that touched something deep inside him that he wasn't altogether comfortable acknowledging. Instead he focused on the obvious—the fact that she was beautiful and eminently fuckable—or would be if she weren't so grievously injured.

He'd heal her as best he could with his strong, but limited skills, then pass her to the experts on Geneth Mar. If he saw her again after that, perhaps he'd be able to act on the unruly desire that coursed through him each time he touched her soft skin, but he would leave that to fate.

So deciding, he stroked her skin one last time and stood from the bed. He took another hit from the field as he raised his shields a split second before he left the room, but he didn't want to take the chance of being unshielded even for a moment away from the protection of the field while they could be under attack. He went quickly to the bridge to rejoin the battle, if indeed it was still ongoing.

When he arrived back on the bridge he found the reflective

field had done the trick. That initial jolt, plus the wave of angry energy Jeri sent out, almost uncontrolled except through her connection with Micah, ended the short attack and left the enemy ships dead in space.

Darak could hardly believe it.

"What did you do?" He turned his questioning gaze to Jeri and Micah, sitting together on the command chair.

"Don't look at me," Micah replied with a tired smile. "My lady got a little angry and she fried them. Dammit, girl," he addressed his woman with a fond smile. "Warn me next time you do that."

She mumbled something against his chest, clearly drained. Darak shuddered to think of the power they must have emitted to drain two such Talented people. He looked at Agnor for clarification.

"What exactly happened?"

Agnor shrugged. "As the captain said, his lady got a little upset when she felt the attack against her sister. The power buildup was like nothing I've ever felt before, but luckily it was directed outward. It didn't hit any of us, except maybe peripherally. But it didn't harm us."

"Of course not, Ag," Micah waved a tired arm. "It wasn't directed at you guys. You weren't fool enough to piss her off." He closed his eyes and snuggled closer to his woman. Something big had definitely happened here to drain them both and disable no less than eleven enemy ships.

"Holy shit."

"Aptly put," Agnor agreed with him. "She's mostly untrained, but she does have power. And when she's angry it seems to grow. This went beyond anything I would have anticipated from either of them, Dar. This was something I've never seen before. Something I've never even *heard of* before."

"It was amazing," Seta agreed with wide eyes. "The way she directed the bolt. It bounced from ship to ship, decimating them in less than a minute. They didn't even have time to retaliate—or to run. They were stung when you put up the field, but that was probably limited to the Talents who were attacking her sister. But this...this...lightning that came from Micah and Jeri disabled the *ships* themselves!"

"Psi energy strong enough to affect mechanical systems?" The thought was amazing. There were stories of Shas who could do that kind of thing, but there were only one or two Shas in each generation and they weren't seen all that often. In fact, for as long as he could remember, there'd only been one old, female Sha who was very reclusive since her mate had died.

Seta nodded, stunned. "I saw it, but I still don't quite believe it."

"They might have just jumped to a whole new level." Agnor's voice was calm, but filled with the awe they were all feeling.

Help arrived the next day, soon after Jeri and Micah woke from their zombielike sleep. Agnor, Darak and the rest of the crew seemed to be tiptoeing around them, but Micah was too busy dealing with the newly arriving Council ships to question it. He'd get around to it, though. As soon as the new ships were in position, they were heading for home. He'd have time on the voyage back to Geneth Mar to get to the bottom of the weird response from his friends.

It took a few hours of concentrated work to get the new arrivals up to speed, but the *Valiant* helped where she could, and within one shift they were on their way. Seta plotted the course, and they made the jump that would take them home. For Jeri, it was the first time she would see Geneth Mar, and

Micah spent a few moments worrying over whether she would like it enough to call it home.

He wanted to build a home there, if she was agreeable, but he hadn't yet broached the subject with her. His family lived there and he had a place with them, but it was past time for him to create a separate place for himself—and his lady—to call home when they were not among the stars. They had many things to discuss, but it was enough for now to know that their love was mutual, deep and abiding. Everything else would work out...somehow.

Jeri spent a few hours sitting with her sister while Micah did his work. Darak kept Jana sleeping for several reasons. First, she had pieces of that stone in her body and he didn't know how it would affect her once she was awake. Second, if she was like other Wizards who'd been separated from the collective, she'd be somewhat lost and unfocused and might be a danger to herself and others with her strong, unrestrained Talent. And lastly, he couldn't bear to cause her any more pain. Letting her sleep through the long journey meant he wouldn't have to see her suffer. He wanted the highest-level experts on hand when she woke and though he'd love to see her pretty purple eyes focused on him, he could forego that pleasure if it meant sparing her even a moment of pain.

"We're almost done here, Jeri." Darak moved into the chamber where Jana lay quietly on the bed, her sister stroking her hair as she sat by her side. "We're on course for home."

Jeri's dark eyes gazed up at him, as if seeking hope. "They'll have help for her there, right?"

Darak nodded and came over to her, putting his hand on her shoulder in reassurance. "The very best people we have will be ready and waiting. Uncle Brandon promised, and when you meet him, you'll understand that he always gets his way. If he wants the High Healers at his beck and call, they come running." His chuckle was meant to comfort and he was glad to see some of the worry leave her beautiful face.

"She looks just like I remember her." Jeri looked back at her sister's peaceful face, lying so still. "Just a little older and a little lost. She was always such a definite person. Always so decisive. She knew what she wanted, and she worked hard to get it. The horses respected her firm hand and loving heart. I'm afraid the Wizards changed her. She led that attack, for heaven's sake. I don't know that Jana. She's not my Jana. My Jana wouldn't harm anyone who didn't threaten someone she loved first." A tear fell unheeded as her brows drew downward in concern. "She defended me a time or two, and herself when necessary, but she wasn't a violent girl, Dar. She was a peaceful soul for the most part, not scared of anything, but not a bully by any stretch of the imagination. I don't see how she could do what she was doing. Attacking innocent people, killing them. Killing *horses*." That last part seemed to shock her most of all.

Darak put his arm around her shoulders and pulled her against his side. "That wasn't her, Jeri. That was the Wizard collective. Somewhere inside this lost little soul is that girl you remember. You have to believe that. And if we all try hard enough—including her—she will be the sister you remember once more. You have to believe that, Jeri."

She surprised him, reaching up to turn his head toward her so she could kiss his lips softly, in thanks. She was more comfortable with him, but still much more reticent than the rest of his people. It touched him that she would bestow a kiss on him when he knew she wasn't in the habit of giving them. It made it special.

"Thank you, Dar. You saved her life and now you're saving my sanity." She chuckled as she rose from the bedside, and he followed suit. "You're a true friend."

He was speechless for a moment, his eyes holding hers. "I'm honored that you feel that way, *dama*." He bowed low, surprising her, he knew. The moment was special. It deserved honor, as did she. He captured and kissed her hand with the utmost respect, his movements solemn and laden with ceremony. "I will value the honor you give me all the days of my life and protect your life with my own."

"Dammit, Dar." Micah's voice came from the doorway as he smiled at the picture they made. "Did you just swear fealty to my woman?"

Darak straightened and grinned foolishly. "Why yes, I believe I did."

"Fealty?" Jeri was endearingly confused. He couldn't resist tugging her close and kissing her on the crown of her head. He let her go just as quickly, laughing at the look on her beautiful face.

"In days of old on Geneth Mar..." Micah clarified as he strode farther into the room, "...warriors would swear fealty to certain people—men and women in positions of power. Basically it meant that the warrior would protect that person with their very lives in return for that person's patronage."

"Patronage?"

Micah smiled at her. "Back then it would mean room and board, provisions, a horse and such. Today?" He shrugged. "Maybe we can fob him off with a letter of reference or something."

Darak sighed theatrically. "I pledge my life and you want to fob me off?"

"I didn't say that," Jeri said, turning in Micah's arms to look at him. "If we were on Pantur I could at least manage the horse."

"Ah, the fair Jeri has a bigger heart than her chosen mate. I knew you wouldn't leave me in the lurch, *dama*."

His eyes were serious even though his expression was teasing. She could feel his discomfort, and she wanted to put him at ease. She moved out of Micah's loose embrace and faced him squarely.

"I never desert my friends, Darak." Her dark eyes held his. "The service you've done me in saving my sister's life can never be repaid."

He shrugged, but she knew her words touched him. "You owe me nothing, *dama*."

"And why are you calling me that? I'm still the same girl Micah dragged off Pantur, much to your dismay." She tried to tease the truth out of him, but it backfired.

"No, you're not." Darak took a deep breath, his whole expression changing. "You've evolved into something that is downright amazing, Jeri. As have you, cousin." His gaze sought Micah's, moving between the two with great seriousness. "The rest of us have been talking. Agnor and Seta are half convinced you're both Shas after what you did to disable those enemy ships."

"What?" Micah was clearly flabbergasted.

"Think about it, cuz. That lightning bolt you two sent out was pure psi energy. It shouldn't have been able to disable mechanical systems."

"Holy shit." Micah was eloquent as he thought through the occurrence he hadn't had time to really dwell on just yet.

"No kidding." Darak looked at Jeri. "The amount of energy you two put out disabled eleven ships—some of them bigger than the *Valiant*. No way could Uncle Brandon have done that, and he's the strongest Talent we know."

"Maybe two Viziers together?" Micah offered, clearly at a loss.

Darak shook his head. "Ag and I searched the records. He's made a study of Talent levels because of his role in testing and training. Only Shas have ever manifested psi energy sufficient enough to affect mechanical systems in such a radical way. Ag 'pathed Uncle Brandon again while you two were asleep. They're sending the enemy ships under seal to him for study. They want to know exactly what you two did to them."

"Oh man." Micah rolled his shoulders uncomfortably. "So this is why everyone's acting so strangely."

"Got it in one, cuz."

"Well you can all just stop it." Jeri didn't like the uneasiness between the two men who had always been the best of friends. "No matter what we can or can't do, Micah and I are still the same people. Dammit, Darak, you will not make him feel like some kind of freak."

Darak laughed. "I'd better be careful. The last time you got pissed, eleven warships stopped dead in their tracks."

"That is *so* not funny." Jeri shook her little fist at him, and he caught it with a grin.

"Be at ease, *dama*. I'm your sworn protector now, remember?" He winked at her when she would have cursed him. "I'll try, Jeri, but it's a little hard to think of your best friend and his mate as two of the most powerful beings in the universe."

"Then maybe..." Micah pulled Jeri back into his arms, nodding seriously at his cousin, "...you'd better not think at all." He pulled Jeri out of the room and toward their cabin, signaling Darak to follow behind. She thought she knew what he had in mind, and it gave her pause, but she trusted Micah and she'd agreed that he was in charge when it came to their pleasures. He would never do anything that she wouldn't enjoy.

Darak paused by the open door to their cabin, resting both hands on the doorframe. "This isn't what you want, Micah. Not for her and not for you. Admit it."

Micah shook his head. "We need this, Dar. Jeri and I both need you, this once, to ground us. To watch over us. To join with us and let us know we're still the same people we were yesterday. To let us know that you're still the same true friend you were to us yesterday, with the same smart-ass sense of humor and an eye for my bride-to-be's butt that makes me want to either pummel you or burst out laughing."

Darak shook his head, chuckling at that last part, and Jeri knew then that everything would be okay. The odd moment was past, now they had to put it in the past for good.

"Well, since you put it that way, I guess I could accommodate the lady, just this once." Darak advanced slowly into the room, allowing the door to swish shut behind him as he began unfastening his worn leather belt. He stopped short of the bed though, to give Micah one last long look. "You're sure?"

Micah nodded once, picked Jeri up by the waist and tossed her into the middle of the huge, soft bed. She giggled as she landed, Micah at her side, already pulling her clothes off.

"I'm trusting you to tell us when we need to shore up our shielding, Darak." Jeri's tone was teasing and she enjoyed the way he looked at her body as Micah revealed it. She licked her lips as Darak did the same, feeling amazingly sexy for the first time in her life. She knew what to expect now and she was looking forward to the things Micah would choose to teach her with Darak's help.

"That's a monumental task you give me, *dama*, when your

beauty is so distracting, but I will endeavor not to let you down." He sought outside himself for a moment, concentrating on the shields Jeri had thrown around herself and Micah ever since that first incident after they'd been elevated. Her shielding skill was so strong and natural, he found no fault. She was still shielding null, which amazed him. With so much more power, she could still hide it completely.

The way she looked at him—so much more at ease with herself and her femininity than the last time he'd been so honored—made him hot. He took his time, baring his chest and enjoying the way her eyes followed him. He'd had more than one woman tell him they enjoyed his muscular form, but with innocent little Jeri, he could see the admiration in her eyes. Along with the lust. It was enough to make him hard. Or at least, harder than he already was.

"Show me that pretty ass of yours, sweet."

Darak saw her eyes widen and shift to Micah for direction. It was a stark reminder that this woman was not his to keep, but rather to help pleasure at the direction of his best friend. It was a hell of a role, but he'd enjoy it while it lasted. He knew the two were so crazy in love with each other that such opportunities would be few and far between—if indeed they came up at all.

"Show him how much you want this, baby." Micah guided her onto her hands and knees, slapping her smooth ass and leaving behind a beautiful pink handprint. His devilish smile shifted to the other man. "She pinkens so prettily, doesn't she?"

"Gorgeous," Darak agreed, finding it hard to speak around the sudden dry catch in his throat as Micah slapped her other cheek. She squealed a bit, ending in a laugh as she signaled her enjoyment of the tender but firm spanks. He had the sudden fantasy of having Micah spank her ass while he was buried in her pussy and he nearly stumbled as he made his way to the other side of the bed, opposite Micah.

Slowly, tantalizingly, he lowered his pants, revealing himself inch by inch to her avid gaze. He stood near her head, purposely giving her a good view and making it easy for her to shift around to take him in her mouth if Micah so desired. How he hoped and prayed Micah did! His cousin was calling the shots here, he had to remember that.

Micah must have sensed his desire. He guided Jeri until she was kneeling across one corner of the bed, her mouth at the perfect height for Darak's dick, while Micah entered her pussy from behind. When she closed over him with a moan, Darak was in heaven.

# Chapter Twelve

"Son of a bitch."

The soft swish of the door opening went unheard, but the three lovers definitely caught the soft curse as Agnor stood shocked motionless in the door.

"Shit, Jeri. Don't stop now." Darak's soft reprimand brought her attention back to his swollen cock, riding hard and deep in her mouth. Agnor watched, transfixed. Then he realized he was staring, and Jeri wasn't used to an audience.

"I'm sorry. I'll come back later."

"Don't go." Micah's command was low but forceful as Darak shot his load down Jeri's throat with a harsh groan of pleasure. She swallowed it, lapping up every drop while Darak started to come alive again under her ministrations. The power levels in the room were astounding. Agnor was feeling a little giddy just standing inside the door. How he wished he could share Jeri's beautiful body with Micah and Darak. They'd shared women between them before. Many times, in fact, when they were younger. It had been some time since the three men had bonded over a woman's joy. In a way, he missed it. But they were older now, needing some emotion along with a hot fuck to make it worthwhile. And emotion the likes of which he saw in this room was rare, indeed.

He watched as Darak left Jeri's mouth and sat at her side,

turning his attention to her nipples, taking Micah's chain from around her neck and attaching it to the points he so lovingly pinched in preparation. Micah was ramming into her pussy from behind and if Agnor was any judge, the man was close. It wouldn't be long.

When Micah came, taking Jeri with him through a prolonged orgasm, the burst of energy that flowed through the room threatened to make him come in his pants. His dick was harder than a rock and ready for action, but he had no idea if he would be invited to join or have to go seek comfort with one of the other women on board or at worst, his own fist.

Micah pulled out, then turned Jeri onto her back, positioning her, spreading her legs and posing her as if for Agnor's delectation. Darak moved silently to the small bathing chamber and returned with a wet cloth, cleaning her folds and rubbing over every inch of her pussy, even pushing his cloth-covered finger deep into her hole, which made her squirm.

Watching was making Agnor squirm as well, as Micah eyed him with a mischievous smile.

"Look, Dar's cleaned her for you. Do you want a taste of my woman's pussy?"

Jeri gasped, her eyes going wide and aroused as he watched her reaction. The arousal clinched it. He'd watched her and dreamed of tasting her for some time now. He knew this was a once–in–a–lifetime chance to have her, with Micah's permission and guidance. This act wasn't about him, Darak or even Micah. It was about her. Giving her pleasure. Giving her new experiences. It was an act of love on Micah's part. Love, trust and total indulgence.

"You know I'm always up for hot pussy, Micah."

Agnor threw off his robes as he advanced on the bed. Decision made, he wasn't one to hesitate or beat around the bush. He saw what he wanted, and he knew his decisive movements were exciting her. He trusted Micah to oversee this first meshing of their powers and assure his safety. Jeri could easily kill him with her expanded powers, but he figured it would be a hell of a way to go.

He settled between her legs, holding her gaze as he moved down, down, down, zeroing in on her clit with unerring intent. He touched his tongue to her and it was as if electric shocks were floating through his whole body. It was an amazing feeling and he wanted more. Using his long tongue, he explored every fold and curve, pushing at her clit and thrusting as deep as he could inside her wet hole.

"She tastes divine," he said, coming up for air briefly, throwing Micah a quick look to make sure all was well. The benevolent smile on Micah's face was a kicker, he thought indulgently. The StarLord shared his lady and was fully aware of what a great privilege he bestowed. The possessive gleam in his eyes was something Agnor had never seen there before with any other woman and it spoke volumes about the love between these two that he so envied.

"She rides cock like a dream too. Don't forget, she's an accomplished horsewoman."

Darak made a strangled noise, and Micah laughed.

For her part, Jeri was pleasantly astounded by the muscular, ultramasculine form Agnor kept hidden under the robes that usually marked a Specitar. His movements were stirringly decisive and his touch as expert as Darak's and Micah's. She never would have thought the usually quiet, respectful man was as wild and skilled as he'd so far proved.

He brought her so close to orgasm with his tongue alone, but Micah stopped her from coming, directing them both as he watched carefully over the meshing of her newly expanded power with Agnor's. Micah touched Agnor on the shoulder, pulling him away from her pussy, moving to her side and bending to kiss her as he did something with his Talent to ease the buildup of her power, dissipating it to safer levels.

"We don't want you frying poor Agnor, do we?" Micah teased her as he lifted his lips and his gaze searched hers. "How are you feeling? Do you want more?"

She smiled at him, tangling her hands in his hair, pulling him down for another kiss before she answered.

"I feel really good, Micah. I'm up for whatever you want to teach me."

He smiled and gave her a smacking kiss. "Then let's put poor Agnor out of his misery and bring you to another level of pleasure."

He rested at her side while he directed to Agnor to take her. She knew this first time he'd watch over them, making sure their Talents meshed rather than clashed. It felt a little more dangerous this time than when she'd first joined with Darak, but perhaps that was because of the rise in power they'd all experienced. She only knew she was glad to have Micah there, guiding her and directing them all. She trusted him with her heart and soul, and she realized she would never do this with anyone else but him.

She didn't really need any man but him, though she knew he enjoyed teaching her the amazing limits of her body's pleasure. She had special places in her heart for Darak and Agnor, but without Micah, she would never have participated in this carnality. He was the one who made her want to explore the boundaries of her sexuality—with him and for him. And she loved every minute of it, just as she loved him.

Agnor settled between her legs, but this time, he braced his strongly muscled arms on either side of her head. He was a tall man, taller than Micah, and she'd thought him lanky, but he was instead, heavily muscled and every inch a dominant male. He smiled at her with a sort of primitive intensity as he came down on top of her, making her squirm with the newness and heated desire that knowing Micah was at her side, watching all, brought her.

"You are beautiful, *dama*. I have wanted this moment since I first saw you."

Agnor's deep voice was soft, almost reverent as he placed nibbling kisses on her mouth before delving deep inside with his talented tongue. His body lowered over her, pressing her into the mattress in a way that made her feel small and cherished, and incredibly hot. He kissed her as if he had all the time in the world, exciting her with his skilled kisses to a fever pitch while his cock rubbed over her slit, spreading her juices and raising her desire, but not yet entering.

"You taste of meadow and sky." Agnor raised his lips from hers, but he didn't go far. His head lowered again, starting a journey to the sensitive areas of her neck and then on to her breasts, licking and sucking, worshiping as he went. When he finally tugged on her nipples with his teeth and lips, she whimpered at the pleasure that was so close.

"It's time, Agnor." Micah spoke quietly, still at her side. "Take her now."

"She's on fire." She looked up to find Darak kneeling at her other side, his eyes entranced, his dick large and long, rising up and ready. Just as Micah's was.

This first joining with a new partner had to be seen to first, before she could do anything about the other two men. She knew their power levels were so high and so new, they didn't dare initiate anything with a new partner in the mix without first meshing their energies. Darak held his cock in one curled fist, mimicking Agnor's motion, watching avidly. It was enough to make her squirm.

While she was looking at Darak, Agnor plunged forcefully home. She went wild, looking from Darak to Agnor to Micah as she panted in shocked passion. Agnor was long and wide and he felt like heaven within her as he moved, hard and fast, taking her over the edge too soon. She came, her inner muscles clutching him tight, but he wasn't finished.

Agnor laughed as he felt her release, leaning down to kiss her steadily, powering through her orgasm and bringing her right back up again to where she'd been—desperate for another release. His pace increased steadily and his expression grew serious as he pressed close but did not crush her.

"Did you enjoy that, *dama*? I love the feel of your tight pussy coming around me. You clench so beautifully." He licked her lips before moving downward. His words were whispers against her skin. "Micah is a lucky man to have both your heart and your luscious body all to himself. I envied him before, but now..." His voice trailed off as he increased his pace again.

"Do it, Ag, she's going to explode again. This time you should go with her." Darak's voice was warning and low.

"He knows what he can handle, Dar," Micah said quietly from her other side. She looked up at him, amazed by the burning desire in his eyes as he watched over them all. Only then did she realize her release could cause some harm to Agnor if he didn't come with her. Micah had explained about how the power built and meshed and released together. But when one partner didn't release, sometimes it could backlash.

She turned her eyes to the man straining above her as he pummeled into her, and reached up with her hands to stroke his massive shoulders.

"Come with me, Agnor. I want to feel you come inside me."

He groaned and grew impossibly harder within her tight sheath. She could feel the tension running through him, echoing her own as she strained toward release. This time when she came he was with her all the way, plunging wildly, deep, hard and fast, in her welcoming heat.

He shouted as he jetted into her, his expression hardening in pleasure as she pulled him closer into her embrace. He came for long, long moments as her own pleasure seemed to go on and on. She felt the slow release of the energies and the wash of pleasure that meshed them together, sealing him to her and vice versa. Nevermore would their bodies or energies be strangers.

She knew a side benefit of this joining would be an increased ability to share energy between them. It was one of the reasons why, Micah had explained, sex among Talents was so open and varied. Those with lesser strength often joined with multiple partners so they would be able to work their Talents together more easily. It was expedient as well as pleasurable.

Agnor rested within her a moment more, rising on his massive arms as if doing a push-up over her smaller body. He stared into her face for a moment before placing a shimmering, gentle kiss on her lips.

"Thank you, *dama*. That was a joining I will never forget."

"Neither will I," she whispered, acutely aware of Darak and Micah watching and waiting on either side.

"But it's not over yet." Micah had their attention as Agnor gently withdrew, rising to kneel between her legs in a rather decadent display. He was semihard again already. And she was surrounded by cock. Bared and claimed. It made her feel wanton and ready, even after the two huge orgasms she'd just had. Micah brushed the hair from her face gently. "Ready for more?"

"More?"

Micah nodded with a sinful smile. "Yes, love. Now that you've joined successfully with Agnor, we three can introduce you to the delights of triple penetration."

"Triple...um?"

Darak laughed and reached out to tug on her nipple as if he just couldn't resist touching her any longer. "Don't worry, sweet. You're going to love it as much as we will."

Agnor was breathing normally again by now and he'd taken the soft cloth from the bedside, wiping his excess from her pussy, gently stroking her with the cool cloth, making her hot. He knew just what he was doing as he rasped the cloth over her clit and stroked her with his long fingers to release his come from her inner depths. He shocked her gaze up to his as he stroked over the bundle of nerves deep inside her channel. He was chuckling in a way she'd never seen the serious Specitar do before and she was glad she could bring him this moment away from the seriousness of his life and responsibilities.

When she was reasonably clean and squirming, Agnor raised his head. "Where do you want me?"

Micah seemed to consider. "At her head, I think. Let's flip her on her stomach first."

Three pairs of masculine hands did the work, turning her gently onto her stomach. She had never felt so pampered.

"How do you feel, my love?" Micah bent low to whisper in her ear.

She moaned as strong hands began rubbing scented oil into the muscles of her back. Agnor, she guessed, while two more long-fingered hands started massaging the muscles in her legs and butt. That had to be Darak, she judged from the strength of his touch. Micah's hands wound through her scalp and rubbed in gentle circles, relaxing her.

"This feels so good." Her words were slurred with pleasure as Darak's hands worked higher, parting her ass cheeks and delving within.

"It gets even better." Darak's chuckle reached her from where he was seated between her legs. "You're so beautiful, Jeri."

"Getting your energy back, love?" Micah whispered in her ear, taking a moment to kiss her face all over.

"Mmm."

He chuckled as he moved back, signaling to the other men his wishes. He moved behind her as Darak lifted her into his arms, facing him. Just that quickly, she found herself settled over Darak's middle, straddling his chest while he played with her clit. Her gaze sought Micah questioningly.

"Feeling up to a nice long ride, my love?" His sexy smile twisted her insides as she nodded back at him. "Good. Let's show Darak what a good horsewoman can do with a stud."

She laughed as Darak's hands clenched around her waist. She steadied herself and took control, positioning herself over him, moving slowly and surely, making him sweat. Her skin was slick with the massage oil and three pairs of hands moved sensuously over her, heightening her pleasure.

With a gasp of delight, she pushed downward, taking Darak's long cock into her body. He clutched her hips with his hands, helping at first, but she moved his hands gently to her breasts, licking her lips as she promised him the ride of his life.

Behind her, she could feel Micah preparing her rear entrance. It wasn't something they did all the time, but she'd come to love the way he took her ass. As he slid home, he signaled Agnor to take his place at her side, his huge erection jutting out, once again fully engorged.

With gentle hands he guided her head slightly to the side until they were in perfect alignment. She needed no further prompting. She opened wide and took him deep in her mouth, sucking and slurping in a way that made his fists clench in her hair. All the while, she used her powerful thigh muscles to move up and down on Darak's hard body, much the way she rode her horses.

It was an intricate dance, made even more so by the addition of Micah's long fingers in her rear, preparing her to take him. When she was ready, he stilled her movements and took a position on the bed, between Darak's wide spread thighs. He was behind her, spreading her ass cheeks and pushing home as she cried out in rapture. Then the dance resumed as she moved up and down on all three cocks. They warmed her, pulsing within her and making her feel so full of life and love, she would never forget the experience.

Micah and Darak came nearly simultaneously. She came hard and fast when she felt the spurts of warmth within her, her entire being filled with the essence of the men who possessed her so fully.

Agnor wasn't far behind as she gave him one last mighty suck, in the throes of her own completion, that made him shout as he came. She lapped at his long dick, swallowing all he offered and licking him until he was clean once more.

Three sets of masculine hands lifted her off Darak and laid her down on the bed, touching her gently as they worshiped her body. They barely took a breather to clean up a bit and regroup before they began kissing her skin—whatever part of her body they could reach. Micah's lips tickled her tummy as he lapped at her navel. Agnor sucked on her toes, and Darak placed the gentlest of kisses on her eyelids, moving down the planes and angles of her face until he reached her lips.

He tangled his tongue with hers, and incredibly, she felt her desire rise once more.

Before long, Micah directed her to settle over him this time while Agnor peppered her ass with spanking blows, heightening both their pleasure.

"I love the way you clench around me when he swats your ass. I've been wanting to try this for a long time." Micah held her close to him as Agnor continued to administer the spanking they both craved with skill and finesse. Jeri marveled at the quiet Specitar's skill. There were hidden facets to Agnor that she was only just coming to appreciate.

Darak knelt at their side. "I'd be happy to help you out in the future when you want to experiment." His devilish wink and piratical grin had her chuckling before the next blow landed, making her yelp and clench once more as Micah groaned in appreciation.

"I'll remember that, Dar." Micah pushed her upwards by the shoulders so that she sat astride his hips, much as she'd done with Darak, but this time her ass cheeks were tinged pink from the spanking Agnor had administered at Micah's direction. She was feeling decidedly warmer in other places too. She didn't think anything could top that last encounter, but she soon realized that was just a warm-up.

Micah called all the shots. At his prompting, she took Darak in her mouth as Agnor took her ass, continuing to swat her from time to time, but with less force. It didn't take much, her skin was so sensitized, and she came over and over again while the three men shafted in and out of her in every possible way.

By the time they had each come again, she was a quivering mass of jelly. She'd lost track of the number of orgasms she'd had and she could barely move under her own steam. The men had to lift her and clean her, caring for her in a way that made her feel cherished and loved. She was barely conscious when Agnor and Darak finally left, many hours since this little interlude had first begun, but she felt Micah settle next to her, cradling her in his strong arms as she slipped into the deepest sleep she had ever known.

Just a few days later, they arrived at one of the elaborate space stations orbiting Geneth Mar. Seta and Trini had helped her find suitable clothing and some serious girl time had been spent cutting and styling her long hair to a more polished look. The other women assured her that the Council would welcome her no matter what, but Jeri felt better with the outer improvements in her look.

She knew she was still a country bumpkin underneath, and she feared saying or doing the wrong thing with a level of nervousness that threatened to make her break out in hives. Micah soothed her, but she was not only going to have to pass muster with the Mage Council, but his family as well. She knew his uncle would be there to meet them and Micah had told her his mother and father were sure to be close behind since the news of his betrothal had undoubtedly reached them by now.

Agnor had been quietly retesting the rest of the crew, though he didn't ask either Micah or Jeri to submit to testing. In fact, Agnor had been incredibly respectful of her in a way she wouldn't have expected since that amazing foursome. She'd been nervous about facing him after that incredible night, but rather than the familiar affection with which Darak treated her now, Agnor was instead somehow more formal and even a little awestruck.

Micah made some oblique explanation about her increase

in Talent making Agnor more reticent when she asked him about it, but she didn't really understand what he meant. The Talent rankings were still new to her, and she didn't quite understand why a powerful Specitar would have such an odd reaction to her.

Agnor wasn't rude. Quite the contrary. He bowed his head a lot when she was near and was doubly as polite as he'd always been—and that was really saying something. Agnor was a polite soul by nature, more concerned with others' comfort than his own, but he took it to new heights and it was perplexing to say the least.

She didn't have too long to dwell on the puzzle because before she knew it, they'd arrived at Geneth Mar. She held hands with Trini and Seta, who'd come to her for moral support while Micah and the other men dealt with the formalities of docking and communicating their arrival. Normally both Trini and Seta would be working alongside the men, but Micah had sent them to her, knowing how nervous she was.

Before long, the *Circe* was fully hooked up to the station, cycling air and offloading waste materials as they did every time they docked. They were also put in queue for automated supply deliveries. Fuel, food and assorted other items that were on the preference lists Trini had prepared were automatically downloaded to the station computer and resupply scheduled. They could be sure of the best in the way of provisions since this was their home port and the captain was an important man.

One of the few StarLords, Micah was well known throughout the Council worlds for his outward deeds and among certain select groups for his less publicized work. Newsbot cameras were already transmitting the arrival of the *Circe* planetside and commentators were speculating on the action the little ship had seen in the recent attacks on Liata.

They'd had to engage the energy shields in order to keep the newsbots from coming too close to inspect the damage on the *Circe*'s hull. Though they hadn't faced much direct fire, some of their maneuvers and encounters with debris in orbit had left their mark on the otherwise gleaming surface of the top-of-the-line ship.

All that would be fixed, now they were in port. While the crew faced testing and debriefing, the *Circe* would get her own sort of once-over. Repair crews were already standing by to swarm over the ship as soon as the occupants left.

Micah commed Jeri in their cabin, signaling it was time to disembark. They'd talked about how this would go, since there would undoubtedly be news crews waiting to capture the moment of their arrival. With a look of dread for her friends, Jeri went to meet Micah at the hatch. Trini and Seta patted her on the back and wished her well, but she had eyes only for her lover as Micah took her into his arms for a quick hug.

"Are you ready?"

She snuggled into him for a moment, then leaned back. "Ready as I'll ever be."

"I'll be with you every step of the way, my love. I know this is new to you, but we're in this together."

She reached up on her tiptoes and kissed him once. "You are the best thing that ever happened to me, Micah."

He couldn't help but kiss her deeply, the fire in his eyes promising more at the earliest opportunity. His woman was in for a long night of loving as soon as they could get away, but first they had to run the gauntlet. There were reports that needed to be made and family that had to be told of their plans.

"All right, you two, we've kept them waiting long enough." Darak's amused chuckle belied his harsh tone.

They sprang apart and Jeri stuck her tongue out childishly

at Darak as he grinned and popped the hatch. Before she knew it, she was facing the group of people waiting in the small reception area set up inside the station for the *Circe*.

"Uncle Brandon, it's good to see you." Micah bowed his head in respect as he walked out of the ship and grasped hands with the man, a slightly older version of himself. The family resemblance was strong.

"Glad to see you, too, boy. I hear you have quite a tale to tell." Brandon nodded to Agnor, who bowed his head in return. "I'm happy to see you safe home once again. And especially to see you've found your heart's desire among the stars." The old man's eyes twinkled at her. "You must be Jeri."

She smiled at him and blushed. It was hard not to respond to the man's direct approach and genuine warmth. She found herself liking the Vizier immediately and her stress level went down just the tiniest of notches.

"It's a pleasure to meet you, Grand Vizier."

"Call me Uncle Brandon, please, my dear. After all, if our friend Agnor is right, you probably outrank me."

Shock made her gasp. She looked from Micah to Agnor and back but the other men only smiled. So this is why Agnor had been acting so funny, she realized. But they couldn't possibly be right. The rank of Vizier was more than high enough to impress anybody. There was just no way.

Then she thought about what she'd done to the enemy ships and she realized that from the crew's reactions, that hadn't been anything they'd ever seen before. She knew her power had grown incredibly since meeting Micah, and even more since the psi wave had hit them, but she'd never expected...

"I see my nephew has been keeping you in the dark. Well, we shall see if our friend Agnor's suspicions are correct soon enough." The Vizier stepped away to speak a few words with each member of the crew, and though the aides with him went to each of them in turn, no one approached her or Micah. She didn't know what that might mean, but it made her nervous.

In short order, the crew had been dispersed with most of Brandon's helpers and he was back with Micah and Jeri. The old man smiled at them, putting Jeri more at ease, but his next words stilled her once more.

"Sha Ellenor wants to meet with you both."

"Right now?" Micah seemed surprised.

Brandon chuckled as he led the way out of the small reception area. "One does not keep a Sha waiting."

They had the run of the station it seemed as Jeri walked quickly to keep up with the two long-striding men. She was entranced by the shops they passed, her eyes following the bright vid displays of women's fashions and accessories in one of the larger stores. She knew Micah and his uncle were talking quietly as they walked, but she let the conversation flow around her. This was her first time on a space station, and this one seemed luxurious to her.

They arrived at a shuttle and she found herself strapped into the seat next to Micah, his uncle across the small aisle and the rest of his people taking seats around. It was a private shuttle, small but fast, and she reached for Micah's hand as the thing shot out of the space station and dived for the blue-green planet below.


Brandon's attention was snagged by the man sitting next to him so Micah turned to Jeri, sitting so pale and scared at his side. She was holding up well under the circumstances. She'd been a farm girl on Mithrak and had never been to a city, much less a luxury space station. Pantur was a rough place and she'd lived out on the plains with the Hill Tribes in a crude tent. The cities below were like nothing she'd ever seen and he couldn't wait to share his world with her.

"You're going to love Geneth Mar, Jeri. There's so much I want to show you." He took her hand in his.

"I feel a little out of my element, Micah."

He bent to kiss her gently. "I know, love. But you have nothing to worry about. My parents will love you because I love you. And our people will love you because of your kind heart. Many of the inhabitants of this world are Talented and anyone with even a hint of it can see your pure heart shining in your eyes." He kissed her eyes with featherlight touches that warmed her from within.

He kissed her deeply then, taking control of her mouth as he often took control of her body. His senses were inflamed just that easily and if it hadn't been for the slight jarring as the shuttle landed, he would have taken her where she sat. As it was, he raised his head reluctantly, facing the teasing smiles of his uncle and his uncle's aides with good humor while Jeri blushed to the roots of her pretty hair.

# Chapter Thirteen

They'd landed on a private shuttle pad near the main Council headquarters. It was set apart in a remote part of the compound reserved for high-level visitors. A small, older woman was waiting for them as they disembarked, her smile wide and warm as she held out her arms in welcome.

Brandon walked up to her and bowed low as she placed her palm over the crown of his head, as if in benediction. One by one the aides with him received the same greeting. But when it came to Jeri and Micah, the older woman paused. She walked up to them and faced them both squarely, looking them over for a long moment.

"Micah, StarLord of Geneth Mar, I haven't seen you since you were a little boy."

Micah began to bow, but she stayed him with a bony hand on his shoulder.

"I am honored you remember me, Sha Ellenor." He settled for a slight bow of his head in respect to the older woman.

It was at that moment that Jeri realized this petite woman had to be the one and only Sha left to the Council, who she'd heard the other crew members speak of in reverent whispers. She was a being of immense power and the highest ranking of Talent known. Her bonded mate had also been a Sha, but he'd died several years before, tragically, and this small woman had retreated from society in her grief.

She raised her bony hands to take Micah's head between her palms. It seemed as if she were somehow reading him as she closed her eyes, and Jeri could feel the hum of power in the air.

"You've grown strong, young Micah. Your parents will be proud." So saying, she released him with a smile and turned her attention to Jeri.

The two women were about the same height, though the Sha was much older, shriveled just a bit with age beneath her flowing pink robes.

"I understand you are from Mithrak, Jeri Olafsdottir."

Jeri gasped. She hadn't heard her full name in more years than she could count. She never used it or even spoke it, lest the Wizards hear of her. But somehow this small woman knew, and Jeri read even deeper knowledge in her compassionate eyes.

"You did well to evade the Wizards and even better to release your sister from their collective." The old woman took her face in her hands as she'd done with Micah and concentrated for a moment. Jeri could feel the probe of her Talent, and she panicked. She put up the wall that had always protected her and moved back away from the woman, her eyes a bit wild.

Micah reached out for her but the Sha stayed him with one raised hand.

"It's good that she does not trust so easily," the old woman said softly. "It's the one thing that has saved her all these years."

Micah moved to stand beside Jeri and took her into his arms, pulling her against his chest as if to protect her.

"She meant no disrespect, Sha Ellenor, but it is her right to refuse the probe."

The Sha smiled benevolently. "You are correct, Lord Micah. No offense was taken. I'm glad to see you've found yourself a feisty mate. You were always a rogue, Micah. Perhaps this little spitfire will be able to keep you in line."

He chuckled. "Or perhaps we'll just feed each other's vices."

"Oh, you have few real vices, Micah. I know that for fact. But she seems your match in every way. Cherish each other while you can. Enjoy each moment and every breath you take together."

The old woman seemed to diminish as the memories of her own lost love came to her mind, and Jeri's heart filled with compassion.

"I'm sorry for your loss, Sha Ellenor." Jeri's heart went out to the old woman. "I thought my sister lost to me. Even now, I don't know if she'll ever be the same as she once was. I understand your pain."

The old woman smiled softly, her eyes kind. "You have a good heart, Jeri. I'm glad to see it." She withdrew, moving away from them as she prepared to go. "Your sister will recover physically, though I fear the stone will always be part of her. It is her heart and soul you must fight for. With love and patience, she will heal and be whole once again."

"Thank you, Sha Ellenor, for giving me hope." Jeri rested her head against Micah's chest, glad of his support during this strange meeting.

They were whisked back into the shuttle, only to land halfway around the planet on Micah's home soil sometime later. His parents were there to meet him, as were most of the rest of his extended family, including Darak, who'd been released from

231

wherever they'd taken him after they left the ship.

Meeting Micah's parents was daunting, but his mother welcomed her with open arms and from then on, things were easier. Micah's father looked much like his son, only older. Looking at him gave Jeri an idea of what Micah might look like in twenty or thirty years. He had that same steady power about him too, a Mage Master of great Talent. Micah's mother held her own place on the Mage Council and was a tall woman with striking good looks and great elegance.

Jeri felt a little bit like a scruffy ragamuffin next to his sisters—one older and two younger—who were as tall and elegant as their mother. But they were warm as well, making Jeri feel welcome and taking her off for a few moments of girl talk while Micah discussed his recent trip with his father and uncles.

Darak came to steal her away, winking broadly as he escorted her to the banquet table that had been set up. Jeri realized only then how incredibly hungry she was as Darak filled a plate for her, chatting about the various characters in the family as they eyed her in return.

"I heard you and the rest of the crew were retested. How did it go?" Jeri asked Darak as they stood eating finger foods that were delicious and in some cases unidentifiable. At least to Jeri, who had never seen such an elaborate buffet.

Darak shrugged. "Ag did some testing before we left the ship. I was close to Mage level before, so I guess that's where I ended up." He looked uncomfortable though he tried to hide it. "I'll have to take a seat on the Council, which will be quite a change. I don't think they're ready for me in that stuffy chamber."

Jeri chuckled. "I have no doubt of that." She saw Micah

bearing down on them and he clapped Darak on the back heartily.

"So I hear we have a new Mage Master of Geneth Mar," Micah teased Darak, who seemed stunned by the news of his rise in power.

"Micah." Darak's tone was chiding and a little panicked. "Tell me you're joking."

"'Fraid not, cuz. The word came down to Uncle Brandon, and he's about to make the announcement. I'd say you'd better get that look of dumb astonishment off your face before everyone else finds out."

"Master?" Darak breathed. "Really?"

Jeri touched his arm. "I've seen what you can do, Darak. The way you healed Tendil and my sister. How could you doubt yourself?"

Darak leaned down and kissed her, taking her in his arms for an exuberant hug a moment before adding his grinning cousin to the mix.

"I can't believe it."

"Believe it, Dar," Micah said encouragingly. "Believe in yourself."


Vizier Brendon made the announcement a few minutes later to much rejoicing among the gathered family. He also mentioned that all the members of the *Circe*'s crew had gained rank in an unprecedented way. Seta was now a strong Dominar, as was Trini, and the two young yeomen had each jumped two levels. Agnor was being seen by no less than the entire conclave of Specitars to see if they could figure out how to classify his incredibly increased powers and he let it be known that the Sha Ellenor had already met with Micah and

Jeri and she would be delivering her findings on their progress soon.

The gathered family members asked Darak and then Micah to say a few words, and Micah surprised Jeri by pulling her into his arms and declaring that their bonding ceremony would be held in just a few days. He kissed her soundly in front of his whole family and she blushed as they made various kind and sometimes risqué comments.

From that moment on, Jeri was taken over by Micah's mother and sisters as they planned the ceremony down to the last detail. Her days at the family compound were spent with the women, but her nights were Micah's. He took her to his private apartments and loved her all night long, taking her to heights they hadn't reached before.

They lay in the afterglow, the retractable ceiling on their tower room pulled back so they could bask under the stars. Micah held her close in his arms at his side, with her head nestled into his neck as they watched the twinkle of the tiny suns so far away and yet so close.

"How are my mother and sisters treating you? I know you've been cornered by them as they plan the ceremony. I'm sorry I haven't been more available for you during the day, but there's a lot to be done before I hand over the *Circe* to Darak."

She leaned up on an elbow, quick as a flash. "You're giving the *Circe* to Darak?"

Micah shrugged. "It's time. The *Circe* doesn't belong to me, much as I might wish she did. She's a spy craft, built by the Council and in their employ. Darak doesn't know yet so don't spill the beans. It's going to be a surprise for our new Master Mage."

"He's going to be floored, Micah. He barely believes he's a Master now."

"I know how he feels. I've been there before myself."

"To answer your question though, your mother and sisters have been amazing. I never thought they would welcome me so readily. Jenet and I are about the same age and we're becoming good friends."

"How about Serina and Alis?"

Serina was his older sister and she possessed a beauty and self-assurance that was daunting. She welcomed Jeri with an open heart. Alis, the youngest, was a devil of mischief and she was fast endearing herself to Jeri's humorous side.

"They've been great, as has your mother. They've made me feel like part of the family already, though I've got a lot to learn. Your mother is teaching me many things I don't know about your culture."

"I'm glad." He hugged her close. "Once I turn over the *Circe* to Darak, we'll have plenty of time for ourselves. And we're taking a honeymoon trip to the southern coast. Just the two of us. I have a private villa there." He moved so that she was straddling his waist as his hands roamed. "We can make love on the beach day and night."

He then proceeded to demonstrate just how they would make love, in many different ways, all through the night.


The ceremony went off without a hitch. The crowd of well-wishers was immense though the ceremony itself was scaled down from what it could have been had his mother and sisters gotten their way. Jeri had insisted on a simple ceremony and Micah was glad. Undoubtedly she'd been told of some of the more excessive ceremonies where the couple consummated the union in front of everyone.

He wouldn't have minded, except for the need to shield everyone present from their expanded powers, but he knew his shy little bride would never go for such a public display. She was slowly getting used to their culture, and he'd already discovered she liked to watch, but she was a long way from putting on a show of her own.

The party went on long into the night and even the next day some of the revelers revived the band enough to do a bit more dancing. Micah and Jeri had one more stop to make before they could go on their honeymoon. Micah had a full month planned at his private island, and he was eager to get there and have his new wife to himself.

There was just one further obligation first. He escorted her to the small shuttle, taking leave of his family with a round of hugs and kisses while Jeri accepted the ribald humor most new brides were subject to with good grace. Her face was red with blushes as she sat next to him in the copilot's chair, and he teased her about it before getting down to the business of flying them to their next destination.

She was interested in learning how to pilot the small craft so they passed the time it took to get to the Council enclave with a rudimentary flying lesson. It wasn't a difficult craft to master and by the time they landed, Jeri was flushed with the success of her first lesson. He was glad she hadn't asked much about why they'd been summoned back to the Council compound. He was nervous about what they might learn, for today was the day he would not only introduce Jeri to the Council, but they'd also receive the results of their recent appraisals by the Sha.

The Council chamber was nothing like Jeri had expected. It was a vast hall, like an amphitheater, with an outer hallway that led to the chamber proper. There were private rooms in the back area, by the access hall, giving each Mage their own private suite for them and their aides. The outermost area was a small box that sat in the theatre itself, with a table and chair, comp and other equipment that might be needed to be heard in the large hall. The whole place was decorated in soothing colors and the energy of the place was dampened in some way that made her feel more comfortable here than she had in a very long time in any public place.

"The Viziers keep a shield up around the place when the Council is in session," Micah explained, knowing her questions before she could ask them.

This new closeness with him was still somewhat startling, but it grew more comfortable with each passing day. She felt she'd finally come home. Wherever Micah was, that was her home. He smiled and swooped to kiss her lips sweetly.

*"You're my home as well, Jeri."* The voice sounded in her mind, and it was undeniably Micah's. She gasped.

"How?"

Micah chuckled, pulling her close for a quick hug. "Agnor showed me a few things. He figured with our increase in power, some other things might've changed as well. I had a very slight telepathic gift before. Nothing to write home about, but it was there. It was hard for me to utilize, so I never really trained it. It hurt when I sent, but I could receive reasonably safely. Ag knew this and would sometimes 'path me when we were on missions. It was a useful little skill."

"But now you can send without pain?"

"Apparently so. Agnor gave me a quick brushup on the technique and since our little jump in power, it doesn't hurt to send. Of course, it's still not my primary skill."

"Do you think I could learn it?"

"Agnor said you might have the Talent. We'll give it a try after we get this over with, okay?"

He squeezed her close for a short moment, then let her go to move into the chamber proper, taking the seat at the table set aside for them. He pulled out her chair, letting her precede him and squeezing her shoulders in reassurance while all heads in the chamber turned to mark their entrance.

Jeri was surprised to see Micah's father and mother in the box next to them, smiling in support. His sister Serina was in the next box and on their other side, Uncle Brendon sat in a separate box, on the fringes of a cluster of other Viziers.

"The Viziers don't always sit in on Council meetings, but they have a reserved area and are always welcome." Micah explained the various tools in the box, message systems and audio pickups, as well as pointing out other sections in the great hall. "The business takes place down on the floor and these boxes can detach and move any of us down there if needed, so don't jump if the box detaches. It can be a little jarring."

"Do you think they'll want us there?" Her voice was a little fearful. The room was immense, and there were so many people watching them already.

"Probably. I'll want to introduce you at least, but there will probably be some discussion of what happened to us at Liata and then some announcement of our new rankings. Don't worry, love. I'll be beside you the whole time. We're in this together."

She smiled up at him and in that moment of unshielded love, a bright light shone on their box and it detached with a jolt from the wall.

"Hmm, that didn't take long." Micah tucked her hand in his and squeezed it in reassurance as her eyes went wide. "Chin up, sweetheart. They won't bite."

She smiled at his reassuring chuckle and it was that

picture of them, united in their love, that most of the Mages present would take away with them as their first impression of the couple. There was silence in the hall as they neared the stage in the center, and Jeri could feel hundreds of pairs of eyes watching their every move. She tried to breathe deeply and concentrate on Micah's warm presence at her side. He was with her. That's all that mattered.

The Master of Ceremonies welcomed them to the floor, introducing Micah and reminding everyone present of his lineage. When he turned to introduce Jeri, he surprised her by using her full name and planet of origin. Several in the audience muttered, she could hear, when Mithrak was mentioned, but she sensed the disapproval wasn't of her or her planet, but of the Wizards and the way they enslaved Talents in their collective.

Jeri's nerves slowly subsided as Micah was asked to give a full report of their journey. He quickly and precisely explained about finding her on Pantur and then the action at Liata. Some of the Mages rang their question bells and asked about her stay on Pantur and how she came to be there, but the questioning wasn't harsh or suspicious, only interested and she found herself going into some detail about her life on Mithrak and her escape to Pantur. Before she knew it, she was feeling more comfortable with friendly questioning and Micah beside her.

When they came to the end of their story, a hush fell over the chamber as a new person walked onto the center stage, stopping before Micah and Jeri. Micah stood and Jeri followed suit, bowing low before the old woman she'd met briefly upon arrival on Geneth Mar. The Sha had come to Council, apparently surprising many within.

All the Mages rose, Jeri realized belatedly, and bowed their heads in respect to the Sha. The old woman acknowledged them with a smile and a benevolent wave, then waited until they'd reseated themselves before addressing the assembly.

"Forgive me for staying away so long, my friends," the old Sha began. "For a long time after my mate's passing I had no hope. But I find new hope for us now, in these two young people." Her arm swept theatrically to indicate Micah and Jeri where they stood off to her side. "For I have seen into their minds and met my match. And more." Her eyes met Jeri's and the woman's smile was brilliant. "In them, I see the rebirth of hope for our people. Two new Shas to protect us and help guide us into the years ahead."

Jeri felt Micah's shock as they stared at the older woman approaching them slowly, her arms open wide as she hugged them both.

*"Don't look so surprised, my dears,"* she said to them privately, startling Jeri a bit. *"You had to have known this was coming. After what you did to those ships? And even before? I studied the records from the Circe after meeting you. You two are stronger even than I and my beloved husband were in our prime."*

Micah bent low to kiss the old woman softly on her cheek, a sparkle in his eye as Jeri did the same. Jeri was crying openly, tears of astonishment and the joy she felt from the cheering Mages running softly down her cheeks.

*"Your lives will be very different now,"* the Sha warned. *"You will be protected and cosseted as you will protect and cosset the people who look up to you and depend on you. It is a weighty responsibility, but I think you two can handle it."*

The Sha turned to address the Mages once more as they grew quiet at her gentle motion.

"Lord Micah, you were bred to command. Your family has a long and proud tradition on Geneth Mar and a love for its people." Her old eyes sought out the boxes where Micah's family sat, and she nodded. "You will be a good and strong Sha, vigilant and experienced in the ways of command." Then she turned to Jeri.

"Jeri Olafsdottir of Mithrak, you are a stranger to our world, born under oppression and forced to hide for most of your life. You have a heart full of compassion and a firsthand knowledge of the right and wrong ways to use Talent. Your love for Micah and your love of freedom will be a beacon for the rest of our worlds to rally behind. We are truly blessed that you have come to us, and the people of our worlds will treasure you both, always."

A huge roar of approval echoed through the hall and only then did Jeri realize there were roving newsbot cameras recording and broadcasting this moment to the rest of the planet and perhaps beyond to other Council worlds. She was nearly overwhelmed.

Micah caught her as she swayed just the tiniest bit, pulling her back against him and wrapping his arms around her waist as they faced the approving cheers of the Mage Council. Never had he felt so light of heart, except perhaps for the day Jeri had told him she loved him. Only that moment could match the joy he felt now directed at them from all these strong Talents.

Suddenly he realized what his new role—their new role— would be. They were protectors and leaders, but now they also represented hope for their people. With two new powerful Shas, the threat against all Council worlds diminished substantially. As they grew into their full power and learned how to harness it and use it, they would be the symbol of protection for the worlds aligned with the Council.

They would undoubtedly be called upon to defend those worlds in the dark times to come. For the attack on Liata was just the first foray, Micah knew, of a much broader plan by the enemies of the Council to expand their influence into Council space and make the Council itself fall, if possible.

That much at least, he had learned from Jana's memories of her enthrallment to the Wizards' collective. She would be either a strong ally or a sleeper agent for the enemy in their midst, but she was being watched carefully. Jeri would keep her close, as would he, albeit for different reasons. Both Darak and Agnor had been let in on the secrets Micah had picked up. He trusted them to look for any sign of problems, and be their backup should he and Jeri be called away somewhere else, which he thought would happen sooner rather than later. Better to attack new Shas who didn't quite know yet what they were doing than go after them later, when they'd had a chance to study and learn to control their immense new powers.

But first, he would enjoy the time they had together. Tomorrow would work itself out. He wanted to revel in the joys of being newly wed to the one woman who completed him in the universe. And he would do so, as soon as he could whisk her away from the throngs of well-wishers and adoring Mages.

As it turned out, their departure for the coast was delayed a day or two at the Council's request. There was a great deal they had to do to prepare the way for two new Shas, and Micah and Jeri's input was required on the decisions, apparently. It was frustrating to Micah, when he wanted to be alone with his new wife.

Before he could do something rash to the aides that insisted on bothering him for every little thing, Darak showed up at the door to the spacious chambers they'd been given. He had the rest of the crew of the *Circe* with him and a supply of food and drink big enough for one final crew party. It was the night before Micah and Jeri were scheduled to finally leave on their honeymoon, and they welcomed their friends with open arms and bright smiles.

At first there was some awkwardness because the crewmembers didn't quite know how to address newly made Shas, but Micah put them at ease in short order. He reminded them that he was still the same man he'd been before, just with a new title. They'd been dealing with the giant leap in their own powers, so they understood perhaps better than anyone how he felt. After Darak poured the first few rounds of drinks, things loosened up even more. And when, inevitably, the group started to flirt and exchange sexual banter, Micah watched Jeri closely to see if she would leave, watch or perhaps even take part.

Micah's tall nephew Kirt settled next to Seta, his tawny hair disheveled as he bent to nip at her shoulder. It was left bare by the typically suggestive top she wore that showcased her pierced nipples. It wasn't long before she guided Kirt's head to her chest, encouraging the young man to suck her nipples. They'd spent a lot of time on the *Circe* pleasuring each other and the young man knew Seta's preferences well. It was only a moment before he had her shifting on the wide sofa, moving around so he could settle between her nearly bare legs.

Darak raised an eyebrow toward Micah and he knew without asking what his cousin was thinking as his gaze shifted quickly to Jeri and back again. Jeri tried not to watch Seta and Kirt on the sofa. The youngster was licking her pussy, eating her out like the old pro he was after spending a few months on the *Circe* with her and the rest of the crew.

Trini moved over to the other yeoman, bending to kiss Welan long and deep, settling on his lap and removing his clothing slowly, one piece at a time.

Micah nodded imperceptibly to Darak and Agnor, settling

one strong arm around Jeri's shoulders. She became aware gradually that Micah was moving her to lie back against his chest, clasping her breasts in his hands as he whispered in her ear.

"Do you want to watch or shall we join in, love?"

Jeri caught her breath and it lodged somewhere in her throat. She knew that Micah was waiting for her answer. She also knew he wouldn't try to influence her either way. She had become more used to the open sexuality of his culture over the past weeks onboard his ship and then the past few days on planet, but she was hesitant to join in the open displays of sexual enjoyment that were common here.

Still, she knew every person in this room. She had fought and worked beside them on the ground and in the skies above Liata. She had laughed and cried with them, and she knew they were Micah's family. Now they were her family too. She loved each and every one of them in a special way. It almost felt natural to think of them sharing pleasure with each other and...maybe...with her and Micah.

She also knew that Micah didn't need for her to do this, though he wouldn't deny her if she wanted it. She'd had some very serious conversations with her new husband about the way she'd grown up and had lived on Mithrak, and then later on Pantur. She knew that he wanted her to open up sexually for her own benefit, not for any need of his own. She'd felt the truth of his words when he'd said that she was the one woman he would want for the rest of their lives, and she felt the same about him.

She really wanted only him, but she knew he wanted to give her the experiences he'd taken for granted growing up and living on a Council world. He wanted her to explore her sexuality, to bring her pleasure and share in her voyage of discovery.

That was the only thing that gave her the guts to speak her mind. Knowing he would enjoy broadening her horizons as much as she would was extra incentive.

"Let's join in this one time, Micah. One time before they pack us off to wherever it is that good little Shas go."

He chuckled as he nuzzled her ear. "As you wish, my love."

Micah shot Darak and Agnor a look they understood well. The men moved the couches back and the huge mattress from the giant bed in the other room was placed on the floor in the center of the sitting room. Sheets and a mound of pillows followed as Seta and Trini took a moment from their pleasures to help the men make the area more comfortable.

Micah called the two yeomen over, taking Jeri's jeweled nipple chain from around her throat as they approached. Both young men had changed so much since she'd first met them. They were truly men now, powerful and confident since the changes and difficulties they'd faced. In their early twenties, they were both well-built, good-looking specimens of the males in Micah's family—tall, handsome, smart and quick to make her chuckle with their witty banter. She felt so different from the shy farm girl who had been so impressed by them, even back when they were somewhat less sure of themselves.

Jeri didn't know what Micah had in mind, but she knew she'd have to shield tightly so as not to hurt either of these young men who were strong, yes, but no match for her new Sha status. She trusted Micah to know what he was doing.

She licked her lips nervously as he handed the chain to the two men who now stood before her with knowing smiles on their handsome faces.

"I think you've earned this little honor." Micah put one end of the nipple chain in each of their hands. "She likes to be bitten. Gently, though."

With a little further direction that made Jeri squirm on his lap, he unlaced her bodice and pulled the sides apart, baring her tightening breasts to their hungry gazes. Kirt and Welan moved forward as one, reaching out with their hands and tongues as Micah moved back, watching with indulgent eyes as the two young men brought her nipples to tight, hard peaks.

She cried out when they nipped her in unison, looking at their dark, laughing eyes, so much like her new husband's. They were slightly younger versions of him and Darak, she realized, with the same devastating sexual skill that would make their mates lucky women someday.

They played with her nipples for a very long time, bringing her to a lovely high peak of pleasure and making her come just from playing with her breasts, as they tweaked in unison. Their bright, sexy smiles made her feel loved—not the way Micah loved her of course, but she felt the acceptance, admiration and love from these people who had become her family, and she took each young man in turn and kissed him deeply.

She was kissing Welan as Kirt squeezed hard on her nipple once more before tightening one end of the jeweled chain expertly. She yelped, and they both chuckled as they switched places, Kirt driving his tongue deeply into her mouth as Welan secured the other end of the chain on her straining nipple.

"Welcome to the family, cousin," Welan whispered into her ear, making her shiver as he delivered one final kiss. Then both young men moved back to Trini and Seta who had been enjoying fondling kisses from both Agnor and Darak.

The older men moved to let the yeomen take over with the women while Micah moved Jeri to the center of the huge mattress. He sat behind her as he played with her tight, bound nipples. Agnor and Darak came to sit on either side of her, reminding her of the pleasure they'd found that one time they'd all been together. She knew this was a farewell of sorts and the thought brought a bittersweet feeling to her. But they were all family. Just because Micah would no longer be captaining the *Circe* didn't mean she would never see them again. It would be less often, and probably not all together in one place, but she would see them from time to time. She and Micah would make sure of it.

# Chapter Fourteen

She realized this farewell gathering was good for them. They needed to celebrate one last time as the group that had weathered such trials and come out on top. They'd grown during their voyage and changed in so many ways. She cherished each and every one of these people, and she never wanted them to forget it, even though she was some kind of important Sha now.

She was still plain old Jeri in her mind, and she wanted to be the adventurous Jeri she'd discovered with these loving people. Already Micah had helped her grow in so many ways. He was her life. As she knew she was his. It was hard not to fall back into her old habits of hiding from the world and keeping a very low profile.

In a way, being a cosseted Sha was going to be hard on her. There was every temptation to retreat from the world, and let them all protect her from afar. But she didn't want to be the timid Jeri anymore. She was strong now and she had Micah at her side. His love made her stronger and together they could face anything that came. She liked that idea and she would try hard not to let the cosseting that came with being a Sha turn her into a recluse once again.

Darak moved to kiss her sweetly on the lips, and she smiled as he pulled back. His kiss was deep, hard, strong and had the tang of possession, though she belonged indelibly to Micah. He knew that well enough. It was just his way. Darak was a very complex man and she understood his need to dominate.

Agnor was on her other side, stroking her skin in that gentle way of his. His touch was different from Darak's direct approach, and different from Micah's knowing hands. Agnor was a gentle soul with the heart of a pirate. She'd already learned how he could make her squirm with his gentle, passionate hands and naughty thoughts. He was perhaps the strongest telepath in the galaxy at this point, and though she had little of that skill herself, he could make his thoughts echo through her mind in a sultry whisper that made her incredibly hot.

Micah hadn't quite caught on to that one yet, but she planned to tell him how sexy she thought it was to hear her lover's thoughts in her mind soon, if he didn't discover it for himself here tonight. She'd nearly forgotten about that little trick of Agnor's, but she knew Micah had some telepathic skill and he'd probably be able to learn something from his friend in this one instance. Jeri shivered in delight thinking about Micah's scandalous thoughts sounding intimately in her mind.

Agnor traced down her body with his warm lips, kissing and stroking her with his long fingers, while Darak left her mouth to follow a similar path down the other side. They both stopped at her toes, sucking them into their mouths as they watched her eyes, using their hands to caress her legs, removing her clothing along the way. Before she knew it, she was bare and her legs spread wide open with Darak in possession of one long limb and Agnor the other.

The kept her writhing in suspense, licking and touching their way up the insides of her legs, letting their hands tangle a bit when they reached her pussy. Agnor flicked her clit with

249

knowing fingers while Darak zeroed in on her ass. She knew he liked that and was glad she would have one last memory to take with her of these special men before she and Micah assumed their full responsibilities as Shas.

Of course, they had a honeymoon planned first, but that would be just the two of them. She was looking forward to spending time alone with him, without distractions and only the two of them making love day and night. But this final send-off with his friends was special too. It made her feel accepted on this new world in a way that was rare and unique.

Agnor plunged his fingers into her pussy as he finally reached her clit with his tongue and she went off like a rocket, held securely in Micah's arms as he watched all that transpired from his seated position at her back. His attention made her hot and honored in a strange way. He was such a special man, and she knew in her heart that he was happy to teach her and share with her the sexual freedoms he'd always known growing up on this world.

She loved having three strong men at her beck and call, and it was something she would never in her life forget. But she would do just as well, she knew, if it were only her and Micah, as it would be for the rest of their lives. There was so much love between them, they didn't really need anyone else to be complete.

As she came down from that first climax, she leaned back and twisted her head to the side, kissing Micah deeply.

"I love you," she whispered.

*"And I love you."*

The low, deep voice was unmistakably Micah's and unmistakably in her mind. Her eyes shot up to meet his as he chuckled.

*"Agnor clued me in on how much you seemed to enjoy a little*

*'pathing with your pleasure."*

She grinned and looked over at the tall, smiling man reclining at her side. "Agnor, I love you."

"Hey, what about me?" Darak winked at her as he came back, having removed his clothing while she recovered from that first shattering peak.

"You know I love you too, Master Mage." She caressed his bare calf with her toes, giving him a daring view of her pussy as he moved closer.

"Master," he chuckled. "I think I finally like the sound of that." His smile was smug and almost comical.

Micah threw a pillow at him that bounced off his nose.

"Hey, is that any way to treat a *master*?"

"You're not *my* master, Dar," Micah joked with the other man. "You're just my pesky cousin, and if you don't get this party started, I'm going to disown you."

"Have you noticed that the man has no patience since he's been made king of the universe, Ag?" Darak jokingly complained to the man across from him, but Agnor was too busy licking Jeri's clit to notice. Darak gave up with a shrug and dived in to make a meal of her chained nipples.

"You have great tits, Jeri," he whispered against her skin, making her gasp.

*"And the sweetest pussy,"* Agnor echoed in her mind.

She went up in flames as his naughty words registered and it wasn't long before she was begging with whimpering cries. The men smiled smugly at each other while Micah orchestrated their positions, taking care of her even in his heightened state of arousal.

Agnor lay down in the center of the large mattress,

obviously happy to have Jeri climb aboard. She went down on his cock slowly, stretching, filling, enjoying the feeling of him inside her tender core. He watched her face with indulgent fascination. She was beautiful to him, a true friend who accepted him with all his little faults and never questioned.

*"My friend Micah is a very lucky man, Jeri,"* he 'pathed to her. Her eyes met his as she came down over him fully. Darak pushed on her back, lowering her over Agnor and she held his gaze as she rested her breasts against his muscular chest.

"I'm the lucky one." Her smile was pure deviltry as she leaned forward to kiss him, her glorious hair spilling all around them, cocooning them in a private world of pleasure.

*"I pray one day to find a mate like you. It is my fondest wish."* He knew he was getting a little too emotional, but this was probably the last time the crew of the *Circe* would be together in one place with the man who had led them for so long and his new mate. He would miss them sorely, though he was glad for them. Still, it made his heart ache with loneliness to think of them staying behind when the *Circe* set off once more, for the first time without Micah at the helm.

Jeri seemed to understand his odd melancholy. She kissed him with a tenderness he'd never before experienced, then pulled back to meet his gaze.

"Micah loves you. That will never stop, no matter where we are in the galaxy. And with your new powers, you can talk to him any time." She gasped as Darak started his surprisingly gentle entry into her ass. "You should 'path him, Ag. He's going to miss you all as much, if not more, than you'll miss him."

He kissed her deeply. *"I will, sweet Jeri. I will. Forgive me for spoiling the mood. I believe you wanted to be fucked?"*

She giggled against his lips as Darak moved just an inch farther inside her back door.

*"I'll take that as a yes. But how do you want it, my lady? Slow and long or hard and fast? Maybe a little of both?"* His voice in her mind made her shiver. *"Ah, definitely both. Well, you have two men in your delicious body already, what's your new husband up to, I wonder?"*

He didn't have to wonder long as Micah's hands reached down, taming Jeri's luscious hair and lifting her by the shoulders to prop her up on her palms. She brought her hands to Agnor's side so she could take Micah in her mouth as he knelt next to them.

Agnor spared one glance at Micah's face and was almost overcome by the love shining in his friend's eyes for his new mate. He wanted to feel that for someone. He wanted that kind of soul-deep love in his life. For now, he would concentrate on this beautiful, kind, giving woman and bring her the greatest pleasure he knew how to give. She was special to him, though he knew she belonged firmly to his friend. Still, not a little part of his heart belonged to her and always would.


Darak slid gently home, taking his time to accustom Jeri's tender anus to his invasion. Gods, but he loved her tight ass.

She wasn't used to being taken in the ass, so he had to be extra careful. He didn't mind in the least, as she was extra tight. She was a special woman. Hot as hell, with a kind, generous heart and a dangerously strong Talent that would bring most men to their knees. She was the perfect match for his cousin Micah. The StarLord had finally found a mate worthy of him and vice versa.

Darak began to move slowly in her ass, knowing he was in charge of this small bit of their shared pleasure. He, Micah and Agnor had shared many women over the years and it suddenly struck him that this would be the last time. It was a sad occasion, but also a good one, for it meant that at least one of them had found the love of his lifetime. It had been a long time coming.

Personally, Darak didn't think he'd ever find a woman he wanted on a permanent basis. He was resigned to the bachelor life, but that was okay with him. Micah was the one who'd gotten depressed and so solitary over his loveless existence. It was only fitting that Micah find a woman who could be truly his for the rest of their lives. Equals in passion, pleasure and power, they would become a force to be reckoned with as they grew accustomed to their new level of power.

Such thoughts were put on hold as he seated himself fully in her tight, tight ass. He groaned out his pleasure at the luscious feeling of her tight hole around him, and her little whimpers turned him on.

Smiling, he swatted her rump, nearly coming from the feeling of her muscles clenching around him. He knew she liked a little roughness in her love play from the last time he'd been honored to join with them, and he vowed to make this final time together one they would each remember for the rest of their lives.

With a little nod from Micah, he swatted her again and all three men enjoyed her little squeak and the responsiveness of her various parts. Agnor seemed content to let Darak's thrusts move them along and Micah gave him the go-ahead with another short nod. He was more than happy to begin the slow digs that would rock them to pleasure.

Reaching around her, he tugged lightly on the chain that connected her nipples, tugging as he increased his pace. He could feel Agnor's excitement through the thin wall that separated their two cocks and he could see Micah's approval as his muscles tightened. Micah had his hands fisted in her hair as she moved back and forth on his cock, and the sight only inspired Darak to move more aggressively.

He was pounding into her ass, and she seemed to love every moment of it. Micah was close, as was Agnor, but it was Jeri that came first in their minds and hearts. Six male hands caressed her, teasing, tickling, and tugging on her various parts until she shivered and clenched around them in a quaking orgasm that lasted for minutes on end.

While Jeri shivered in one, long, continuous climax, she carried her men with her, one by one. First Agnor, then Micah and last of all, Darak, they paid homage to her with their bodies.

Now that they'd jumped in power, there was little recovery time needed before the four of them were at it again. Jeri briefly noticed that the other two couples had taken the big couches in the room, watching the foursome in the middle and finding their own paths to pleasure.

Jeri realized she didn't mind them watching. They were her family from the *Circe*, and she'd watched them many times while aboard. It was only fitting that she take her turn as the center of attention, even if only for this one last time.

Agnor took her in the ass this time as Darak cleaned himself up, then found his way into her pussy. Micah sat back to watch and after Agnor came with a shout, he took the other man's place in her ass. They loved like this, separately and together, long into the night, and when morning came there was no doubt left in anyone's mind that they would remain friends forever, even with the new rankings of power that separated them.

Before everyone left the sumptuous suite, Micah made sure

to impress upon them that they were to contact him at any time if they wanted his help or just to hang out. He still considered them his closest friends and family and wanted to be sure that becoming a Sha wouldn't interfere with the relationships he considered the most important.

Darak was the last one to go, and perhaps the easiest to convince, since he wasn't much for ceremony or position anyway. Jeri was glad to see that these two men, these best friends, would remain so. True, many things had changed and they were being swept along with the changes occurring around them, but this one friendship would never change. She left them to their goodbyes, knowing that Micah wanted a moment alone with his cousin.


"How does it feel to be a Master Mage, Dar?" Micah poured out two measures of Aurellian brandy and gave one to his cousin.

"Weird as hell, I have to admit." He downed a bit of the brandy and sat on the sofa across from his cousin.

"Yeah, I know how you feel."

"I bet you do." Darak chuckled.

"So isn't it about time we made you a StarLord as well?" Micah asked the newly minted Master Mage, shooting him a mischievous look.

"You think they're fool enough to make me a Lord?"

Micah just nodded. "Yes, I think I am fool enough to do it."

"You?"

"Who do you think makes these sorts of recommendations? I'm a Sha now, cuz. Some folks actually listen when I speak." Micah chuckled at Darak's surprise.

"You wouldn't."

Micah only smiled and nodded. "Already did."

"Holy shit."

"Hang on, Lord Darak, you're the new captain of the *Circe* as well."

"No way."

"What did you expect? I couldn't turn her over to just anyone. I trust only you, Dar, to take care of her and her crew."

Darak looked stunned as he sat for a moment, taking it in. "I can hardly believe it, Micah. But I swear to you that I'll make sure you never regret your trust in me." His gaze rose to his cousins and for the first time Micah saw the real feelings Darak kept so well hidden. He loved the *Circe* and her crew, as much if not more than Micah did himself. He could see it in Darak's eyes and it gave him comfort. Giving the ship to Darak had been the right decision.

"Take care of her, and her crew, Dar. That's all I ask."


The small craft glided low, coming in for a gentle landing on the wide beach. Jeri could see an immense and breathtakingly beautiful house in the distance, but even more breathtaking were the stretches of green grass dotted here and there with horses. Beautiful horses, she could tell even from this distance as they lifted their heads in greeting. She stepped off the small shuttle on Micah's arm, breathing in the fresh, hay-scented air. It was like coming home.

"Your wedding present, my love." The sweep of his arm indicated the island paradise and the herd of beautiful horses. Some were old, retiring to this warm climate to live out the rest of their lives in luxury, some were just born, frolicking in the tall grass with their mothers. It was a family place, and she looked forward to having her own family, with Micah, as tears of joy came to her eyes.

"I love you, Micah. With all my heart."

"As I love you, Jeri. For now and for always."

# About the Author

Bianca D'Arc has run a laboratory, climbed the corporate ladder in the shark-infested streets of Manhattan, studied and taught martial arts and earned the right to put a whole bunch of letters after her name, but she's always enjoyed writing more than any of her other pursuits. She grew up and still lives on Long Island, where she keeps busy with an extensive garden, several aquariums full of very demanding fish and writing her favorite genres of paranormal, fantasy and sci-fi romance. You can learn more about her books on her website, located at www.biancadarc.com.

*Most lovers kiss. This one pounces.*

# Cat's Cradle
*© 2010 Bianca D'Arc*
*String of Fate*, Book 1

As bad days go, this one qualifies as one for the books. Elaine knew being late for her jiu jitsu class could earn her a reprimand from her sensei. But the sensei's not there. And suddenly, neither is her car. Even walking home becomes problematic when she stumbles onto things that most definitely do go bump in the night. One of whom is too handsome for his own good—and too sexy for hers.

An *Alpha Pantera* Noir—black panther shifter—Cade operates on his immense skill, superior strength, and dominant personality. There's something about this small spitfire of a human woman that threatens to bring him to his knees. She blundered into the middle of his mission to transport his queen to safety, and now it's his responsibility to keep Elaine safe as well. Except no matter what he does, danger finds her at every turn.

Thrust into a world where the supernatural is commonplace, Elaine finds her considerable martial arts skill tested to the limit—and her ability to resist Cade crumbling by the second. But when nothing is as it seems, the last things she can trust are her own instincts...

*Available now in ebook and print from Samhain Publishing.*

*Demons in a feeding frenzy drive the*
*world-weary Markhat to the brink...*

# Hold the Dark
## © *2009 Frank Tuttle*
### A *Markhat* Story

Quiet, hard-working seamstresses aren't the kind that normally go missing, even in a tough town like Rannit. Martha Hoobin's disappearance, though, quickly draws Markhat into a deadly struggle between a halfdead blood cult and the infamous sorcerer known only as the Corpsemaster.

A powerful magical artifact may be both his only hope of survival—and the source of his own inescapable damnation.

Markat's search leads him to the one thing that's been missing in his life. But even love's awesome power may not save him from the darkness that's been unleashed inside his own soul.

*Warning: This gritty, hard-boiled fantasy detective novel contains mild romance and interludes of suggestive handholding.*

*Available now in ebook and print from Samhain Publishing.*

# SAMHAIN
### PUBLISHING

*It's all about the story...*

## Romance

## HORROR

*Retro* ROMANCE

www.samhainpublishing.com